The Bloody Harvest

By

C.W. Whitehair

∞INFINITY
PUBLISHING

ISBN 0-7414-6719-4

Printed in the United States of America

Published September 2011

INFINITY PUBLISHING
1094 New DeHaven Street, Suite 100
West Conshohocken, PA 19428-2713
Toll-free (877) BUY BOOK
Local Phone (610) 941-9999
Fax (610) 941-9959
Info@buybooksontheweb.com
www.buybooksontheweb.com

Chapter One

On March 17, 1862, Federal soldiers under the command of Major-General George Brinton McClellan boarded transports in Washington City, carrying them to Hampton Roads and Fortress Monroe, Virginia. After disembarking, General McClellan's 100,000-man Army of the Potomac began marching up the Virginia Peninsula with the intentions of capturing the Confederate capital of Richmond.· It was believed by politicians and the military establishment in Washington City that if Richmond were seized, the Civil War would come to an end.

*   *   *   *

During the late afternoon of Saturday, April 5, 1862, Jacob was at the Trader's Bank in Richmond, Virginia. His position as chief cashier carried enormous responsibilities. Jacob was placed in this position because of his high ranking, thirteen months ago after leaving Loudoun County, Virginia, just before the commencement of the war. Jacob's elevated position with the bank was because of his higher educational standing, intelligence, integrity, and that he had proven beyond a doubt that he was a capable leader. Most importantly, Jacob had earned the unquestionable and unchallengeable trust of the bank's president and many of its employees.

Jacob's duties, such as today were of the most secret nature. He was promoted to chief cashier six months ago because of his aggressive style, using wisdom to the fullest, and exhibiting shrewdness in issues concerning bank business. Most importantly, he had won the confidence and admiration of high officials within the Confederate government. Jacob carried out and fulfilled his obligations meticulously and with the greatest dedication to the vocation.

Jacob sealed an important document and placed it in the inner pocket of his frock coat. After walking from the office, he paused long enough to inform a clerk that he was leaving the building.

After leaving the bank, Jacob paused along the street in front of the financial institution and lit a cigar. The afternoon breeze felt good blowing across his olive skin. Quickly looking around his surroundings, Jacob noticed a poor young man of color looking in his direction from across the street. Jacob took a long gaze at the medium sized, older individual, who when noticed, turned and continued to proceed in the direction of 15th Street pushing his cart full of produce. Jacob knew him as Hezekiah.

Jacob turned and walked toward 9th street where the Confederate War Department was located. For days, the city had been in a state of anxiety because General McClellan's large Federal army was only sixty miles away near Yorktown. Restrictions were implemented where no citizen was allowed on the city streets without special permission after dark. The sale of liquor had been suspended. Additional militia had been called upon. All military furloughs were cancelled. Some of the city's ladies had been requested by the authorities to stitch together sandbags to be used by the 10,000-man Confederate force on the Virginia Peninsula under the command of General John Magruder. The strictest measure upon the citizens was the implementation of martial law by the provost marshal, Brigadier-General John Winder. Even with its enforcement, many of the city's residents were going about their business as usual. The only difference being that there were many more citizens than usual milling around and trying to gather the latest news on Federal forces challenging General Magruder's small army. Jacob's observations and thoughts were not only on the events in the city, but also on his family's welfare on their farm in northwestern Loudoun County. They were behind Yankee lines.

Jacob came to the corner of Main and 11th Street. Several soldiers from the provost detail were randomly stopping citizens and checking their passes. At first, he ignored the line and continued to walk toward his destination. One of the soldiers stepped away and gestured for Jacob to pause. The Corporal looked sternly at Jacob when asking for his pass.

Pulling the document from his coat, Jacob handed it to the soldier. The soldier's eyes moved steadily over the paper. He continued to glance up at Jacob's physical description to see if it matched the description written on the pass.

Jacob turned his attention to the American Hotel to see if there was anyone he knew. The Confederate soldier looked up from the pass. When Jacob was about to speak, he heard another individual call his name.

Jacob looked to his right and noticed a tall Confederate officer in an open carriage driven by a coachman. Jacob recognized the officer as Colonel Alfred Palmer. Colonel Palmer was the officer in charge of the Confederate telegraph office where important messages were received and sent to cabinet members, government officials, and the commanding officers of the two largest Confederate armies in the field. Over the last six months, Alfred Palmer had proven to be a loyal friend and an important associate. His shrewdness, proven character, and unquestionable integrity was well respected in Virginia. Colonel Palmer was from an aristocratic family along the James River near Charles City Court House. He served from 1856 until 1860 in the Virginia legislature and was well-educated in Virginia politics.

The Corporal quietly returned Jacob's pass. Jacob turned, saying, "Colonel Palmer, it's good to see you."

"Yes Jacob, the feeling is mutual. Where are you heading to?" Colonel Palmer asked.

"I have business at the War Department."

"With Secretary Randolph, I assume?"

"Yes sir."

"Well young man," Colonel Palmer answered, "I'll save you the trip. I have just learned from a clerk at the telegraph office that Secretary Randolph is at the Spotswood. I am on my way there now to speak to him. Would you care to join me?"

"Thank you sir. I would appreciate the ride," Jacob smilingly answered.

"The good citizens of Richmond are concerned, and concerned they should be. I am sure in those gatherings they are talking about McClellan's forces marching up the peninsula," Colonel Palmer said, his gray eyes steadily looking along the street.

"Sir, I am sure that with the arrival of General Joe Johnston's army, we should more than have the ability to turn back McClellan and his army. No matter how many Yankees he has with him. Most assuredly sir, the citizens' mood will turn to one of jubilation with the arrival of our troops. Their confidence will soar like an eagle," Jacob confidently answered.

"This is why I wanted to speak with the Secretary. I have learned the first of those men from General Longstreet's division are nearing the city from Fredericksburg and they should be here sometime tomorrow. When they arrive, we will have to rush them down the peninsula. I just hope they arrive in time." Colonel Palmer again paused and shook his head. "It's going to be close, Jacob. This fighting could decide the war." Pointing in the direction of Capital Square, he continued to pour out his frustrations. "If only those politicians up there at the capitol building would have decided to act earlier to forcibly enlist men for the army, we might not have found ourselves in this fix. But no, they have to fight and fuss over nothing and leave the welfare of the nation hanging." He turned and looked at Jacob. "And with a large army at our doorstep, they still can't make a decision."

"How many troops do you think General Longstreet will bring with him?" Jacob curiously asked.

"His division consists of six brigades and Walton's artillery battalion."

"I have a close friend, Benjamin Kelly, who is a lieutenant with Company A of the 8th Virginia Infantry."

"The 8th is with George Pickett's splendid brigade," Colonel Palmer answered as the carriage came to a halt in front of the five-story Spotswood Hotel."

After stepping from the carriage and entering the newly constructed hotel, Jacob looked around and noticed that the lobby was filled with people. The Spotswood was much like the Willard Hotel in Washington City; it was a place the most notable politicians patronized. When Confederate President Jefferson Davis arrived last year with his family, the hotel served as their residence until they moved to their present location at 12th and Clay Street. Many notable generals, gentlemen of notoriety, and upper class spent time gossiping and sipping mint juleps. Jacob knew the patronage was mixed with profiteers and spies, looking for opportunity and information that could be passed onto Federal authorities in Washington City.

Both Colonel Palmer and Jacob looked around the elegantly furnished hotel to see if they noticed the Secretary of War. Colonel Palmer silently gestured with his hand to follow him. They proceeded until they came to the dining room where Secretary Randolph, a great grandson of former president, Thomas Jefferson was seated. Before the war, Secretary Randolph had served as a commissioner for the new Confederate government, interceding with the Lincoln administration for the release of United States forts within the new boundaries of the Confederacy. He fought at the Battle of Big Bethel during the first year of the war and was rewarded later with the rank of Brigadier General before assuming the cabinet position in President Jefferson Davis's government.

Secretary Randolph wiped his mouth with the linen and looked up at Colonel Palmer and Jacob. "Gentlemen, I have been expecting both of you. Please be seated. We have much to talk about."

Immediately, a waiter appeared. Colonel Palmer and Jacob ordered bourbon. Secretary Randolph turned his attention to Colonel Palmer. "I have been concerned about the fighting along the Tennessee River around Pittsburgh Landing between Grant's and Sidney Johnston's boys. As I understand from an earlier telegraph, Johnston hasn't been able to bring all his forces into play because of numerous delays."

"I know, "Colonel Palmer calmly answered. "But, Sidney Johnston is the right officer with the greatest tactical experience between the two to win this fight."

"Well, let's hope that Grant is too drunk to fight," Secretary Randolph replied with a humorous chuckle.

"Yes sir, let's hope for just that," Colonel Palmer added as everyone broke out in laughter.

Once everyone was composed, Secretary Randolph asked Colonel Palmer, "I assume you have news of General Longstreet's arrival?"

"Yes sir. Longstreet's division will be here by tomorrow," Colonel Palmer enthusiastically answered. "The General informed me he would send a telegram later letting me know all the details. The rest of Joe Johnston's forces are also on the move, and are following Longstreet."

Secretary Randolph was quiet as he turned his attention to Jacob. He asked, "Did you bring the draft?"

"Yes sir," Jacob softly replied, pulling the envelope from his coat pocket and handing it to the Secretary.

Secretary Randolph was quiet as he inconspicuously placed the envelope in his interior coat pocket. He stroked his beard and looked up at Jacob. "I understand you are from Loudoun County?"

"Yes sir, I live a short distance from Harpers Ferry."

"I ask because you must know the area quite well."

"I know it inside and out."

Secretary Randolph smiled and continued in a low tone. "I would like to employ your services as a courier to get a message through to someone of importance in Washington City,"

"Jacob, we trust your loyalty. Can you help us?" Colonel Palmer swiftly added.

"What about the other couriers?" Jacob inquisitively asked.

"Son," Secretary Randolph answered, "unfortunately one of them was captured by Federal authorities while in Washington City after a female Pinkerton agent tricked him into giving her valuable information. After this happened, things became more complicated for us. Agents were compromised as well as couriers. We don't know how much he may have said to her. Our whole operation might be in jeopardy. No one knows you. Can you help us?"

Jacob was quiet as both men looked anxiously at him for an answer. Many thoughts about the perils and dangers raced through his mind.

"We will send you through Federal lines by a different route." Secretary Randolph promised.

"And we were thinking since you know the Northern Virginia area, you would be the best choice," Colonel Palmer confidently added.

"It might give you a chance to see your folks since you'd be in that area and you could also give us some idea of what the Yankees were up to and any other news of value," Secretary Randolph said.

Jacob knew the message must be very important and that they were desperate for assistance in its delivery. After gazing at the two men, Jacob took a sip of bourbon and reluctantly nodded his approval.

A smile beamed across Colonel Palmer's ruddy complexion as Secretary Randolph said, "Tonight, sometime around

7 o'clock, come to my residence. There will be someone there of importance who will explain to you this undertaking."

"What about my position at the bank? What will they say?" Jacob anxiously asked.

"I'll take care of that, don't you worry about a thing," Secretary Randolph assured.

Jacob looked at Colonel Palmer and then at Secretary Randolph. He smiled and held up his glass with the others and proposed a toast, "To a prosperous and successful endeavor for the Confederacy. And may we teach old Abe Lincoln and his friends to stay out of Southern affairs."

Chapter Two

After leaving the Spotswood Hotel, Jacob returned to the bank to finish paper work. He was writing figures in the ledger book when the clock on the wall chimed. Jacob looked up from his work and noticed it was 6:45 in the evening. He closed the book and carried the document to the bank's vault. He took his coat and hat and said farewell to the guard and then departed the front entrance.

Outside, the gaslight lamps were glowing as dusk was settling in over the city. Jacob's mind was consumed in thought over the undertaking Secretary Randolph had in mind. He was inexperienced and had never attempted to penetrate Yankee lines and he was concerned over how this might be accomplished. What pretense could he use to cover his identity and true intentions if confronted by Federal authorities? Jacob reasoned within his mind that all would be revealed to him once he arrived at the Secretary's residence.

Jacob walked casually in the direction of 7th and 8th Streets where Secretary Randolph's residence was located. He knocked on the door and waited, looking around the deserted street. Promptly, a servant opened the door and greeted him. The servant took his hat, gesturing to follow him into the parlor.

When Jacob walked into the room, Secretary Randolph rose from his chair by the fireplace and approached with a warm greeting, "Jacob, I am glad that you could join us."

The Secretary dismissed his servant. Jacob noticed there was another individual dressed in civilian attire, rising from a chair opposite Secretary Randolph.

"Jacob, I would like you to meet Captain William Norris of the Signal Corp," Secretary Randolph said.

Without hesitation, Jacob extended his hand and William did likewise, exchanging greetings. The Secretary walked over to a table and began pouring several brandies.

"Jacob, the reason I asked Captain Norris to come here this evening is to lay out your assignment. What we are requesting of you is of the utmost importance and could be highly dangerous," Secretary Randolph said.

"Jacob, I'll get right to the point," William said. "We have an agent, working in Washington City that has been of the greatest importance to us and on more than one occasion she…"

"She? A woman?"

"Yes Jacob, a woman. She has returned to us valuable information that has served our noble cause. Currently, she is among the most elite in Washington society where she enjoys the respect and admiration of all. She has worked her way in among the highest authorities in the Yankee government. At the present, she has been keeping company with an influential senator, whose name I won't mention at the moment. But we know he is quite fond of her. Therefore, he has been very generous in his conversations with her."

"I thought some of those politicians would have learned their lesson after Rose Greenhow pulled off the same scheme," Jacob replied.

"Well apparently, they didn't learn their lesson. And this lady through this senator has access to Secretary Stanton and others of value in the Yankee government," William quickly added.

"Jacob, politicians are like army officers," Secretary Randolph smilingly answered. "When there are attractive ladies around, they will do all or anything that is needed to win their admiration and attention."

"What am I supposed to do?" Jacob asked.

"A gentleman will arrive at your boarding house and he will use the ruse of bank business. This will keep down any suspicions regarding your true intentions. He will pass a document with important information that you will be carrying to Washington City. You will then depart for the train depot where you will meet an accomplice. They will be your guide," William said.

"Once I arrive in Washington City, how and where will I meet this lady of interest?"

"She will place an advertisement for a laborer in the Evening Star. You will answer that call and you will be dressed accordingly for the role," William answered.

"And if she doesn't carry out her part or she gets caught, then what?"

"Oh, she will," William replied with a smirk on his face.

Once Jacob finished speaking to Secretary Randolph and William Norris, he departed. He approached Saint Paul's Episcopal Church, where two soldiers were standing near the entrance to the Monumental Hotel, which was used as the office of the Comptroller of the Confederate States government. Without warning, a familiar faint voice coming from near the rear of the church building caught his attention. Jacob looked to see what the two soldiers were doing. They appeared to be occupied in conversation. Jacob quickly slipped to the rear of the church and noticed it was Hezekiah. He was the person of color from across the street at the bank earlier in the afternoon.

"You're on time tonight," Jacob whispered.

"Yes'um. I'se been awaitin' on ya for nearly twenty minutes, Hezekiah replied rubbing his gray beard. "Dis time, yose is da one dats late," Hezekiah answered in his slow graveled drawl.

"You must get this message to the mistress tonight. It's the only chance we'll have. Tell her I've learned from Colonel Palmer that the leading elements of Johnston's army will pass through here tomorrow. Longstreet's six brigades will probably be the first division to arrive along with Walton's artillery battalion. They will be rushed down to

Yorktown. She will need to get this information to McClellan as soon as possible."

"I'se see."

"Can you remember all that I've told you?"

"Yes'um. I'se doesn't forget anything," Hezekiah softly answered.

"Also tell the mistress that I must go to Washington City on business. I'll be in touch when I return." Jacob noticed the bewilderment in Hezekiah's expression.

When Hezekiah began to walk away, he turned and said in a concerned tone, "Ya's be careful Mr. Jacob. Ya's be real careful. Cause da rebels will be harsh on ya if they catch up with ya."

"I will," Jacob answered, watching Hezekiah push his cart into the street toward the Monumental Hotel. Jacob smiled, knowing Hezekiah was very intelligent and could be deceptive if needed. Over the past year, Jacob had come to respect the mistress' servant for his unquestionable integrity, devoted loyalty, and sacrificial courage. If captured, the Confederates would kill him.

When Hezekiah was approached by two rebel soldiers, he was commanded to stop and be questioned. One of the soldiers pulled back the blanket to examine the contents in the cart. Jacob knew Hezekiah was experienced in this role and was confident he knew what to say and how to act. With both soldiers' attention occupied, Jacob inconspicuously slipped out into the street and walked in another direction away from the two soldiers.

For some strange reason, Jacob did not know why, the venture up North troubled him. He knew he had to prepare for the unknown.

Chapter Three

Twenty-six year-old 1st Lieutenant Benjamin Kelly of Company A, Hillsborough Border Guards, the 8th Virginia Infantry, was quietly sitting along the front of an open gondola car behind a locomotive engine of the Richmond and Fredericksburg Railroad. The train was speeding south and was within an hour of arriving at the western outskirts of Richmond where the soldiers would depart and move through the city to help reinforce General Magruder's forces at Yorktown.

Benjamin rubbed his hand across his clean shaven face. His dark-brown piercing eyes looked at the men that made up his company. He thought of how many of these men had been serving since the beginning of the war. He could still recall the previous spring on April 19, when they proudly departed Hillsborough, not far from his family's 250-acre farm in an area known as Between the Hills. Dressed in their new gray-swallow tail coat uniforms with three rows of Virginia buttons on the kite shaped red breast, the eighty man company marched to the Fair Grounds in Leesburg to the sound of the fife playing "St. Patrick Day in The Morning." The men had dispersed of the colorful uniforms and were now wearing the regulation gray or just civilian blouses and trousers. A year later and after hard service at battles such as Manassas and Ball's Bluff, the men had become hardened veterans of war.

Like some in his Company, Benjamin was very opinionated concerning his Southern views. He didn't believe President Lincoln or any Federal government had the right to dictate to the states what they could do in governing their people. Benjamin hated to leave his family and farm, but his passion to protect those rights compelled him to Confederate service. He enjoyed working on the farm and one day he hoped that he would inherit the property and possess the ability to financially purchase other farms in the immediate area.

Time was slowly passing with little to do for the men on the train but sleep or try and write a correspondence home. Many were silently thinking about their wives, sweethearts, and families they left behind. For Benjamin, he wasn't any exception. He recalled that after two soldiers from the celebrated Louisiana Tiger battalion were executed for desertion, he had received a thirty-day furlough for re-enlisting to return home and marry a young lady that he had been fond of since their youth.

Rachel Harrison Kelly had lived with her Aunt Jane and older brother Luke on their farm next to Benjamin's family. Rachel was a young lady of twenty-two with long blond hair who had for many years held his heart captive.

Benjamin's wedding day came to mind. It was a moment in his life that he cherished with the utmost fondness. He could still visualize in his mind the day they exchanged vows and the heartfelt expression on Rachel's face. His heart was moved with expression as she softly spoke with tearing eyes, gripping his hands in hers tightly to affirm her love and commitment to their new life-long relationship. When she kissed his lips at the conclusion of the ceremony and caressed his face with her hand, he knew he must prevail and return to her.

Benjamin's time was short. They shared words of encouragement, of an everlasting hope, of their undying love, and the vision of having a large family. Rachel's words continued to echo in his mind. His heart was still wounded when he recalled the morning he had to return to his regiment. The sad expression and tears, filling her pale-blue eyes as they stood on the front porch of his parents' home was more than he could endure. Never had his family and two younger brothers witnessed such an expression of emotion as tears flowed freely down his cheeks and he quietly stepped back from her embrace.

Once the locomotive's whistle began to blow, Benjamin's mind returned to his surroundings. He could see off in the distance the many church spires and buildings, indicating that they were on the very outskirts of Richmond. As he looked around the train car, many of the men broke their silence and began to anxiously anticipate what would happen once they arrived in the Confederate capitol.

When the train came to a slow halt, Benjamin was one of the first men to step down from the train car. He immediately received an order from Captain W.R. Bissell to place the men into rank and form up with the rest of the regiment.

Chapter Four

Around 11:30 in the morning, Benjamin and the rest of the 8th Virginia began moving through Richmond along Broad Street. Regimental bands struck up patriotic songs such as the "Bonnie Blue Flag" and "Dixie." Word spread among the citizens like wild fire that Longstreet's men had finally arrived. The city's mood began to brighten and became one of jubilation, and hope. The oppression that had laid siege to the city had lifted. The soldiers' appearance was ragged, faces sunburned, the clothing soiled with red Virginia clay, and spring flowers stuck in some of their hatbands, but they were a happy sight to the citizens. These men represented their salvation from General McClellan's invading legions and deserved to be treated as royalty. Before churches had concluded their services, parishioners were rushing home to get food to share with the hungry soldiers. Men, women, children, and servants jammed Broad Street with baskets of food to share with the soldiers.

Benjamin noticed one soldier in particular was eating a piece of bread while the bayonet on the end of his musket rifle was carrying ham. The ladies, waving their white handkerchiefs and shouting expressions of adulation, were received with warmness by the Confederate soldiers. Many of the officers returned the affectionate compliments by saluting with their swords.

There was a sense of patriotic pride consuming Benjamin's heart after noticing and experiencing the outpouring of affection and gratitude from the Richmond citizens. Again, he quickly thought of home and how he wanted his children one day to grow up in surroundings where they could enjoy all the freedom and liberties that he was fighting to protect. He knew this war had been surfacing for years and with the failure of compromise, he believed such as others that it could only be resolved by the shedding of blood.

Once Benjamin's regiment arrived at the Rocketts Wharf to board steamboats that would carry them down the James River, he heard a voice shout his name. Looking around to see who was calling, he noticed Jacob, his one time close and dearest friend.

The 8th Virginia was pausing and Benjamin went over to speak to Jacob. He approached with a smile and embraced Jacob. Benjamin stood back and said, "It's been almost two years since you left the valley. We haven't heard a word from you. What happened to you?"

"I am sorry I didn't keep in contact with you. Many times I've wanted to write, but just couldn't find the time with my position at the bank."

"The bank?" Benjamin answered in an astonishing tone. "With your training and military knowledge from West Point, I thought you would have pledged your allegiance to the Confederacy. All this time, I thought maybe you had snuck off to Harpers Ferry and joined the 1st Virginia Cavalry against your father's wishes."

"No, I had enough of fighting the Cheyenne in Kansas with the 1st Cavalry. A man thinks twice about his immortality when he has been hit in the chest with an Indian's arrow. It's something that still troubles me from time to time."

"I can still recall the many evenings you, Luke, and I spent down along the base of the Short Hill fishing along the banks of Piney Run. Afterward, we would fry them up and joke around. But then, sometimes the conversation got serious. Sometimes too serious."

"Yeah, Luke was always good at helping to give advice on those little discussions," Jacob said with a smile. "Those days were before the war and the cares of life. We enjoyed some of the best times that anyone could have experienced.

Now look, we are engaged in a great war with too many uncertainties."

"Unfortunately families are divided and fighting against each other," Benjamin sadly replied. "Some of the men in my company have cousins and in-laws that are with McClellan's army. It's tough on them knowing they might be shooting at family. This war is tough on everyone," Benjamin began to smile. "But, we don't have that problem. We have always seen eye to eye on matters."

Jacob paused and avoided the comment. He wanted to know about his family. "How is my sister Sarah and parents doing?"

"I saw them back around Christmas time when I returned home on a short furlough. They were well and in good spirits when I delivered a fruitcake to them. But like other families, the war has lasted longer than what they anticipated."

"That relieves my mind to know things are well with them."

Jacob was anxious to know about Rachel. Through most of their youth, Benjamin and Jacob had been rivals in their efforts to win her affection. Nothing had been said thus far about her.

Suddenly, Benjamin removed his gray brim hat and ran his hand through his long ash-blonde hair. Benjamin sighed and somberly said, "Jacob, there is something of importance that you must know before I leave the city. And I'd like to be the one to tell you."

"What is it?" Jacob asked.

"Back in December when I returned home, it wasn't just for a visit with the family, but it was to marry Rachel," Benjamin said. Benjamin's tone was compassionate when he continued, "I am sorry, but when you and Rachel broke off your engagement and without a word to her why you left the area, she was devastated. She waited on you for little more than a year to return. Maybe if you would have sent her a word or two, it would have mattered, but when she heard nothing of your whereabouts and your family didn't know where you had disappeared to, than she gave up all hope and began to move on with her life. Jacob, what else was she supposed to do?"

"I understand. She didn't know. I was to blame,"

"Are you angry?" Benjamin asked.

Over the music of several regimental bands playing Dixie and the noise of the citizens shouting, Jacob shook his head and quickly replied. "No, no, you nor anyone else is to blame. I wish Rachel and you nothing but the best and all of God's blessings. She is my loss and your gain. She'll make you a good wife. I know where you are going the fighting will be hell. Just take care of yourself and don't try to become some kind of hero, understand?"

With a concerned expression on his face, Benjamin turned and headed with the rest of his company for the ship. He was troubled by the news he shared with Jacob and his reaction. He didn't think Jacob would rush home and confront Rachel over the issue. His intuition continued to plague him over his suspicions of Jacob's expressions and revealing disappoint-ment. Jacob should have been over Rachel by now, but it was apparent he still possessed strong feelings for her. Benjamin was sure he could trust Rachel and she was committed to their relationship. Another issue puzzled him greatly. Why didn't he already know? Why did Jacob's family not tell him? His thoughts continued to trouble him over this mystery.

Jacob gazed after Benjamin, as he crossed the plank onto the ship's deck. The anguish Jacob was experiencing was deep and painful. He turned and began to walk away with tears streaming down his cheeks. Benjamin was correct. Had Jacob communicated with Rachel through some kind of correspondence, she might have waited for him. He felt so foolish that he had allowed the lady of his dreams slip away. Although he wanted to race from the city and back to Loudoun County to see Rachel, he didn't desire to place her in such an uncomfortable position and maybe destroy any relationship with Benjamin and her. Still the desire was burning within his heart to see her.

Jacob looked up, paused, and noticed President Jefferson Davis standing on a balcony, waving his hat and shouting to some Mississippians, "God bless you, boys! Remember Mississippi!"

For now, the war goes on. Jacob was determined to do his best to accomplish the purpose set before him. Jacob hoped that Benjamin would come through this campaign uninjured. It would be devastating to all if something were to happen to him.

Chapter Five

It was near dusk when a well-dressed, middle-aged gentleman of prestigious appearance arrived at Jacob's boarding house. With only a nod, he delivered the documents to Jacob's care just as Secretary Randolph had promised. After closing the door, Jacob placed the envelope in his coat pocket and walked into the parlor. He picked up yesterday's copy of the Richmond Dispatch lying on a nearby table and began to read information he already knew. Two agents, both Federal spies were condemned to die by hanging at the fairgrounds yesterday, but the punishment was not carried out as scheduled. Jacob knew in order to save their own lives they implicated Timothy Webster, the chief agent working for Alan Pinkerton and the Federal government. He was sure Confederate authorities were after Webster all along because he possessed the greatest experience among Federal agents and he had also carried important mail for Secretary Randolph's predecessor, Judah Benjamin. It was the usual practice of Pinkerton to open the mail and make copies, and then resealed the contents, delivering it through one of his undercover agents to the Confederate agent that was supposed to receive it. The Yankees knew through Webster's work all of the Confederate plans that would be carried out. They even knew the identity of some of the Confederate agents and arrested or killed them.

Jacob thought of his own dilemma if captured. Rebel authorities would execute him if they knew he was betraying them. His mission was risky and many would be surprised if they really knew who he was working for and the assignment that was entrusted into his hands. Jacob returned to his room where he slowly walked over to a table near the bed. He looked down at a small box, which had not been opened since leaving Loudoun County. It contained valuables, but there was something of far more importance and interest in the box. Jacob took a deep sigh as he placed the box in his hand. Jacob opened it and removed a photograph. Jacob felt the warmth of tears streaming down his cheeks. The photograph was of Rachel. It was the first time since leaving home that he had looked upon her face. Jacob sat alongside the bed and began to think about the times they shared together. One time in particular, while they were both still in their teens, stood out in his mind. It happened while they were sitting along Piney Run during the fading autumn afternoon hours. Jacob noticed Rachel gazing into the water and watching a fish swimming below the water's surface. She took a piece of bread and tore it into small pieces. Jacob remained quiet, gazing at her natural beauty. He was fortunate because even then, he was sure of Benjamin's interest and love for her. All through their youth, Benjamin and Jacob had competed for her affection. They struggled at times with their relationship.

Jacob watched Rachel tossing the bread pieces into the water. She smiled as the fish swam frantically from one side to the other after the morsels. He remembered asking her what was so funny. She replied the fish reminded her of him. When he asked in what way, she looked into his eyes and said, "It reminds me of your vain-less attempts at escaping my love for you." She slowly turned and looked at him, continuing, "Because I do love you, and I always have." Her voice was filled with compassion and sincerity. Her eyes revealed a joy unspeakable, something he hadn't witnessed or known since the beginning of their relationship. Even while he was at West Point and later in the west, she faithfully wrote and constantly reaffirmed her love and loyalty. Her commitment was unquestionable. Now through his own thoughtlessness and carelessness he had lost her to Benjamin. How could he have let her go, or face her again.

Jacob returned the photograph to the box and placed it on the table. After regaining his composure, he glanced at his timepiece and prepared to leave for the Virginia Central depot.

*   *   *   *

Once Jacob arrived at the busy train depot, he looked around at the many people going about their business. After lighting a cigar, Jacob walked in the direction of the waiting train. After boarding, he found a seat near the front of the coach. The train coach was almost full. As the train began moving, a young lady with long brown hair approached and softly asked, "May I join you?

"By all means," Jacob replied, looking up and gesturing for her to be seated. After she was comfortable with her carpetbag on her lap, Jacob continued, "If I may, I would like to introduce myself. I am Jacob Martin."

"Jacob. What a rare name. It is a pleasure to make your acquaintance," the lady answered.

"And if I may ask, what is your name?"

"Miss Sarah Robins."

"Sarah. It's a very beautiful name, biblical. Your mother used discretion and chose wisely."

"Yes, I guess she did."

"Are you going to visit her?" Jacob asked, glancing in Sarah's direction.

"No, I haven't seen my mother in sometime."

"Oh. I see," Jacob said, looking at her somber brown eyes.

"Well, to be honest with you, she's been deceased for sometime," Sarah softly replied.

"I'm sorry," Jacob sighed after feeling like he had made a fool of himself.

Jacob knew by Sarah's social graces and appearance that she was well educated. She appeared to be proper in manner, but there was something about her that appeared to be questionable. Jacob didn't know what, but his intuition had always served him well concerning people. Another question that surfaced was why did she ask to be seated with him when there was another empty seat in the front of the train coach?

"Where are you traveling to?" Sarah asked.

"I am going as far as Gordonsville," Jacob swiftly replied.

"Wife I assume?" Sarah asked with a smile.

"Oh no. I'm not married or that sort of thing, I have a brother I'll be spending a few days with," Jacob confidently replied.

"Why isn't he in the army fighting like all of the other brave men from Virginia?"

"He's much older than me and suffers from the consumption. I don't believe the army would want someone like him for military service."

"What if I were to tell you that you were lying to me," Sarah retorted in a whisper, "That your real destination is behind Yankee lines and you are carrying something of importance to Washington City."

Jacob was stunned by Sarah's revelation. He looked at her. How did she know? Who was she working for? All of these questions at once raced through his mind. No one was supposed to know of his assignment except Secretary Randolph, Captain Norris, and Colonel Palmer.

"Who are you?" Jacob asked in a sharp whisper.

"I will be your lovely accomplice," Sarah said as she pulled out a piece of paper and handed it to him. As Jacob glanced at the note, Sarah continued, "Captain Norris decided that I would be going to Washington City with you."

Jacob was puzzled and was sure she noticed his expression. Sarah said as she destroyed the note, "It's only because of my previous experience and knowledge at playing this game,"

Jacob didn't plan on an accomplice traveling to Washington with him. He didn't question her role, but instead played along with the plan. His own scheme would have to be altered, but that was the way it was with the world of espionage. Maybe she would be useful in helping to get past General Richard Ewell's men along the Rapidan River.

The train's whistle began to blow. Sarah took Jacob's arm and smiled, "You're new at this."

"Quite so, I wish that I hadn't gotten so involved in this."

"Maybe I make you nervous. I know you didn't plan on a woman to be your accomplice, but there will be less suspicion if I travel with you. Just remember to act natural once we come into contact with the Yankees."

"Well, I hope you're good at this."

"Believe me, I am," Sarah replied in a serious tone.

Once Sarah and Jacob arrived in Gordonsville, he took her hand and assisted her down the steps of the train coach onto the depot's platform. Jacob could not help but to look at her petite shapely form. She smiled knowing his thoughts.

Chapter Six

The waters of the James were calm and darkness made it difficult for Benjamin to recognize the outline of the dwellings along the river's shoreline. As he leaned over the ship's railing, the small homesteads and plantations reminded him of the warmness of home and family. He especially gave thought to Rachel. He could vividly visualize the warmness of her smile, the soft touch of her hands, and the sincerity in her eyes. He was never one to show his inner feelings and affections, but that had all changed in his relationship with her. He looked forward with constant anticipation when he would see her again. Should there be a continuation of the conflict after this coming fight then hopefully his army would move back into Northern Virginia where he could be close to home.

As Benjamin continued to ponder on home, he felt an anguishing void in his heart slowly wearing him down. Sometimes the idea of leaving the army without leave had entered Benjamin's mind, but he felt ashamed at such thoughts. Earlier in his life, his father had taught him a man's word was his honor, and his pride wouldn't allow him to seek that direction. Besides, he was an officer and was expected to set an example of leadership for those he had been entrusted to command in battle. Still, like everyone, he played with the thought only out of desperation because of his separation from Rachel. Like all soldiers, he was hoping for an end to the war. Just yesterday, some of the men in his company had expressed in conversation that maybe this would be the decisive victory the army needed to convince the Lincoln government to give up its efforts of subjugation of the Confederacy. If so, then they could all return home and be with their families. From their words, he knew that it was keeping their hopes alive.

From behind he heard a voice calling, "I can guess what's on your mind."

He turned around and there stood 1st Sergeant James Bell from Purcellville, which was near Hillsborough. Benjamin shook his head and answered, "As always, you're predictable." Benjamin paused and continued as James approached and stood near him gazing into the water. "I was just standing out here for a moment and getting my mind off the war. It's peaceful and I can hide within my thoughts about home and forget about all the fighting and bloodshed that I've experienced."

James sighed and answered in a sincere tone. "It's only natural that a soldier thinks of home, wife, and young ones, especially when you're about to go into battle. When I re-enlisted for the duration of the war and went home like you to see my family, I didn't want to return to the army. The homesickness I endured over the first eight months after leaving the area was more than what I had bargained for, and my thoughts were seriously on staying behind with the family. But after witnessing the execution of those two Louisianans, it changed my mind. I returned to take my chances, knowing that if I die then it is with honor. Besides, it would only be a matter of time before being captured and returned to the army and risk suffering execution like those poor men. At least this way, I have a fighting chance of returning home and seeing Lucy and the kids."

"Yeah, you're right. I guess I have much to be thankful for and like you want to protect it. For me, I married a girl that I have always been in love with. She comes from a good Christian upbringing and her brother is a preacher. So I would not do something like deserting. It would be so foolish."

Taking a match and striking the heel of his shoe to light his pipe, James swiftly replied, "In this type of business it's always good to know that you have a preacher in the family."

"My only concern is that Rachel is behind Yankee lines. And I pray to God no harm comes to her or my family. That worries me more than fighting the blasted scoundrels. I am just concerned maybe some of the soldiers will get out of hand and their officers won't have any control over them. The Yankees will surely know that most of the families living in the area are fighting for the Southern cause and might try to extract some measure of revenge against us," Benjamin answered in a troubled tone.

"Yeah, I share your fears," James replied as his brown eyes were on Benjamin. "Since General Jackson was defeated at Kernstown several weeks ago and General Banks has chased him up the Valley, the whole area has been left wide open to the Blue Bellies. But I think the Yankees will leave the civilians alone." Both men were silent, then James added in a more serious tone, "And you must get your mind off home because the fury of war will continue once we are off of this ship tomorrow. Death respects no one,"

"I know. I have a duty to do, but the thought of killing still lingers, seeing men dropping and torn apart by cannon canister, fighting hand to hand until death decides the victor. The first time I shot and killed a Yankee in battle, I struggled with the guilt for days. Maybe he was like me. A wife or kid to return to or a sick mother at home waiting. For days after Manassas, I could still see the tormented expression on his young face and the anguishing sounds coming from his lips as death claimed him. I assumed by his youth that he still had a lot of life to live, but now he is rotting in some grave. Maybe he spent some evenings thinking of his family as I've been doing? But now after so much killing and maiming, the guilt has turned to numbness and callousness within my own heart. And now tomorrow or the next day or the next week, there will be more sacrifice of life and who knows how many lives this war will require before it's all over."

"I know how you feel, but you can't stop. You've got to keep going," James replied after taking a puff from his pipe. "But I keep telling myself that this fight is a noble one, and it's for my family so that they will not have some Blue Belly government telling them how they can live their lives. You can't lose sight of that principle. If you do, than you'll give up fighting and die for nothing."

"Than I guess we need to be bold and brave on the field to make sure those rights are protected," Benjamin quickly replied with a tone of pride in his voice.

James remained silent and continued to gaze at Benjamin. He didn't doubt his loyalty, courage or ability, but he wanted him to get his thoughts on the fighting that would be ahead.

As Benjamin and James were turning around to go and get something to eat, a soldier came up and handed each of the two men mail that had arrived before departing Richmond. Anxiously, Benjamin took his letter and walked away from James to read it under the light and to have some privacy. He glanced at the date on the envelope. Apparently, the correspondence was written before the army departed from Northern Virginia. He opened the envelope. It was from his wife.

Rachel wrote:

My Dearest Benjamin,

I wanted to write you a few lines and let you know we are all doing as well as can be expected. Your father and your brothers Buck and George are doing a good job of keeping up all the chores. I don't mean to distress you, but Buck wants to join your regiment once the army returns to the area. Your father has given his blessings with great joy and pride on the matter, but I feel hesitant about his enlisting. I don't know why I feel this way. Maybe it is because of his tender age.

I have some good news to share with you. Yesterday I went to Harpers Ferry and saw Doctor Marmion and he gave me the good news that we are going to have a baby. When I found out the news, your father went to each of the neighboring farms with fresh pies that your mother and I baked and gave one away to each family as he shared the tidings. On Sunday when Luke allowed him to make the announcement at Ebenezer, the congregation began to Praise the Lord with all their heart and offered to help make some of the clothing.

I know this news will brighten your day and help you to look forward to our reunion. Stay safe and well my love. As I understand from news in the valley, a great many of the soldiers in the army are sick with the jaundice and dysentery.

All of my love I send to you and pray that you keep me in your thoughts and prayers, as I will keep you in mine.

Your Loving Wife
Rachel

Immediately, Benjamin began to celebrate Rachel's news by yelling in a loud tone. He went first to James, who was still reading his correspondence a few feet away. Then he raced to some of the other men and officers of his regiment as they came onto the ship's deck to investigate why all the commotion. Once informed, they extended their congratulations to their friend and leader.

Benjamin was caught up in the bliss of the moment. For now, the war and its traumatic effects were far from his life, and it was a time to rejoice and share the tidings of great joy with everyone. He cherished this moment and the rights and wrongs of the war didn't make any difference. The news he cleaved to and for the coming campaign against McClellan's army would be his purpose and determination of returning home.

Chapter Seven

Darkness was settling in and the air was chilled when Sarah and Jacob left the depot at Gordonsville. Without hesitation, they headed toward the Exchange Hotel where they planned to have dinner and spend the evening before continuing their journey the next morning to Washington City.

After renting a room on the second floor in the back of the hotel, Sarah and Jacob quietly went about their business. As Jacob began to glance at a newspaper that he picked up in the hotel lobby, Sarah quietly sat on a chair opposite him. She laughed at the thoughts rushing through her mind.

"What's so funny?" Jacob asked, putting down the paper.

"I need your trousers," Sarah demanded.

"You need my what?" Jacob asked in an astonishing tone.

"Your trousers. Take them off," Sarah insisted in a serious tone.

"What for?" Jacob asked in an irritated voice.

"Don't ask questions, just do what I tell you."

With an angry expression, Jacob grudgingly removed his trousers and handed them to Sarah. Without a word, she ignored him and ripped open the inside seam. Afterward she looked at him, demanding, "The envelope! Give it to me!"

Without a word, Jacob removed the contents from his coat pocket and handed the document to her. He watched as she meticulously began to sew the envelope into the seam, creating a small pocket in his pants. "Why are you doing that?"

"We will be stopped by General Ewell's men and may be questioned."

"But they are friendly."

"I know, but still there is a risk! But worse yet, once we cross the Rappahannock and are among the Yankees, they will surely be suspicious of anyone traveling. They can and probably will search us. You can't take chances or trust anyone when you're doing this sort of thing," Sarah replied, looking up from her work. She continued as she followed her sewing pattern. "If we are caught with the documents, than we will end up in jail or even prison. I suspect with the importance of the envelope that you're carrying you might even get hung since you're a man."

Jacob jumped from the chair and replied in an irritable tone, "That's comforting to know."

Jacob knew Sarah's intentions and why, but again played naive to the scheme. He knew why Sarah didn't want to confront Confederate soldiers. They would allow them to pass once the army's provost marshal had telegrammed Richmond authorities concerning the nature of the mission. Until then, they would be certainly detained since they carried no verification of their identity. Once the word was passed to pickets, it would still take too much time. Even after they were successful, it could still be possibly a treacherous undertaking. This was because of the possibility of spies infiltrating the Richmond intelligence network, and also there were surely to be Unionist Virginian spies among the army and surrounding area. They couldn't afford to be identified and their mission jeopardized.

"I knew I shouldn't have taken part in this scheme. It's too risky for someone of little experience such as I," Jacob said in an anxious tone.

"That is why I am here. I am very particular with whom I work. I don't work with just anybody. I am sure I am educating you for more trips to the North. I learned from an acquaintance this morning that you are very respected among the government authorities and they'll use you until they have reason to believe that the Yankees suspect you of any transgression or you just become reckless. But if that happens, it might cost you your life. So use good judgment, patience, and keep your mouth shut to those you don't know, and trust no one."

As Sarah handed Jacob the trousers and looked coldly into his eyes, he knew he was dealing with someone who knew how to play the game very wisely. She was shrewd in all her activities and in all probability was deadlier than a rattlesnake in her cunningness. Sarah had apparently become very experienced at secret activity in a short time.

*　　*　　*　　*

Early the next morning, Jacob went to the stable and rented a horse and buggy. As he loaded Sarah's carpetbag onto the back of the buggy, he thought of his plans to cross the Rappahannock at Fredericksburg and head directly north to Alexandria. Jacob just didn't know how he would escape Sarah and place the information that he was carrying into the hands of Federal authorities. Jacob had only been used for intelligence within Richmond and was inexperienced at such duties as carrying messages north. His thoughts were broken when Sarah departed the hotel entrance.

"Are we ready?" Sarah asked.

"Yes, everything is loaded," Jacob answered, taking Sarah by the hand and assisting her into the buggy.

Once they were on the move, Jacob looked ahead along the road. "Sarah, since we are going to meet Federal troops anyway after we cross the Rappahannock, I was thinking we should head north by the way of Fredericksburg."

"No, no, we won't do that."

"Why?" Jacob surprisingly asked.

"Because we are going to go a different way."

"Which way, if I may ask?"

"Through Culpepper Court House."

"That will put us behind schedule. It is a roundabout way. I am suppose to be..."

"I know when you are supposed to be in Washington, but I am the one with the experience and I'll be the one to get you there. We have to take extreme caution and not give anyone the impression of what our intentions are. Besides, you'll understand once we get to Culpepper Court House."

Jacob didn't dispute Sarah's request, but quietly complied with her demands. He wanted to learn for the future should this war continue and relay the knowledge to his authorities in Washington City. It was his fullest intention to play the game to its completion.

Chapter Eight

Once near Culpepper Court House, Sarah pointed to the direction she wanted to follow. Jacob was curious because thus far on the trip, she hadn't revealed any of her intentions, but kept their conversation general in nature. Jacob thought she could have played the role of courier without his assistance because she was making all the decisions and he was being kept in the dark and had contributed little to the journey. It must be, Jacob thought, there was some truth in Sarah's statement that Captain Norris and Secretary Randolph were interested in him continuing clandestine activity and Sarah was the one they had chosen to teach him. She must be very skilled.

It was near 3:00 o'clock in the afternoon when Jacob glanced at his timepiece. The pace had been slow from Gordonsville. Suddenly, Sarah and Jacob came to a quaint little homestead about a mile from town. Once in front of the house, they noticed several slaves working around the barn. Jacob brought the horse to a halt and assisted Sarah from the buggy. They headed in the direction of the house. Once they were near the porch, an elderly lady came rushing from the dwelling with arms outstretched. "Molly, Molly my child."

Jacob knew Sarah was using a different name in order to protect her identity. Was this being done because of the two slaves within listening distances? Did these people really believe Molly was her real name?

Without hesitation, Sarah rushed and embraced the lady. "Aunt Clara!"

With all the commotion, Jacob noticed an elderly gentleman departing the dwelling. Once he recognized Sarah, his eyes began to brighten; his expression glowed with excitement as he rushed to embrace her. He was introduced as Uncle William Huffman. While the others were speaking to each other, Jacob looked around and noticed one of the slaves was casually gazing in their direction while continuing to feed some chickens. Jacob was sure he was listening for information. Jacob turned his attention to Sarah speaking to her aunt and proceeded to follow them into the house.

After entering the house, Clara said, "Ya two must be hungry. Be seated while I dish ya up sum rabbit stew."

Jacob looked around and noticed William looking out the window at the two slaves working. He turned around and took a sip of coffee and a bite of the rabbit meat. He didn't get involved in the conversation between Sarah and Clara, but instead continued to watch William from the corner of his eye. Finally after eating much of the stew, Jacob said, "Mrs. Clara, I must say this is very good and filling."

"Well young man, I'm glad that ya's like it. I have more."

Clara began to stand when Jacob gestured with his hand, "No, no, I'll get it myself. Just stay seated."

After walking to the fireplace and scooping up some of the stew, Jacob turned and asked William while returning to the table, "Something caught your attention?"

"You know how it is," William answered in an abrupt tone as he turned and looked at Jacob. "Those two darkies out there have been hired out from Mr. Derry to do some of the chores around here. I'm getting too old to run this place any longer and so is Clara. You can't trust the darkies for nothing because they'll carry the least little information they learn to that traitor, and I am sure their curiosity is up with you two here."

"How do you know he is a traitor?" Jacob curiously asked.

"He asks to many questions."

As Jacob sat down, William turned his attention once more to what was happening out the window.

After more conversation, the discussion turned serious. Clara said, "Molly, eat up, ya's gonna need ya strength.

Everything is ready for tonight. William will sneak ya all across the river."

"We need to get moving after we rest for a couple of hours and feed and water the horse," Jacob said.

"William turned. "No, you can't do that. The darkies will become suspicious since they know that Molly is kinfolk. They will want to see what she's up to."

"I see. I guess it would look funny if we only stayed a few hours."

"By dark, they'll return home. When they come tomorrow, ya gonna be gone," Clara swiftly added. She stood and walked over and pulled a stone from over the mantel of the fireplace. She approached the table with a wooden box. She opened it and handed Jacob and Sarah a slip of paper. "Once ya cross the river, destroy ya passes that was given to ya before leaving Richmond. These are ya passes that we stole for ya to travel the rest of the way."

"For their benefit, we have to make it look real the rest of the day," Sarah said as she smiled at Jacob.

After removing Sarah's trunk from the buggy and settling in, Sarah suggested, "Why don't we take a stroll around the pond to pass the time. I have something in mind."

Jacob silently nodded his head in agreement, knowing her intentions.

As Sarah and Jacob leisurely walked along the pond, he noticed Sarah was quiet, gazing intently at the water. "If I may ask you a question, other than serving the Cause, why does an attractive lady such as yourself get mixed up in such a risky occupation?"

Sarah glanced at Jacob and smiled. "I guess I like the adventure and challenge of the unknown."

"There has to be more to it than those reasons. You could find something else to do that challenges you, like teaching rather than spying on people." Jacob paused, looking into Sarah's eyes. Jacob continued, "And the name Molly. Who are you and why are you doing this?"

"My real name is Sarah…not Molly. Those people are not related to me in any fashion. They are just my associates. They operate a place of safety and smuggle medicine or agents to the north when needed. I deal with them from time to time, just like now." Sarah's smiled and her expression was mischievous as she continued to gaze at Jacob.

"Like I said, there is more to it than what you are telling me. If we are going to work together then you are going to have to learn to trust me."

"You really want to know what compels me to do what I do? I'll tell you. My father and youngest brother were serving with the Richmond Grays of the 1st Virginia Infantry and were killed nine months ago at Manassas by those Yankee savages," Sarah angrily replied in a whisper so that she wouldn't be overheard.

Without warning, Sarah embraced Jacob and passionately kissed him. She broke their embrace and smiled. "After all, we have to make it look real, don't we? And if this war continues and there are more missions to be made, you'll be required to do the same thing as I did."

"With you, I think there is more to this than meets the eye."

"And you're going to tell me that you're not attracted to me?" Sarah replied laughingly.

"I would be lying if I said that I wasn't, but this isn't the time nor the place. We have to get going."

Sarah took Jacob by the arm and smiled, "Another time, another place."

Sarah was so believable in her role Jacob didn't know if this was all a pretense or if she was sincere. Jacob knew he must guard his actions and meticulously choose his words because she was deadlier than he realized.

Chapter Nine

Jacob was lying on a bed in one of the upstairs bedrooms, pondering on what his next move would be once they crossed the river near Washington City. He knew couriers were not necessarily privileged to secret information but only responsible for delivering its contents. He couldn't allow the documents he was carrying to fall into the enemy agents hands without discovering and revealing its contents. With the information, they would possess specific instructions on how to continue their clandestine activity within the highest ranks of the Federal government. Jacob was curious of the envelope's contents. If he opened it, memorized its contents and resealed it without difficulty, when the time came, he wouldn't have to consider other alternatives.

Those alternatives, Jacob thought, would be how he would be forced to deal with Sarah. Jacob felt an attraction to her, but she could be using her graciousness and flamboyant ways to seduce him into opening the envelope, testing his loyalty or believing that he was sincere in his efforts to help the Confederacy. Maybe, she was an agent playing both sides of the game. Time might cause her to reveal her hand once they neared the Potomac River on the outskirts of Washington City. Maybe Sarah was sincere in her efforts for the Confederacy. If so, he might be forced to do something drastic in order to escape her.

It was nearing 7 o'clock in the evening when there was a rap at the bedroom door. Jacob rose from the bed and opened the door. Much to his astonishment, there stood William with a cold expression dressed in a black suit with a white collar around his neck to indicate that he was a minister.

"Is it time?" Jacob asked.

"Yes, it should be quiet in the area. No one should be traveling the roads at this hour."

"But what about us? If we run across some of our boys patrolling the road, won't they have questions?"

"For thirty years, I've been preaching the Gospel, and tonight isn't any different. There won't be any questions the way I am dressed," William said with confidence.

"Preaching where?"

"At the Confederate camp less than a mile from the river. Now come on, it's getting late and we must get started," William replied.

After grabbing his bag, Jacob followed William down the narrow stairway to the kitchen. He noticed Sarah was dressed in men's trousers and shirt with a haversack. When Jacob went to pick up her trunk, she swiftly replied, "Leave it."

Looking into her eyes, Jacob noticed a determination and fire. There were two sides to Sarah. One, she was a lady of culture when needed, and the other, she was quite devious.

"Now Molly, take care. We want ya to come back and see us real soon, ya hear?" Clara said as she hugged Sarah.

Jacob said his farewells and followed William and Sarah. He knew now why they had stopped at this place. It was to receive the passes to travel through Northern Virginia when encountered by Federal troops and to evade detectives. They were sure to be scouring the area along the eastern area of the state.

Once Sarah and Jacob were aboard the two-horse wagon on the road heading north toward the river, Sarah asked, "How will you get us across the river, William?"

"I will not be the one," William answered.

"What? I thought you were going to help us," Sarah quickly replied.

"I will, but you must listen. Just before I get to the first picket post, I'll let you two off the wagon. The area is heavily wooded and will give you someplace to hide, but you must stay as quiet as possible while moving through the underbrush. Stay put and don't cross the river until I have the men shouting praises unto the Lord."

"Why wait for you to do that?"

"At that time, the pickets along the river will be preoccupied by all of the noise. When you cross, do so about 100 yards west of their campfire. It is a fording area. Once on the other side of the river, you will find several horses tied to a tree out of sight of the pickets."

Sarah and Jacob waited over an hour before they heard the last hymn, "Rock of Ages" being sung by the soldiers attending William's tent meeting. Afterward, the men began to follow his lead of praising the Lord. Jacob gestured to Sarah and they began to move through the undergrowth, while listening to the men in worship.

Once Sarah and Jacob arrived along the riverbank in the vicinity of the fording area, he could see by the glow of the campfire that the pickets' attention was distracted as William had said. Jacob looked across the river and noticed the opposite area was heavily wooded. If they crossed unnoticed by the pickets, they could easily disappear into the forest. Thus far, the Confederate underground and how they operated impressed him.

"You better remove your trousers," Sarah softly said.

"I know, so the documents don't get wet."

Quietly, the couple waded through the water and occasionally glanced toward the campfire to see what the pickets were doing. Sarah kept her haversack above the water to make sure it stayed dry. When they arrived on the other side, both were cold from their experience, but knew they couldn't light a fire. Sarah said as she embraced Jacob. "Hold me, I am so cold."

"Are all of your trips this interesting?"

"No, I very seldom have traveled this way. I am mostly alone."

"Why? You give me the impression that you're very experienced at this trade."

"This way is seldom used by us and least expected by the Yankees. But you already know why we couldn't go the other way. This route will be frequently used by some of us until it is safe to use the Port Royal route across the Rappahannock. And still some of our agents and couriers will continue to take their chances," Sarah replied as she broke their embrace, adding, "We need to find the horses and get moving."

Jacob looked around and off in the distance on a ridge half way up the hill were two horses. He pointed to them as Sarah stood behind a tree and removed her wet trousers, putting on a dry pair.

Once Sarah and Jacob were mounted, they rode off into the night in a northerly direction until they came to the outskirts of Warrenton Junction.

Chapter Ten

Sarah used the same alias she portrayed at the Huffman's, only this time, the gentleman operating the safe house was a physician by the name of Thomas Mason. He only knew Sarah as her assumed name, Molly. At his home, Sarah and Jacob were given dinner, clean-dry clothing for change, and most importantly, some intelligence concerning Federal cavalry patrols in the area. Jacob went to his bedroom, but Sarah sat near the warm fireplace and spoke with the physician. After a little time had gone by, Jacob left his room and stood at the top of the stairway and listened to Sarah and Thomas's conversation.

"Molly, I can't tell you how good it is to see you again," Thomas said in a serious tone.

"I guess it's been almost a year since I passed this way," Sarah replied as she watched the flames dancing in the fireplace.

"I won't press the issue, but as before, you know I am quite fond of you."

"Oh dear, such flattery," Sarah replied as she turned and smiled, continuing, "but you know with this terrible war going on that it's no time to let's say, have a serious encounter."

"Molly, Molly, just like always, trying to evade my quest for your love," Thomas said smiling and adding, "But you know I won't give up."

"We have to move on with more important issues. Now what about the passes?"

"They're in my possession. I will give them to you before you leave along with a map in case you have to go by a different route because of troop movements. I took great pains in having one sketched for you."

"Good because I want to get an early start and finish this business by tomorrow evening," Sarah answered as she threw her pass that Clara gave her into the fire.

"I don't know much about your friend. Can he be trusted?"

"There are some people in Richmond that think so. That's why I am with him."

Thomas stood and placed his arm along the mantel of the fireplace. He turned to look at Molly. "For some reason, there is something about him that I don't trust, that I don't feel right about."

Sarah laughed and answered in a joking manner, "Maybe it's because you feel I am attracted to his good looks. Well if you really want to know, I am. It just won't stand in the way of my work. Trust me." Again Sarah laughed and added as she held up her hand, "I am confident that I have him wrapped around my little finger."

"I sure hope for the sake of the Confederacy and yourself that you do."

Sarah and Thomas were unaware that Jacob was standing in the upstairs hallway next to his bedroom, listening to every word and pondering on his next move.

*   *   *   *

After a few restless hours, Jacob was up and ready to begin the final journey. It wasn't until dawn that Sarah and Jacob finally departed from Warrenton Junction with a buggy loaned to them by Thomas. They continued to travel steadily without any detours or interruption until they came to Fairfax Court House.

As Sarah and Jacob slowly rode into the village after being confronted by pickets, their attention was attracted to a regimental band playing the patriotic song, "Rally Around the Flag." Jacob glanced around and noticed there were a number of houses and gardens located around the two-story dwelling known to the locals as the Fairfax Court House.

From what Jacob observed, Federal soldiers were marching on one side of the courthouse grounds, apparently drilling, while some cavalrymen were standing near their horses on the other side. Jacob assumed they were couriers. Occasionally, one of them turned and spoke with one of the other soldiers standing guard duty around the brick structure. He knew from all appearances that the courthouse was being used as army headquarters, and with several soldiers within the cupola on the roof, it obviously was used as a signal station. To his amazement, they were not confronted by a Federal cavalry patrol on their way to the village. Jacob didn't know why. He knew they were less than twenty-five miles from Washington and the patrols should have been constant. Now that Jacob was close to his destination, his thoughts were continuously on how he would elude Sarah and escape into the city alone.

Sarah was experiencing an uncomfortable feeling with the presence of Federal soldiers. Something was not right. Turning and glancing at Jacob, she said, "Act natural and don't do anything that will arouse their suspicion. If you do, it's all over for us."

"They'll want to know where we are coming from. This village isn't that big and they'll know we are not from here. What do we tell them?"

"You'll have to be the one to answer that question since it would be the proper etiquette." Sarah paused and asked, "Did you remember the name on your pass?"

As she silently glanced at Jacob, he nodded.

Sarah and Jacob came to the double-porch, three-story Wilcoxon Tavern at the corner of Main Street and Chain Bridge Road, where he brought the horse to a halt. Looking toward the entrance of the tavern, he stepped from the buggy and walked around to assist Sarah from her seat. When they came to the entrance, one of the soldiers asked, "May I see your pass?"

Jacob pulled the document from his pocket and quietly handed it to the soldier. While the soldier examined the pass, Jacob glanced at Sarah and noticed she had a very calm expression on her face, but her eyes were continuously on the soldier.

"I don't believe I've seen you people before," the soldier commented.

"No, probably not. We are from Warrenton Junction," Jacob answered, noticing the star on the soldier's blouse, indicating he was with the provost detail.

"What brings you to Fairfax Court House?"

"My wife and I are on our way to Washington City because her Aunt Lily has taken sick and might be dying."

The soldier nodded his head and allowed Sarah and Jacob to pass without any additional delays or questions.

On the inside of the tavern, and after a long journey, Sarah and Jacob ordered something to eat.

"You were very believable out there," Sarah casually said.

"I'll be glad once this trip is over and we are in Washington. We should cross Long Bridge before dark."

"We have to. I don't want to take any chances."

"Then we had better get started."

Sarah quietly nodded her head in agreement.

Once Sarah and Jacob departed, he noticed that the soldier who had questioned them earlier was looking in their direction. Jacob and Sarah continued to look forward.

After leaving the edge of town, Jacob noticed many white tents populating the nearby area. This was the camp of Federal soldiers. Their guns were stacked in a circle. The smell of campfires burning with dinner cooking, caused an aroma to fill the air.

Shortly, Sarah and Jacob came to a crossroad where he paused.

"Why are you stopping?" Sarah abruptly asked.

"We are still in sight of the camp," Jacob said glancing at her. "Now if I am not mistaken, you don't want to give those soldiers any reason to be suspicious, do you?"

"No, you're right. I guess I am in a hurry," Sarah answered as she placed her hand on his arm.

Once Sarah and Jacob started moving again, he heard the swift clatter of horses approaching from the direction of the village. He glanced at Sarah. She had a concerned expression. They did not turn to look and see who was approaching at such a fast pace.

"I am sure they are after us," Sarah said.

"What makes you say that? What are we going to do?" Jacob asked.

"Answer their questions and cooperate. It might not be anything. After all, there weren't any pickets on this side of town. Maybe they just want to check our passes."

One of the soldiers rode alongside the buggy, gesturing with his hand and demanding that Sarah and Jacob halt. Without hesitation, Jacob complied with his command.

Immediately, Jacob looked around and noticed there were four cavalrymen. An officer rode up to him. "Sir, Madam, my name is Second Lieutenant Roberts of the 2nd New York Cavalry."

"Yes," Jacob calmly answered. "Why are you stopping us?"

"I would like to see your passes?" Lieutenant Roberts requested.

Quietly, Jacob handed the officer their passes. After a few moments, the officer looked up from the identification documents and glanced at his Sergeant. He looked in Jacob's direction. "Where are you coming from?"

"Warrenton Junction."

"Your pass says that it was signed by Captain Murdock."

"Yes sir, that's correct."

The officer sighed. "I am sorry to delay your journey, but you must return to the village with me."

"What is this all about?" Jacob irritably asked as a soldier dismounted and checked the inside of his coat for a weapon while another searched Sarah's basket that she was carrying in her lap.

"That's what we want to know. Now, if you will, please do as I say and turn the buggy around and follow me."

Jacob quietly complied with the request. He looked at Sarah, who continued to remain calm.

Chapter Eleven

On the return to Fairfax Court House, Sarah and Jacob were quiet and didn't converse in any manner because of the Federal cavalrymen surrounding their buggy. Once they came to a halt near the entrance to the courthouse, they drew the attention of many of the soldiers around the structure.

Upon entering the courthouse, Sarah and Jacob were escorted by Lieutenant Roberts to separate rooms on different floors of the building. Jacob was sure an informant had tipped off the Federals, but the question was who? They did everything to keep down suspicion. With Sarah's caution, meticulous skills for this trade, and knowledge of how the game of covert activity was played, he found it unacceptable that she had so easily made a mistake. Unless it was as he had assumed earlier, that she was playing both sides of the game and really believed he was committed in his convictions and was a Confederate agent. Time would tell. Jacob had to exercise patience and see what happened. As for the correspondence he was to deliver, it still remained in the lining pocket of his trousers where Sarah had placed it at Gordonsville.

Time passed and Jacob was growing restless. Jacob believed Federal authorities had questioned Sarah first. He looked out the window and noticed the sun was beginning to fade. According to his timepiece, it was after 6 o'clock in the evening.

After closing the timepiece, Jacob turned his attention to the sound of the key unlocking the door to the room. Lieutenant Roberts and another soldier entered. The officer commanded Jacob to follow.

Jacob complied and was escorted into another room where an officer of higher rank was seated with an individual dressed in civilian attire standing near his desk. Several additional privates were standing near the door's entrance and watching his every move.

The officer looked up from scribbling on some paper and commanded in an abrupt tone, "Sit."

Jacob quietly sat as the officer pushed the papers to the side. "I am Colonel Morgan Lyons," pointing to the civilian gentleman, he continued, "and this is John Carpenter, Chief of Detectives from the Pinkerton Agency in Washington City."

With eyes on the officer, Jacob remained silent and nodded his head in acknowledgement, waiting for him to continue.

Colonel Lyons got right to the point of the interrogation and asked, "Who are you and what are you up to?"

"As it says on my pass, I am George Arnold from Warrenton Junction," Jacob angrily answered.

"According to your pass, you received this from Captain Murdock at Warrenton Junction?" Detective Carpenter asked as he walked to the front of Colonel Lyons' desk.

"That's correct."

"You know that passes are only good for thirty days and no longer. When did you apply for this one?"

"You can tell by the date..."

"I am well aware of the date written on it. I am asking you," Detective Carpenter rudely interrupted.

"Yesterday," Jacob replied glancing at Colonel Lyons' grim expression.

"Captain Murdock hasn't been at Warrenton Junction in over a month," Colonel Lyons said in an irritable tone.

"Though you're right about the date. It says April 7, 1862. Now I am convinced you are hiding something from us. It also means these documents are forged," Detective Carpenter added.

Jacob was surprised and realized he had been double-crossed, but by whom? What would be his next course of action? No one had any knowledge but only a selected few officials why he was in Richmond in the first place. If he exposed his identity, than it would make it almost impossible for him to continue any covert activity in the future.

"Son, you're in a lot of trouble and you have a lot of explaining to do," Colonel Lyons said. "Now we want the truth. Maybe it will make things easier for you."

Jacob was concerned about Sarah. Jacob calmly asked, "What about my wife? Where is she?"

"She is being well provided for," Colonel Lyons replied.

"We have already spoken to her. She was most uncooperative and very un-lady like," Detective Carpenter added in an irritable tone.

"That's because we know nothing. Here in Virginia, our liberties have been stripped from us. We have no rights. Wouldn't that make you mad if you were a lady?"

Jacob was quiet after answering. Whether the colonel realized it or not, they had given him some very important knowledge that told him she was in all probability as he had assumed, a Confederate agent. Jacob knew now whatever he said in his defense they wouldn't believe that he was a Federal agent working for the War Department. Jacob still had a plan and it would resolve his eluding Sarah.

"Tell us what you know. It might go easier on you," Colonel Lyons demanded.

"Like I said, I am George Arnold. There must be some mistake."

"There is no mistake," Detective Carpenter irritably answered as he drew closer to Jacob's face in the attempt to intimidate him.

"Maybe some time in confinement, thinking about the possibility of imprisonment for spying will soften you up and make you let's say, more agreeable," Colonel Lyons added in a threatening tone. He sternly gazed at Jacob and then looked at one of the guards. "Take this man back to his room and if he attempts to escape, you have my orders to shoot him!"

The guard carried out the order by approaching and nudging the back of Jacob's neck with the butt of his musket.

Jacob rose and quietly departed the room with the sentry. He glanced out one of the windows and knew that under the cover of darkness he would have the advantage over his adversaries in an escape.

When the guard opened the door, Jacob quietly entered the room. He immediately glanced out the window where he noticed another sentry nearby walking his post. Time was on his side. All he had to do was wait patiently until the right moment. Jacob sat on the floor and closed his eyes and briefly rested for what was to come.

*　　*　　*　　*

It was late and completely dark in Jacob's room. He noticed through the window the village of Fairfax Court House was quiet and from the little light from the moon, he could tell, there were not many people around. He noticed the military drilling near the courthouse building had ceased and from the sound of the music most activity of any kind was taking place within the soldiers' camps.

Jacob rose to his feet and lit a small candle on a stand. He crouched below the window, looking to see where the outside guard was located. He was pleased the guard wasn't near the window to see what was about to happen. He began to put his plan into effect by crying out in pain. At first there wasn't a response, and as he continued, the guard outside the door demanded, "What's going on in there?"

"I'm in pain! It must have been that lousy food I ate for supper. I need help!"

Jacob continued to moan in agony, waiting for the guard's response. When there wasn't an immediate response, Jacob fell against the stand with the candle and crashed to the floor. Quickly, but quietly, he rose and hid behind the door.

Immediately, the guard came rushing through the door into the dark room. When he did, Jacob quietly closed the door and jumped the guard from behind, overpowering him with his strength and easily subduing him.

As the guard lay unconscious, Jacob began to remove the soldier's uniform from his body. He searched the uniform trouser pockets looking for his purse or some means of identification just in case he needed the information such as name and company. After removing his own clothing, and the envelope from his trousers lining, Jacob swiftly dressed in the soldier's uniform. Fortunately, they were both about the same height and weight. Jacob picked up the musket lying on the floor.

When ready, Jacob slowly opened the door and glanced around to see if another soldier was nearby. Convinced that it was safe to proceed, he headed directly toward the entrance of the building. After opening the door, he noticed several soldiers along the stairway on the veranda casually talking.

Jacob paused and studied his surroundings. He noticed some of the soldiers assigned to sentry duty were still awake and sitting around the campfire waiting their turn to assume the duty. Others were standing their post at various locations around the courthouse. He stepped out the door entrance and began to walk by the two soldiers, ignoring them. A sergeant called out, "Hey Laddy. Where are you going?"

Turning around, Jacob looked at the soldiers and answered, "Back to camp."

"Were you on guard duty?" The Sergeant asked.

"Yes sir," Jacob calmly replied, knowing he had to carefully guard his words.

"Well Laddy, I must admit, I don't remember you. You are not from my Company," the Sergeant replied in a suspicious tone as he approached Jacob to get a better look.

"I am from D Company."

"D Company? Laddy, A Company, my Company has the Provost duty. What were you doing in there?"

"I was sent with a telegram for Mr. Carpenter and was told by the clerk he was gone." Jacob continued the ruse, "I temporarily had to relieve Private Slater, who I happen to know was delayed."

"That's my bloody job," the Sergeant angrily answered.

"True, but when one must unexpectedly relieve himself," Jacob replied laughingly, "he looks for help. I just happened to be there to assist."

"Go on, get the bloody out of here you dang fool."

Jacob didn't look back, but knew the two soldiers were still watching him. He wondered if the old Sergeant was still suspicious and would call him back for further interrogation. At the bottom of the stairway, he turned and headed toward camp. Once Jacob was out of sight of the two soldiers and the sentries around the courthouse, he disappeared into the night.

Chapter Twelve

After leaving the courthouse building, Jacob moved in a northward direction on foot until coming to the first farm. While everyone was sleeping in the farmhouse, he stole a horse and continued rapidly in the direction of the Potomac River where he hoped to cross the river at Rowser's Ford near Dranesville, Virginia into Montgomery County, Maryland. Jacob had a Unionist friend by the name of Samuel Chambers that owned a farm along the river on the outskirts of Washington City where he would be able to get something to eat and some information. It was the long way, but he couldn't afford to be detained by a Federal cavalry patrol. He was sure the Federals had sounded the alarm at Fairfax Court House after his escape. They would be waiting for him if he approached by way of Long Bridge like his original intentions. Jacob would use Samuel to slip him into the city unnoticed past Federal pickets.

It was after midnight when Jacob arrived at the Chamber's homestead. The house was dark, giving the appearance of lifelessness. Jacob walked onto the porch and knocked at the door. After several minutes had passed, a middle-aged gentleman with a long dark beard and a balding head slowly opened the door. He noticed he had a revolver in his right hand. Jacob spoke his name.

Samuel took a long look and opened the door the rest of the way and glanced around outside before closing it. He gestured for Jacob to follow him to the back of the house.

Once Samuel and Jacob were in the kitchen, Jacob asked, "What's going on? Why all of the mystery?"

"Old man Henley has been watching this place lately."

"Who is he?"

"Oh, he lives down the road a piece. I suspect that he and his son Owen are working for the rebels. At times, I've noticed one or the other passing along this road. More so than they used to. Owen hangs out along the river, acting like he is fishing, but I know he is watching to see who comes and goes from here."

"Are you sure they are spying?"

"I'm afraid so. They know about me."

Jacob took a long gaze at Samuel and knew by the tone of his voice and his actions that he was greatly troubled. "How did they find out about you?"

"It's a long story. Several months ago, while in the city at the National Hotel, I met a lady that was a lot younger than me by the name of Molly Wells."

"Hold it right there!" Jacob said. "Is this Molly that you call her have long brown hair, dark eyes, medium height, and shapely. Maybe 22 to 24 years old?"

When Samuel didn't reply, but instead hung his head, Jacob walked to the far end of the room in frustration knowing the female's identity. He turned and said, "She is an agent for the rebels. Does she positively know about you?"

Samuel quietly nodded his head and walked over to the table and poured a drink of whisky. He downed the glass and wiped his mouth, sighing.

"How does she know?" Jacob asked in an irritated voice.

"I was there with fresh tomatoes and corn. I was keeping my ears open for anything that might be of use since it was once an establishment where many Southern Congressmen had patronized. I had finished my delivery; I had a few drinks in the bar. I was trying to listen to other conversations or pick up some rumors. Anything of use. When it seemed like it was going to be a slow night, I left the establishment when suddenly I bumped into her in the lobby. I apologized, helped her gather her things that she had dropped, then departed.

Samuel somberly continued. "Once outside, I lit my pipe and was heading for my wagon. I heard her calling. When I turned around, she was standing there. She asked me if I was missing anything and immediately I patted my pockets with my hands and she held up my change purse. We began to laugh and one thing led to another. The next thing I knew, we were exchanging conversation like we had always known each other. We returned to the lobby and sat for a spell exchanging a few laughs and talking. After that night, I saw her several times the following week, and then she just disappeared."

"What did you talk about? What did you tell her?" Jacob said angrily.

"I didn't tell her I was spying, believe me," Samuel pleaded.

"What did you do to make her believe you were working covertly?"

"You have to try and understand when a man loses his wife and is alone for several years, his desires and emotions build up. He tries his best to impress someone, especially as attractive and young as Molly."

"Her real name is Sarah and I guess at this point, it doesn't matter how she found out," Jacob snapped. "I have run into some problems and I need you to get me through the picket lines into the city."

"When?"

"We need to leave immediately. I don't want anyone to know that I've been here or that I have been seen with you."

Chapter Thirteen

While Jacob was changing into some civilian clothing for the trip into the city, Samuel went into the barn to saddle several horses. Samuel knew the immediate area and the surrounding trails to get him past the Federal pickets. He did this because he didn't have a pass in his possession and any delay could be crucial in his timing. Jacob was already a day behind schedule because of the Fairfax Court House situation. With the cover of darkness, and the lateness of the evening, no one would know his intentions.

Once ready, Samuel and Jacob departed the homestead and rode across the fields in the direction of the river where they eventually disappeared into the wooded area on a secluded path only known by Samuel. It ran parallel to the Potomac.

Within the hour, Samuel and Jacob were near Georgetown, proceeding near the area of the Aqueduct Bridge where the Frederick Road crossed Rock Creek and into Washington City. It was near this area they left the road and crossed over a field that overlooked the bridge, well out of sight of Federal guards picketing the area. They continued in a northeast direction until they crossed Rock Creek. They then proceeded toward their destination, which was 1325 K Street. The residence was the home of one of the most powerful men in the Lincoln cabinet, Secretary of War Edwin Stanton.

Samuel and Jacob arrived in front of the Secretary's residence and Jacob noticed several Federal soldiers posted at the front entrance to the three-story brick dwelling. While Samuel stayed mounted, Jacob slowly dismounted and approached one of the sentries. The guard commanded, "Halt there!"

"I am friendly," Jacob answered, complying with the order.

"Who are you? What are you doing here this hour of the morning?"

"I am Captain Jacob Martin of the United States Army. I have very important documents for Secretary Stanton to see. It is of the utmost urgency that I see him immediately."

When the guard paused in apparent indecision, Jacob ordered, "Now Corporal!"

The soldier kept his eyes on Jacob while ordering a private, "Go and get Lieutenant Stanley."

Shortly, the soldier appeared with the officer. Lieutenant Stanley walked from the entrance of the residence and asked in an abrupt tone, "What is the meaning of all of this commotion this early in the morning?"

"I am an officer with the United States Army and I have important information that only Secretary Stanton should see."

"Did you check his pass?" The officer asked as he turned and looked at the corporal.

"No sir."

"Let's see it," the officer requested turning toward Jacob.

"Instead, if you'll allow me," Jacob replied, "I'll show you."

Jacob removed his timepiece and its back cover. He removed a piece of paper that had been folded up within and handed it to the officer.

The officer's eyes glanced over its contents. It just simply said, "Believe the bearer," signed Abraham Lincoln. The officer handed the paper back to Jacob with an expression of relief and said, "Follow me sir."

Once on the inside of the Secretary's residence, Lieutenant Stanley escorted Jacob to the parlor. Immediately one of the servants entered the room and was asked to awaken Secretary Stanton.

Lieutenant Stanley and Jacob remained standing without conversation. Jacob walked to the fireplace and gazed at the family photographs covering the mantel. He knew the Secretary had lost his first wife and child. Currently, Secretary Stanton was married a second time to Ellen and they had a son by the name of James.

Jacob continued to gaze at the family heirlooms, he knew before the war, Secretary Stanton had been a successful attorney and had made a reputation for himself when he defended New York congressman Daniel Sickles against murder charges. Sickles had shot and killed Philip Barton Keyes, the son of Francis Scott Keyes after Sickles caught Keyes with his wife in an adulterous affair. During the trail, Stanton was the first to used the defense of temporary insanity and Sickles was acquitted of the charges against him.

Jacob also knew Stanton was a Democrat in a predominantly Republican Administration. He had only been on the job for the last three months and was possibly unaware of his role within the military.

Lieutenant Stanley walked over to the fireplace and said to Jacob, "I hope whatever is in your possession will be enough to keep Mr. Stanton from throwing both of us out of this house and keep us out of jail."

"I heard he was difficult to get along with." Jacob replied gazing at the officer. "But whatever I have in my possession, Mr. Stanton will have to decide its importance."

"That's right! I will!" Secretary Stanton said in an irritated tone as he entered the room. "What do you have for me that is so important to awaken me at 3:30 in the morning?"

As Jacob approached Secretary Stanton, he pulled from his coat the envelope and handed it to him. Immediately, Secretary Stanton handed the envelope to Lieutenant Stanley. The officer glanced at Jacob as he carefully opened the document. Once opened, Lieutenant Stanley handed the paper back to Secretary Stanton. The Secretary quietly read the contents while the officer and Jacob stood nearby. Once finished, he removed his spectacles and rubbed his eyes. The secretary glanced at Jacob and said, "It's not written in code."

"That's strange," Lieutenant Stanley answered.

"Apparently Mrs. Greenhow was the only one who knew how to write and decipher the code. She didn't have the opportunity to teach someone else how to do so before being arrested."

"And then too, maybe she just didn't trust anyone," Lieutenant Stanley swiftly replied.

"Who are you delivering this to?" Secretary Stanton asked.

"A lady by the name of Amanda."

"Where does she live?" Lieutenant Stanley asked.

"I don't know. She was supposed to have a request for a laborer in yesterday's Evening Star. I have been instructed by Captain Norris in Richmond to answer it. He gave me specific instruction as to what she'll say in order to know that I have this information for her from Secretary Randolph."

Secretary Stanton turned to the officer and asked, "Go and get the paper. It's in my library on the desk." Turning his attention again to Jacob, he continued, "I see, and you will be the one to do so. For your information, this Amanda as you call her is to find out if McDowell's Corp will be joining McClellan forces or staying around the Washington fortifications. She is to be diligent and at once send a courier with information by the most practical route when his intentions are known. Also the rebels would like to know a fairly good estimate of McClellan's present troop strength on the peninsula." Suddenly, the Secretary threw the paper on a nearby table and shouted, "I am curious where she is getting her information."

"I know in part," Jacob answered.

"Who! I want to know who would be so treacherous and commit such atrocities!" Secretary Stanton shouted.

"All I know is that he is a senator. For some time, she has continued to have a relationship of some sorts with him and has obtained valuable information that has previously been sent back to Richmond."

"That greatly troubles me," Secretary Stanton answered in a angry tone.

Secretary Stanton and Jacob's attention were drawn to Lieutenant Stanley as he entered the room with the paper in his hand. When the officer pointed to the column, the Secretary glanced over its contents. He said in an emotional tone, "The request is in here," the Secretary added as he handed the newspaper to Jacob. "We need to find out who the scoundrel is so I may severely deal with him."

Secretary Stanton paused and quietly paced the floor, looking over the paper that was to be delivered to Amanda. He turned and looked at Lieutenant Stanley, handing him the paper and asked, "Could you reseal this?" Again he began to pace the floor, then turned and said to Jacob, "After Lieutenant Stanley gives you the envelope, I want you to find out who she is getting her information from. Afterward, I want you to return here again late at night by the back entrance. I am sure the rebels have someone constantly watching my home to see who comes and goes."

"Yes sir, I will. I am sure she'll be giving me information to take back to the rebel government."

"And I need to see it," Secretary Stanton answered as Lieutenant Stanley handed Jacob the resealed envelope.

"What do you feel the mood is in the rebel capital?" Lieutenant Stanley asked.

Pausing and looking quietly at the officer and Secretary Stanton, Jacob confidently replied, "Jeff Davis and the generals feel more threaten by navy warships coming up the James and bombarding Richmond more so than McClellan or McDowell's forces uniting."

The Secretary quietly nodded in agreement and with a grim expression, he departed from the room. Tomorrow Jacob knew he would have a greater understanding of who Amanda was and who was supplying her with information.

Chapter Fourteen

Early the next morning, Jacob arrived at a three-story house at 390 16th Street, carrying over his shoulder a pick and shovel. After glancing across the street at the gardeners working around St. John's Church, he turned his attention to his surroundings and glanced at the newspaper. He walked to a tree in front of the dwelling and paused, looking, then walked up the stairs and knocked on the door several times. As he waited for an answer, he knew Amanda would have certain questions to ask to ascertain his identity as a Confederate agent. Captain Morris had given Jacob the key answer before leaving Secretary Randolph's residence.

Again Jacob knocked. This time an elderly male servant opened the door and he held up the paper pointing to the advertisement. "I am answering this announcement. Who do I speak to?"

The servant quietly gestured for Jacob to enter the vestibule and wait. After a few moments, the servant returned and asked Jacob to follow him into the parlor. Once he entered the room, he gazed at the lady sitting on the sofa, dressed lavishly with a headpiece of daisies covering her auburn hair. After she excused the servant, she said in a soft and congenial manner, "Good morning, my name is Amanda Wilson."

"Good morning ma'am, I am Jacob Martin."

"I understand you are answering the announcement that I placed in the Evening Star?" Amanda asked as her green eyes glanced at Jacob.

"Yes ma'am. I would have been here sooner, but I was delayed. Everywhere I go, someone wants to see my pass. I guess I am still not use to such loss of liberties."

"I see. But you know these are very perilous times that we live in." Amanda answered as a female servant entered the room and poured her morning tea.

Jacob withheld his answer until the servant had finished and departed. He calmly answered, "Yes, but we are looking for better times."

"And to what shall we look?"

"To the thirteen stars."

Amanda's expression changed to relief as she rose from the sofa and approached. She softly said when she came near, "What are you carrying?"

Jacob pulled from his haversack the envelope and handed it to Amanda. She glanced around to see if there were any other servants nearby, then she opened the document. Jacob stood quietly near as her eyes carefully followed each line. When Amanda was finished, she walked over to the fireplace, tossed the paper into the blazing fire and watched until it was totally consumed by the flames. When she was satisfied of its destruction, she walked over again to where Jacob was standing and said in a serious tone, "As of now, I don't have an answer, but I should know something within the next couple of days. Until then, you must stay busy working outside digging a small drain ditch that will run away from the rear corner of the house. The water does build up at times and it would be a service to me. At nights, you can stay over the carriage house in the rear. But stay out of sight unless called for. Understand?"

Quietly nodding, Jacob turned and walked outside to the area in the rear of the house where Amanda had instructed and began the labor to cover his disguise.

*   *   *   *

Darkness had settled over the city and Jacob was sitting in his room, looking out the window in the direction of Amanda's house. Throughout the day, he had kept his eyes on anything that would give him any information on how the

Washington spy-ring functioned. He knew the residence with the fence around it several doors down was the former home of the Confederate spymaster, Rose Greenhow. Before the outset of the war, Greenhow had mingled and developed close relationships with the most elite in Washington society. With the outbreak of the conflict, Greenhow used her wily ways to garnish information from Washington politicians and army generals to pass on to Confederate authorities in Richmond.

Now imprisoned at the Old Capital on First Street, Rose Greenhow was awaiting her freedom, but the spy-ring that she had mastered was still thriving and functioning in its covert activity to gain valuable intelligence. Amanda was apparently a lady who had learned the trade well under Mrs. Greenhow and maybe was operating the spy-ring in her absence. Jacob had to find out. By his first impression of her, she played the role to its fullest with her flamboyant demeanor and gracious ways.

As the hours passed, Jacob kept the room dark without candlelight to give Amanda the impression that he was tired and sleeping, but he had other intentions in mind.

It was 8:30 in the evening by Jacob's timepiece when he noticed an enclosed carriage come to a halt in front of Amanda's house. He couldn't see who the individual was, but he thought it might be the person who had inadvertently been giving Amanda valuable information. He waited for another twenty minutes until he knew she was occupied, then walked down to the lower level. Pausing, Jacob looked around to see where the servants might be. He didn't know with certainty their loyalty to Amanda, but he had learned not to trust anyone.

Looking into the nighttime sky, Jacob noticed the moon was hidden behind the clouds. Glancing at the house and noticing that a light was burning in the kitchen area along the back porch, he proceeded with caution in that direction, but stayed out of its direct reflection. Once by the porch, there was a stairway he noticed earlier during the afternoon. This would give him access to the upper porch and possibly entrance through the door on that level of the house. Jacob looked around and slowly climbed the stairway to the upper porch. There was only one light burning. He paused and cautiously looked into the room and noticed it appeared vacant. He continued until coming to the door that would give him entrance into the house.

Jacob attempted to lift the latch, and much to his surprise it was open. The upper level was dimly lit by gaslight. He quietly closed the door. He continued to glance around and memorize the layout of the upstairs area. Softly, Jacob walked along the rug covering the floor until coming to a bedchamber in the front of the house. The door was wide open. He glanced into the room. It too, was also dimly lit, but lit enough to reveal its lavish decorations and heavy drapes covering the front windows. This must be Amanda's room.

Jacob turned and walked the short distance where he noticed a stairway leading to the first floor. There were voices, one male and the other female, coming from the dining area. He assumed Amanda was entertaining a dinner guest. This would be a good time to search her room for any valuable information since she was preoccupied.

Returning once more to Amanda's bedchamber, Jacob began to look through her dresses, drawers, and wardrobe, but turned up nothing that would implicate her or the identity of the individual she was gathering her information from. He turned and noticed several decorative bonnets. One was on a table the other in a hatbox. Jacob examined the green bonnet on the table, but when he pulled the blue one from the box, he noticed the lining where the seam came together had been cleanly separated. His suspicions were aroused.

Suddenly without warning, Jacob heard the sound of footsteps approaching through the hallway. It was more than one person. He quickly looked around for a place to hide, but there was none to be found. By instinct, he crawled under the bed because there was a large spread covering its sides. It might be Amanda and her guest. He must remain calm.

Chapter Fifteen

Once Amanda and her male guest entered the room, she gazed at her guest as he slowly closed the door. She knew her intentions were being accomplished by the pleased and content expression on his face. As he removed his frock coat and vest, Amanda looked into the mirror to make sure that her auburn hair was in place. She gazed at her companion in the mirror and asked, "What time will Abigail be arriving tomorrow from Boston?"

"On the late afternoon train."

"I guess we won't be seeing each other for awhile?" Amanda asked as she turned to face him.

"No, it wouldn't be safe."

"Oh Harry, I am so tired of this kind of a relationship with you." Amanda answered in a frustrated tone. "You just use her to maintain your righteous image among your colleagues on the Committee for Military Affairs and the President. What about us?"

Harry slowly approached and quietly placed his hands on Amanda's shoulders. Without another word, he passionately kissed her.

Amanda abruptly broke their embrace and said, "That's not good enough. I want more."

"Right now I can't give you more," Harry somberly answered. "If I am suspected of infidelity it will cost me my position and reputation. That will mean my chances of running for the presidency someday will be tarnished."

"And I guess you feel they need you more than I do?" Amanda snapped as she walked near her bed.

"The war is at a crucial point. Jackson has been making serious threats in the Valley and that's why McDowell's Corp hasn't been given orders to join McClellan on the peninsula. We don't know what the rebels' intentions may be. McClellan has 100,000 men and he still continues to ask for reinforcements, but for now, he'll have to do with the troops that he has." Pausing and shaking his head in frustration, Harry continued, "I must admit I have a lot to deal with at the moment. What happens along the peninsula could determine the outcome of this war."

"I am sorry," Amanda said approaching Harry. "I guess I was only thinking of myself." Pausing and quietly brushing her hand across his cheeks, she continued in a soft tone, "Your concerns are my concerns my love. Do you think the President and Secretary Stanton will agree to eventually allow McDowell to join with McClellan?"

"They are like everyone else in the administration. They worry about Jackson. What if he is reinforced and drives against Banks, defeating him and crosses the Potomac into Maryland?" Amanda was silent as Harry continued to pour out his frustrations, "Well, I'll tell you. At that point there is nothing to stop him from capturing Washington and all of us in the government. Let me ask you, how embarrassing would that be to us as a nation with our friends like the British or French?"

At the thought of such a scenario, Harry turned from Amanda and walked over to a table in the sitting area of the room and poured a whiskey. He gulped it down in one swallow.

Amanda came near and embraced him, knowing she had accomplished all that was requested of her by the Richmond authorities. She said as she looked into his eyes, "Everything will work out. For now my love, you must forget about the war and politics."

As Harry and Amanda began once more to kiss, there was a knock at her door.

"Who is there?" Amanda asked.

"It's Sissy."

Amanda opened the door and asked, "What is the matter?"

"Dere's a gentleman in da parlor dat needs to speak to Mr. Harry. He says it's important."

"Tell him that I'll be right there," Harry answered.

"I wonder what this is all about?" Amanda anxiously asked.

"It must be important when I am called upon this hour of the evening. Maybe it has something to do with what we were just speaking about."

Harry put on his vest and coat and proceeded to the downstairs with Amanda following closely behind.

Jacob looked out from under the bed to make sure they were gone. He rose to his feet and proceeded into the hallway. Jacob was tempted to try and discover in which location of the house that Amanda's library was located. He wanted to investigate to see if she had any incriminating letters, recent stolen documents, identities of her Washington associates, and most of all her cipher for sending coded messages. After evaluating further risk of discovery, he decided to depart from the way he entered.

Chapter Sixteen

The next morning after breakfast, Jacob continued digging the trench for water drainage. No sooner had he begun than he was summoned to the house by Amanda. Jacob knew she would want him to depart as soon as possible for Richmond with the information she had received from Senator Harry Putman the previous evening. The question that concerned him the most was would he be able to pass by Secretary Stanton's residence with the intelligence.

Immediately, Jacob entered the house and was escorted to the library. Once he entered the room, he found Amanda hastily writing on paper.

Amanda didn't look at Jacob, but was aware of his presence. She asked in a soft tone as she continued to write her lines, "Jacob, did you sleep well last night?"

"Yes ma'am."

"Did you have plenty to eat this morning?"

"Yes Ma'am."

"Well then, you must return to Richmond immediately," Amanda answered, looking up from writing.

"I am ready to leave now if need be."

Amanda folded up the piece of paper and handed it to Jacob, commanding, "Return this to Captain Norris." Jacob quietly turned to leave when Amanda continued, "I have someone in southern Maryland who will help you cross the Potomac."

"I didn't come that way because I was informed right now it might be too risky since an agent was recently captured."

"True, the risk is high, but this must go through by express. It is the shortest way with contacts that you'll need to complete the assignment. When you arrive at Pope's Creek, you will inquire of Mr. Thomas Jones and he will assist you and place you in touch with the name of the next contact you will need to know." Amanda laughed, then continued in a serious tone, "It's apparent you don't know anything about this type of duty?"

"No, actually, I am nothing more than a banker in Richmond. For some reason, there are those in Richmond who believe for some unknown reason that I would be good at doing this. But the truth is, I am afraid of getting caught and detained like I was at Fairfax Court House."

"What did you do that the Yankees allowed you to leave?" Amanda said as she stood and approached Jacob.

"I escaped after they apprehended me for not having a pass. Someone, who, I don't know double-crossed me. It grieves me that I had to leave an associate behind…female at that."

"That happens because there are as we say in this game, double agents. You must be suspicious of everyone you come into contact with. You trust no one or it might cost you your life. As for your associate, they will probably release her after they warn her by reading the Articles of War and promising to severely punish her if caught again." She paused and advanced closer to Jacob. She smiled and continued, "I don't know why, but I am very fond of you. You have an innocence about you that is very attractive to me. But unfortunately, we don't have the time to let's say, get better acquainted. For now, you must go and get this information to Richmond."

Jacob gazed at the concerned expression on Amanda's face and the sensitivity her eyes revealed. He assured, "Don't worry about me, I'll get through."

"Take care of yourself, you hear. And come back soon."

After departing the house and gathering his tools, Jacob departed for Secretary Stanton's home. He took a longer way so he wouldn't arouse suspicion since both homes were on the same street. Jacob wanted to make sure he wasn't being followed and careful not to raise suspicion. When Jacob arrived, he found the Secretary had already departed for the War Department. It wasn't his intention to go there because he didn't know if enemy agents were working within the department that might reveal his identity to the Washington underground. Jacob was certain the building was being observed by Southern agents to see who comes and goes. He sent a sealed envelope to Secretary Stanton. It was a request that Amanda would not be arrested at this time until more information could be garnished concerning the names of her associates within the spy ring. He also included Senator Harry Putman's name. A trustworthy courier carried all the information to Secretary Stanton.

When finished, Jacob mounted a horse and headed in the direction of Pope's Creek. Once he arrived, he easily found Mr. Jones, his contact, who ferried him across the Potomac River. After crossing to the Virginia shore, Jacob was told where he could get another mount. This time his contact was a lady. She supplied him with dinner and another horse. Jacob continued until crossing the Rappahannock and into the town of Port Royal. After briefly resting and receiving shelter from the heavy rains at the home of a local physician, he rode swiftly over the last eighteen miles arriving in Richmond in less than twenty-four hours. Jacob found Captain Norris and delivered the information he was carrying to him. Jacob cooperated fully in order to win their confidence and to be used for future excursions to the North. On this particular journey North, he had learned many valuable lessons and some of the tricks of the trade in espionage.

Chapter Seventeen

Operations for Confederate forces were not unfolding as envisioned by Richmond authorities during April of 1862. Along the Tennessee River at a place called Shiloh, the Confederate army under the command of General Albert Sidney Johnston was defeated after gaining what appeared to be a victory the previous day over General Ulysses S. Grant's Federal army. In the fighting, General Johnston was mortally wounded and died shortly before the fighting concluded on the field of glory.

In the east, Joe Johnston's Confederate army eventually reinforced General John Magruder's forces at Yorktown, but with McClellan's massive Federal legions, the rebel army was compelled to give up the historic town. During the retreat toward Williamsburg, Johnston's forces under Generals Longstreet and Hill fought a valiant rear guard action, but still continued the slow retreat along the Virginia Peninsula toward Richmond. The cautious McClellan slowly and methodically followed his foe.

In early May, the Federal army continued its move up the peninsula and their warships steamed along the James River toward Richmond. Out of great fear, farmers and refugees from all along the peninsula streamed into the city looking for shelter from McClellan's invading legions. With the Yankees at their doorstep, panic began to spread among the citizens within the city. Anxious expressions about the uncertainty of events were evident upon the faces of men and women, young and old alike. Some of the city's residents fled the capital, leaving their homes deserted. One of those individuals was Varina Davis, President Davis's wife. Wagons with valuable possessions were seen heading south, while canal boats headed west carrying individuals with their trunks and possessions. Contempt for the Yankees increased as citizens swore loudly their cries of oaths and bitterness toward the invaders. Men in and out of uniform were seen heading toward the river to repel any kind of invasion. Would the city's population collapse and break into lawlessness? Could the inadequately equipped Confederate army prevail against the Yankee invaders?

Off in the distance, Richmond's citizens could hear the muffled sound of artillery fire eight miles to the southeast at a curvature in the James River known as Drewry's Bluff. Would this be the decisive battle that would determine the fate of the Confederate capital and the Confederacy?

The fighting at Drewry's Bluff continued most of the day with some damage inflicted on the Federal warships. The five ships, including the Monitor, were not able to penetrate the Confederate fortifications. Naval forces, which were on a 100-foot high cliff, fired well-aimed heavy cannon fire at Fort Darling with deadly accuracy. The selection of old sunken ships in the river formed a barrier that helped the Confederates turn back the attack and stall the Federal invaders by water. For now, Richmond enjoyed a brief reprieve.

As McClellan's Federal army continued to advance on Richmond from the southeast, McDowell's 40,000-man Federal army was marching from Fredericksburg to the north. There was hope of uniting the two armies, but the continuous looming threat that Stonewall Jackson's army posed in the Shenandoah Valley with several recent victories caused President Lincoln and Secretary of War Stanton to call McDowell's forces back to Fredericksburg.

Once the Federal army under McClellan was near Richmond, Joe Johnston looked for an opportunity to strike the Federal forces a blow. It came on May 31, when McClellan split his army. Johnston's Confederates attacked two Federal Corps that appeared isolated south of the Chickahominy River in an uncoordinated effort. The Confederates were successful, but the casualties were high. Between both blue and gray, there were 11,000-men that lay as casualties on the field. This was the greatest sacrifice of life since the war began in the east. During the battle, General Joe Johnston was severely wounded and now a new commander, General Robert E. Lee, assumed the generalship of the army.

Before the war, Lee had been trained as an engineer at the United States Military Academy at West Point, New York. During the war with Mexico, Lee served gallantly under General Winfield Scott. In 1852, he was appointed the Superintendent at West Point until he became colonel of the 2nd Cavalry. General Scott was very fond of Lee. At the outset of the Civil War, Scott offered Lee the command of the Federal army. Instead, Lee refused General Scott's request and pledged his allegiance with his native state of Virginia. Now, he was placed in command by President Davis of the 60,000-man Confederate army facing McClellan on the outskirts of Richmond.

Lee quickly took the intuitive. On the afternoon of June 26, Confederate forces attacked the Federal Army's V Corps under General Fitz John Porter, which held the army's right flank north of the Chickahominy River near a small hamlet known as Mechanicsville. The fighting was vigorous and uncoordinated. Stonewall Jackson's army from the Valley was supposed to play a role in the offensive, but didn't participate in the effort.

After the fighting that raged throughout the afternoon around Mechanicsville, the 8th Virginia of Pickett's Brigade rested. They were ordered to draw eighty rounds of ammunition and to cook three days rations for the fighting that was sure to come the next day.

*   *   *   *

That evening, Benjamin Kelly was sitting around the campfire looking aimlessly into the flames. He had participated and witnessed heavy fighting at Williamsburg and Seven Pines. Some of his friends in the regiment and the brigade were now casualties of war. There were only 219 men left out of the 544 present for duty in December of '61.

For a brief moment, Benjamin thought of Rachel. He knew she must be worried over the news that was surely being received at home concerning the fighting between the two armies along the Virginia Peninsula. The loneliness he experienced and the void within his heart was agonizing. Almost constantly during his spare time in camp or on the march, he continued to send correspondences home, hoping with each passing day, Rachel would know he was still alive. Not a day passed that he didn't anxiously await news from his wife or the family.

Benjamin's thoughts were interrupted when he heard the voice of James Bell asking, "I bet you I know who you are thinking of?"

Looking up from the flames and turning around, a smile crossed Benjamin's face as he answered in a low tone, "Yeah, my wife and family. Every time we go into a fight, they are the last ones on my mind before the business of battle with the enemy."

James knelt down next to Benjamin and gazed for a long time at the flickering flames. He answered somberly, "I know. With every passing moment we have time, I try to drop Lacey a few lines to let her know that I am doing fine…the woman worries too much. And then too, maybe I am worried that I won't see her again. So Benjamin, it's only natural to feel the way that we do. It doesn't mean we are any less of a man than the most brave among us because I am sure they think and feel the same as we do. To worry about a destiny that we can't control is the human thing to do."

"For a man who claims he doesn't have much book learning, you sure have a way of looking at life."

"I've learned the hard way, through experience," James answered with a grin. "I know according to the Good Book I only have one day at a time. I've learned to appreciate what life has to offer and give for that one day."

"A lot of us need to learn the Way. As I look across the faces of these young men in the regiment, barely out of their teens, I see some try to appear courageous and noble, and speak the words to reinforce it, but I know they are hiding their fears of the uncertainty of battle and maybe their own death. And still the others you can tell by their somber expressions. It's like reading a book. They are scared, not knowing if they'll die in this fight or if they'll live to see another day, or like us, their family."

"It makes good sense to me, especially knowing a lot of good men got killed out there today," James replied as he stood to his feet.

Benjamin looked up as he removed his skillet with its bacon. He said, "I appreciate our little chats. You have a way with words that I don't."

Quietly gazing and nodding at Benjamin, James took a puff from his pipe and turned around, walking toward another group of men cooking their rations.

* * * *

The next morning when the Confederate army was ready to seize the initiative and attack the Federal V Corps behind its strong fortifications, they discovered Porter had already retreated and gave up the ground he had valiantly held the previous day.

Immediately, General A. P. Hill's 12,000-man division began the pursuit of Porter's Corp, moving eastward down the River Road. On Hill's right and closest to the river was James Longstreet's division.

"Keep the men moving! You officers, close up those ranks," General George Pickett shouted.

Benjamin saluted Pickett as he passed by the officer sitting on his charger along the road. He turned and shouted,

"Let's move it boys. Let the general see what A Company of the 8th can do."

General Pickett smiled at Benjamin as he approached and rode along side of the 8th Virginia. Pickett asked, "Where do you hail from Lieutenant?"

"Loudoun County, sir."

"Well Lieutenant, I must say you keep your men in good order. If the rest of the army is as disciplined as yours, then maybe today will be a good day to beat the Yanks. I hear your boys from Loudoun County are good in a scrap?"

"We have yet to run from a fight and are always ready for one."

"I am sure we'll have our hands full, but I want you to remember that we have to drive those people off Virginia soil. Exhort your boys to do so. Tell them the Yankees are invading our land, state, and nation. And what they'll be doing is freeing their loved ones and family from tyranny."

"Yes sir, I will. These men are the best Loudoun County has to offer."

Again, General Pickett smiled and saluted. He turned his horse around and returned to his aides and staff waiting for him in a field just off of the road.

It was difficult for Benjamin to remain focused when there was the possibility a great battle would be fought today. His mind was constantly on Rachel, but at this time, who wasn't pondering on a loved one that they had left behind in Loudoun County. As difficult as it was, they must somehow stop thinking of them because off in the distance, he could hear the rumbling sound of artillery and musketry. He observed the haze of cannon and musket smoke lifting over the wooded area to his front. According to his timepiece, it was 4:00 o'clock in the afternoon. The word was passed along the line to close it up and move at the double quick. Benjamin knew this was it. A great battle was to be fought before the sun would set today.

Chapter Eighteen

The roar of artillery and musketry from the area of Gaines' Mill seemed to increase with every step that Benjamin and the 8th Virginia took in their rapid advanced toward the direction of battle. During the whole time, Benjamin was waving his sword and exhorting his men to follow him and move quickly along.

Finally, Pickett's brigade passed through a wooded area where they paused in an undulating field. There was heavy timber on all sides. There, they formed in line of battle.

Benjamin inspected the alignment of his company. He passed by his men with sword resting on his shoulder. He witnessed the somber, cold, and determined expressions covering the faces of the harden veterans that had served with him since the opening battle at Manassas. Some of the newer men of the regiment and in his company appeared to be restless, exhibiting the nervousness and anxiety that comes with the unknown and uncertainty. He noticed one young soldier by the name of Arden. Tears flowed freely down his cheeks. Benjamin paused and looked the young man in the eyes, asking, "Soldier, why the tears?"

Over the bursting sound from artillery shells exploding in the air, the soldier answered, "It is all wrong, it is all wrong sir, I shouldn't be here."

"Arden, you have a job and duty to do just like the rest of us. Every man standing here is counting on you to do just that."

"I know, but I am thinking of my Mary Ann at home. I received a correspondence from her the other day telling me that I am the father of a baby boy."

"That is all the more reason you have to pull yourself together, so that you can return home and see your son."

"Sir, I have this strange feeling that won't happen. That's why the tears. I'll never lay eyes on my son."

Benjamin remained silent. He knew how the young boy felt because he was also trying to hide his true feelings. War and soldiering wasn't an easy occupation and wasn't one that anyone would be fond of pursuing. He placed his hand on the soldier's shoulder and calmly said, "I know how you feel. I will do my best to look out for you and to make sure you'll return home to your family."

The brigade was ordered to advance and to make a vigorous demonstration to take some of the pressure off of Hill and Ewell's divisions to their left. The order was passed along the line. Battle and regimental flags were fluttering in the afternoon breeze, the drum and fife were playing the patriotic tune, Dixie, and the men stepped off with their officers in the lead to meet their adversary. Suddenly from across Boatswain Swamp, Benjamin and his company were exposed to a furious-raking cannonade and musketry that sent many from the brigade to the ground as casualties. Without hesitation, Benjamin continued to lead his men forward. He saw some begin to shriek under the heavy fire from the Federals along the hillside. He grabbed one soldier by the shirt and pointed with his sword, saying, "There is the enemy up there, now do your part to your country and if you must die, then let it be with honor."

The soldier still wasn't persuaded. He began to turn back when Benjamin took the blunt end of his sword and struck the private in the back of the neck. As the private was recovering from the blow, Benjamin took and grabbed him by the sleeve of his shirt and nudged him forward shouting, "If you turn back, I'll kill you myself!"

An angry expression covered the soldier's face, but he complied with the order. Most of the men from the company witnessed the incident and their respect grew for Benjamin as a leader.

With his sword waving and exhorting his men forward under the hailstorm of shrapnel and shell, Benjamin moved to the front rank of his regiment. When near the Swamp, which wasn't much more than a slow-flowing marshy stream, the Confederate battle line paused and answered in response to the Federal barrage with a well-directed volley.

After several volleys of musketry from both sides, the attack was called off and Pickett's brigade was ordered to retreat or be destroyed trying to take the hillside. The demonstration in force was costly to the brigade.

Once the men of A Company were reassembled after the attack on the Federal forces occupying the hill, Benjamin looked around and noticed the cost had been heavily paid . with the price of blood and life. He noticed James was bleeding from his forehead. He approached while James was wrapping a handkerchief around the injury.

"Are you all right?" Benjamin asked as he removed his hat.

"Yeah, it's just a scratch. I'll survive."

"Hopefully, all of us will do just that unless this hot June sun gets us first," Benjamin said after taking a drink from his canteen.

"That was a costly effort that gained nothing."

"I am sure we'll go again. This attack was just to test their strength." Benjamin said as he looked on the blackened stained face of his comrade.

"They'll probably reinforce this side of the field. I understand from some of the others the fighting has been severe to our left."

"We'll hold our own. Get some rest while you can."

Benjamin walked among the men and noticed Arden sitting on some grass with his body resting against a log. He approached and said, "I see you made it through."

"Yes sir. This one I did, but what will the next attack hold for me?"

"Not one of us can answer that question. We are only guaranteed one day at a time and we must live it to the fullest."

"Well sir, with all due respect, I'd rather be elsewhere if this is to be my last day."

"And so would I. But we have an obligation to defend our wives, sweethearts, loved ones, and kids so that they can live in freedom and without some Yankee government telling them how they should conduct their lives and what they can do with their property."

"I must admit sir, I am not as much into this war as you are."

"Then why did you join?"

"My father is a prestigious attorney in Leesburg. I didn't want the citizens of Leesburg and my Mary Ann thinking I was some kind of a coward. Do you realize the shame that would be placed on me. On my son? I would dishonor my family's name and my sweetheart. I could never obtain the respect of anyone again."

"There are a great many men fighting today that are just like you.

Benjamin and Arden's conversation was interrupted when James walked up to Benjamin and said, "Captain Bissell wants the company to fall in."

Benjamin began to walk away when he suddenly paused, turned and said, "Arden, take care of yourself." Pointing with his sword, Benjamin continued, "I'll see you on that plateau after this fighting is done."

Arden smiled as Benjamin turned and walked away.

*   *   *   *

It was near 7:00 o'clock in the evening and the sun was descending on the western horizon. Again Pickett's brigade was assembled for another assault behind a low-lying ridge west of the Federal fortifications. This time the attack was to be a general advance by all of the various Confederate divisions within the army on the Federal forces. The 8th Virginia was on the far right of the brigade. Thus far, the fighting had been a series of uncoordinated assaults that had proved costly. Pickett's brigade would attack with James Archer's brigade on their left and Cadmus Wilcox 's brigade on their right with Roger Proyer's brigade in the second line following. They would have to cross over a quarter mile of ground that was planted in wheat and entirely open to Federal artillery. The ground would slope down to Boatswain's Swamp, which they would have to re-cross and move up the hillside where there was a triple row of defenses shielding the Yankee defenders.

Once the Confederates were in range of the Federal artillery, the cannons began to open with shot and shell. Benjamin could tell as he looked around that this was beginning to take an appalling effect upon his brigade. As far as he could see, Confederate forces were rapidly advancing. This offensive, he thought, would determine the victor of this engagement. He continued to shout loudly to his men to close up the gap where the wounded were falling.

When Benjamin's brigade was across the stream and within striking distance of the Federals, Colonel Hunton ordered his men to fire. The first volley had a horrible effect on the Yankees that were sheltered by a deep ditch. As some of the soldiers attempted to reload their muskets, they fell as casualties from the Yankee volley that followed. Even though Benjamin was shouting orders, he still noticed the agonizing cries of pain on the faces of the fallen.

As the Rebels continued in broken ranks once more, Benjamin heard the missiles of death whizzing around his body, but any fear that attempted to surface in his mind was quickly overcome by the powerful determination to defeat and crush the Yankee army.

Soon, the 8th was upon the ditch with many of the enemy firing from behind its earthen shelter. Benjamin saw the frightened and hesitant expressions on some of their faces.

He raised his pistol and fired deliberately several times in succession. His anger still wasn't quenched over the loss of some of his men that had already fallen in battle. The soldier that he fired at was now lying prostrated over the mound of dirt.

Suddenly, the air was filled with the sound of the Rebel Yell. It was an intimidating noise and had its effect on the Yankees. The sound was so shrill coming from the men that at times it was louder than the sound of musketry.

Finally, Benjamin and the rest of Pickett's brigade were on top of the Federal defenders. Without hesitation, Benjamin witnessed white handkerchiefs, men rising to their feet and holding their weapons above their head in a gesture of surrender. But the deadly work wasn't finished nor was the battle won.

Benjamin and the rest of his regiment realigned their battle line, again they stepped off to challenge the second row of fortifications, which was made up of fallen trees and timber. They moved forward at the double-quick. The Yankee defenders poured a storm of lead into the Rebels' faces. Many of the men staggered, including Benjamin, who had been hit in the upper left arm. He wasn't ready to give up the fight and fall, but instead, he continued to wave them forward with his sword, believing that with a little more encouragement, the fortifications could be captured.

When the Federals sensed the determination of the Confederates to drive forward, they fled from the protection of the natural fortification. The momentum was on the Confederates' side. Soon after the second line gave way, the third line held by Yankee defenders on the brow of the hillside were soon caught up in the panic.

Once on the crest of the hillside, Benjamin quickly examined his wound. He was bleeding at a steady rate. He applied some pressure with a handkerchief as he continued forward in front of his men.

James noticed Benjamin was injured. He quickly approached and asked, "You are hit! You must go to the rear for help!"

Over the sound of artillery and musketry, Benjamin shouted, "No, it's not that bad. Besides, I want to be in on the capture of those artillery pieces over in the peach orchard behind that house."

"You are in no condition!" James shouted noticing the fire in Benjamin's eyes.

"Tell the men to move faster."

A section of four guns suddenly roared in succession across the plateau. Benjamin heard the little canister balls hitting the ground to his front. Suddenly, he fell to his knees in excruciating pain. He looked and noticed the blood pouring from his upper right arm. He fell prostrate to the ground and rolled over on his back. His eyes followed his men as they continued forward, shouting the Rebel Yell and firing their weapons like demons. The haze of battle, the smell of gunpowder, the cries of the wounded filled the air. Looking to his side, Benjamin noticed Arden lying face up, motionless and not breathing. Benjamin's heart sank and tears filled his eyes. He struggled and pulled from his coat pocket a photograph of Rachel and held it close to his chest. As the second column of Confederate soldiers approached, they were careful to step over him and not add to his injury. He gazed at Rachel not knowing if this was going to be the end of his life. Without warning, he lost consciousness, but his hand held its tight grip on the photograph of the lady dearest to his heart.

Chapter Nineteen

It had been several months since Jacob's journey to Washington City. He didn't remain idle after returning to Richmond. During the last several months, he continued his work at the bank, but more so, his real vocation of keeping his ears and eyes open for valuable information to pass on to authorities in Washington, or to the Mistress. Jacob received most of his information through Colonel Palmer, who considered him a trusted and loyal friend. Often as on this particular afternoon, Jacob planned to walk over to the telegraph office and speak to Colonel Palmer. He was going to inquire about the latest information in the fight between Generals Lee and McClellan.

After leaving the bank, Jacob looked around and noticed ten wagons carrying wounded soldiers down Main Street to a hospital. He had heard the news of the severe fighting at Gaines' Mill. Walking but a short distance, he paused and listened to a young man sitting along the street singing a very sad song about death and leaving a wife and children behind. It wasn't going to be a short and swift war like everyone had concluded at the outbreak. It was already becoming a long and dreaded affair. Jacob could only imagine the unspeakable void, the inner pain, and horrifying anguish that families were experiencing with the loss of a loved one in this conflict. The young man's music caused all these feelings to surface within his heart. The emotions that Rachel was enduring, he thought, must be placing her in a position of great anxiety, knowing the fighting around Richmond was causing many casualties, and Benjamin might be one of them.

Once Jacob arrived at the telegraph office, he inquired of Colonel Palmer's presence. He was immediately led to the colonel's office. After entering, Jacob noticed the colonel standing very erect with his hands behind his back and looking out the window.

Colonel Palmer said as he continued gazing, "The wagons carry on day and night bringing our boys back after they have nobly defended our soil. Often I wonder how many lives will have to pay for our freedom and at what cost will it take to drive off the Yankee invaders. My own son, Jimmy, is fighting with Kemper's Brigade of the 11th Virginia from our hometown of Lynchburg. Just before the fighting at Gaines' Mill, I knew he was all right. But thus far this day, I've heard nothing…even after dispatching a courier to find out his welfare."

Turning around toward Jacob, and in a quivering voice, Colonel Palmer continued, "In my heart, I fear something has happened to him. From all I understand, the fighting was furious. I understand many of the boys are still lying injured or dying on the field. I pray to God he is not one of them. What would I tell his mother. Oh God, what would I tell her."

"Sir, do you know how Pickett's men fared in this fight?" Jacob anxiously asked.

"The cost was heavy. Even Pickett was wounded in the fighting."

"Then I must try and find my friend, Benjamin Kelly."

"That's right, I remember you speaking of him."

"Sir, if you'll excuse me, I must go."

"By all means." As Jacob turned and began to leave, Colonel Palmer called out, "Does he have a wife and children?"

"He has a wife and they will soon be parents."

"I hope your friend survived."

Once Jacob departed the telegraph office, he began to anxiously look in every hospital that he knew was open in the city. After several hours of constantly looking, he came to a makeshift hospital down on Main Street in the Kent and Paine's dry-good store.

Before entering, Jacob paused and looked at some women, white and black, cutting clothing to make bandages, then boiling them in a large kettle of hot, steaming water. Then his attention was attracted to several attendants that brought their team of horses to a halt carrying the wounded in an ambulance wagon.

Jacob watched as they jumped from their seat and began to unload some suffering Confederate soldiers. Several of the soldiers screamed with pain as a doctor swiftly approached and said, "We are full! We can't take any more of the wounded."

"Then what are we supposed to do with them?" one man asked.

"Take them to Chimborazo Hospital at the eastern end of Broad Street."

"We've been there. They won't take anymore."

"If you leave them here, I am afraid they will die. I am short staffed and no room. Now do what I say."

A nurse came running out of the building, frantically calling for the physician. He turned around to hear her plea, "Doctor, you must return quickly."

Without another word, the physician swiftly re-entered the dwelling. The two attendants defiantly stepped to the back of the wagon and continued to unload the wounded soldiers, dumping their bodies from their litter and letting them lay on the dirt street without any type of bedding to make them comfortable. Afterward, they mounted the wagon and headed down the street.

The soldiers' agony was apparent by their moans and cries. As some of the ladies gathered around and attempted to make them comfortable, Jacob noticed a pail of water sitting nearby. He took the pail and its dipper and knelt down beside each soldier and carefully lifted each ones head to give them a drink of water. When he came to one soldier to give him a drink, the young boy of about fifteen just gazed quietly for the longest time at him. As Jacob looked into his green eyes, the boy finally attempted to speak.

"Tell my mother that I love her, and I'm sorry for runnin' away from home and joinin' the army," the lad said in a whisper.

"What's her name? Where does she live?"

"The young boy didn't respond to Jacob's questions. His motionless eyes gazed off into the heavens. Jacob knew he was dead.

Jacob rose and took off his coat and placed it across the boys face and body. He did this not only for privacy, but also to keep the flies off him. He looked at the despair on the face of one of the ladies.

"We will take care of him and see that he gets a decent burial." one lady said.

"What about his family?" Jacob asked.

"We don't know." She pointed to the building and continued loudly, "There are many of our boys in there that are going to die and we don't know who their kinfolk are. We can only do the best we can do to save their lives."

Jacob knelt down and searched the lad's pockets for some kind of identification, but there wasn't any to be found. Tears began to fill his eyes as he stood. Jacob turned and walked into the store knowing the boy's family might never know what actually happened and have the opportunity to bury him.

There were many men lying on cots and on the floor in the downstairs of the dwelling when Jacob walked through the front entrance. Jacob looked off to the back of the room where surgeons were performing the ghastly work of amputating an arm. There were no barriers for privacy. He held a handkerchief to his face because the smell in the room was offensive. Jacob looked upon every face, but didn't see Benjamin.

After sometime searching, Jacob was exhausted physically and emotionally. Maybe, he thought, Benjamin wasn't wounded or injured after all, but instead was still fighting. If that were so, maybe everything he was doing was in vain. It wasn't enough. His determination to discover Benjamin's fate compelled him to continue his quest.

Chapter Twenty

Jacob observed a young girl bandaging a soldier's leg. Another nurse was covering a soldier's face with a blanket. The scenes were depressing. Turning around again, Jacob noticed there was a second floor to the makeshift hospital. As he approached the stairway, he continued to hear the suffering of soldiers on the second floor. Once at the top of the stairway, he noticed the same deplorable conditions that he had witnessed on the first floor.

Jacob walked to the center of the room, continuing to examine each face. Suddenly, he noticed a young man with a stubble face that looked a little like Benjamin lying in the corner of the room next to the window. He walked over and observed the figure for a moment and when he was sure that it was his friend, he knelt by the cot.

"Benjamin, it's me, Jacob."

Slowly and wearily, Benjamin opened his eyes. He smiled when he recognized Jacob. Benjamin said in a whisper, "Jacob, It's you."

Jacob looked around and found some water in a pail nearby. He put some in the dipper and gave it to Benjamin to drink. When Benjamin had his fill, he wiped his mouth with Jacob's handkerchief. Jacob noticed the right arm was bandaged, but hadn't been amputated.

"Have you seen the surgeons?"

"Yes, from what I understand, I was fortunate. Some of the pieces of shrapnel passed through the arm and didn't damage the bone. I am in this condition because when I was wounded the first time, I kept moving with my men instead of seeking help. When I was hit the second time near the same area of the arm, I collapsed because I had lost so much blood."

"You always were stubborn as a mule."

"It's called pride. Something we all can't live without."

"I guess you'll be here for awhile. I will see you get something to eat everyday and you're cared for."

"Thank you. I appreciate your sacrifice and loyalty to our friendship." Benjamin whispered.

"We were always like brothers when we were growing up."

"And even after we became men. I will always cherish and call you my brother, no matter what happens between us."

"We need to send Rachel a correspondence and let her know that you're going to be all right." Jacob said to change the subject from the guilt he was experiencing.

"I know she must be worried sick by now with the knowledge of the fighting that is being published in the newspapers up north."

"I will go downstairs and see if I can get some paper and we will write it together since you are unable to do it yourself."

When Jacob returned from getting the supplies that they needed, he sat next to Benjamin's cot and asked, "What do you want me to say."

Benjamin began to speak his heart:

"My Dearest Rachel,

I am sure by now that you've heard we won the battle at Gaines' Mill, but the affair was costly in casualties to the 8th Infantry. By God's will and my love for you, I have survived, but was wounded in the upper arm in the battle. I am in a hospital in Richmond and hopefully my duration will be short.

I want to tell you the whole time before the battle, I found it difficult to think of the deadly work ahead because of my loving thoughts for you and our child to be born. I wish that I could see you now and hold you in my arms and reassure you that all will be well with us and I'm coming home. When I was lying on the field of glory, wounded, you were the first person on my mind. I held your photograph in my hand, crying and thinking I would never see you again. I know you have never seen me in that state of emotion, but when you feel your time is up in this world, you begin to feel guilty and sorrowful over all that you have sacrificed. Sometimes I feel I should have not joined the army, but instead stayed home, especially after you accepted my proposal of marriage. I feel so foolish now for doing so.

Tell mother and father I am well and I send my love to them and my brothers. I ask you and my folks as well as Lucas and the church to keep me in your prayers.

Your Loving Husband
Benjamin"

Jacob quietly watched as Benjamin covered his eyes and began sniffling. He knew he was struggling emotionally with his feelings and the separation from Rachel.

Once Benjamin was composed, he asked, "Can you get that to Rachel?"

"Yes, I will see that it is delivered."

"But they are behind enemy lines."

"I know, but I have my ways," Jacob answered, knowing he would use Hezekiah and the Union underground in Richmond.

"I remembered when you were seeing Rachel how envious I was of you. I thought you were the luckiest man in the world, and all of a sudden, without warning, you're gone and she is grieving. May I ask what happened that you suddenly disappeared, not telling anyone, not even me, your best friend why you did that?"

"It's a long story and now isn't the time. Besides, you need your rest to recover your strength. Sometime when you are better, we will talk about it. I promise," Jacob replied after standing to his feet.

"Does it have to do with Rachel?" Benjamin called out.

Jacob turned and gazed at Benjamin. He answered reassuringly, "No, it has nothing to do with her. What Rachel and I had is gone. She is your wife now and she deserves you more than she ever deserved me. As I said to you several months ago when you told me she had married you, it was my loss and your gain. You deserve her because you are a man with integrity, a good heart. She is a very sincere and loyal lady whom I am sure loves you very much. And knowing Rachel as I do, she will always be committed and love you all the days you are on the earth."

"I want to thank you for sharing your feelings with me."

"We are older now," Jacob laughingly replied, "the days of competing for everything, even Rachel, is a thing of the past. Trust me."

"You're right. I guess I had to know."

Jacob turned and walked away knowing he had lied to his best friend. As for Rachel, he was determined within that no one now or in the future would ever know his truest love and affection for her. It would always remain his secret even though she was still continuously in his thoughts and a part of his life. The anguish he still experienced would always be repressed until he could discover some way of dealing with it. For now, his prayer was that Benjamin would give up the war and return home to Rachel.

Chapter Twenty-One

Five days had gone by since Jacob first found Benjamin wounded at the dry-goods store. During that time, he had delivered on his promise of providing breakfast and dinner from the boarding house where he was living. It was around 6:00 o'clock in the evening when Jacob arrived, carrying Benjamin's dinner. As he began to ascend the stairway to the second floor, he experienced a very strange feeling in his heart. He didn't understand nor did he question it, but continued to the second floor.

When Jacob turned toward the front of the building, he noticed a lady leaning over Benjamin. He knew now why he was feeling so strangely, it was Rachel; she did the unexpected and came to Richmond. Jacob approached slowly with the small crock of beef soup. There was a variety of mixed feeling taking place in his heart. This was the first time he had seen Rachel since unexpectedly leaving home. What would he say, especially since she was married to his friend?

As Jacob approached Benjamin and Rachel, he knew any feelings for her had to be subdued, and the attempt to act as naturally as possible must be maintained.

When Jacob came to the side of Benjamin's bed, Rachel turned and looked up at him. Her eyes met his and she gazed intently at him for the longest time. He noticed her beauty was just as natural and attractive as it was when he left home. His first impulse was to embrace her, but decided against the idea because he had to be cautious of Rachel's feelings and the respect and brotherly love he felt for Benjamin.

"Rachel, how are you doing?" Jacob asked in a soft tone.

"I am doing as well as can be expected," Rachel answered turning away and looking at Benjamin.

"My friend, I brought you some of Miss Phelps's soup," Jacob said as he handed the crock to Rachel.

"Thank you so much," Benjamin said as he looked at Jacob.

"Rachel, when did you arrive? Jacob calmly asked.

"About an hour ago," Rachel replied as she began to feed Benjamin.

"How did you manage to cross Federal lines?"

"The Yankees cost me every dime I possessed to buy my way through their lines," Rachel answered in a defiant tone.

"I will return your money to you."

"No, that's not necessary," Benjamin swiftly answered.

"Benjamin, as soon as you can travel, I want to take you home with me where I can take care of you," Rachel said gazing into his eyes.

"That means I'd have to leave the army. My enlistment is for three years and if I am found capable of returning to the army and serving, I'll have to do just that." Pausing and caressing her face, Benjamin slowly and softly continued, "As much as I want to be with you, I have an obligation to defend the wife and family that I love, Virginia where we were born, and our rights as citizens of this state. Neither of us want our family to live under a government that will always be telling us what we can or cannot do."

"I don't care about our rights and the Yankee government. All I want is to have you home safe with me. You're going to be a father soon. Doesn't that mean anything to you?" Rachel replied as she began to weep.

"Having a family with you means everything in this world to me, but I am fighting to protect the ones I love and cherish the most, and the family that we will soon share. I don't want my men to suffer for what I failed to do by not fighting in this noble cause. I have the power to help bring about change for not only us but also for them and that begins by defeating the invaders of our land. If we can accomplish that goal then the Lincoln government must leave us alone and negotiate for peace."

Jacob looked at Benjamin and Rachel. He knelt on the side of the bed and said, "I understand from Colonel Palmer that Pickett's brigade got pretty cut up yesterday at Gaines' Mill. Your regiment, the 8th lost 50 to 55 men in the assault along Boatswain's Swamp. As I see it, you're very fortunate to be alive."

"What are you saying?" Benjamin asked.

"What I am saying is I feel that maybe you should consider giving up being a soldier, resign your commission and return home permanently with Rachel. She is right. You are about to be a father and begin the responsibilities of raising a family and you can't do that if you're marching all over Virginia with the army."

"Yes Benjamin, please listen to Jacob and consider that option?" Rachel eagerly said.

Benjamin remained silent and glanced at Rachel, then Jacob.

"Your odds of surviving this war are against you," Jacob continued.

"Is that why you didn't join with us?" Benjamin swiftly asked.

"No, I realized at the beginning of the war that the South wasn't prepared economically or with manpower to fight a prolonged war. Benjamin, the North possesses all of the industry and factories to build cannons, muskets, and medical supplies. Besides, their resources for manpower are much larger than ours. They will be able to replenish their manpower more readily and easier than us. Since Southern conscription, many of the boys have run off to the mountains to hide to avoid serving, or once in the army, they deserted as soon as they had the chance. In some cases they refused to fight at all, even when threatened with the sword. This war has gone on longer than anyone anticipated and the odds of winning are against us."

"Please Benjamin, listen to what Jacob says," Rachel cried.

Benjamin shook his head in frustration and answered softly, "I can't let my men down. Many of them gave their lives yesterday for all the things that I believe in. Should I not be a part of avenging their blood? Should I not fight to insure their families live in freedom, the very liberties that they sacrificed their lives for?"

"You are still as stubborn as you always were."

"No, it's the principal."

Seeing the uselessness of continuing the conversation, and darkness settling in over Richmond, Jacob turned and asked, "Rachel, do you have some place to stay tonight?"

"Yes, at the American Hotel."

"Would you see that she gets there safely?" Benjamin asked, continuing, "I don't feel right about her walking the streets alone and it's getting dark."

"If that is all right with you?" Jacob asked, turning and looking at Rachel.

"I guess so," Rachel reluctantly answered.

Kneeling over Benjamin, Rachel kissed him on the lips and said while she caressed his cheek with her hand, "Get some rest, I'll see you early in the morning."

Quietly, Rachel stood, turned and walked away with Jacob. Without a word, she paused and looked back at Benjamin. She noticed he was looking at her. At the moment, her heart was frayed with grief and anguish over seeing her husband in this type of condition, but she was thankful to God that he was alive and she had the chance to be with him.

Chapter Twenty-Two

After departing from the dry-goods store with Rachel, Jacob turned and noticed some Confederate guards escorting a large number of Yankee prisoners to the old warehouse at Cary and Dock Street. The structure had been converted into a prison last year. Jacob paused and knew from an inspection last month with Colonel Palmer the conditions in the warehouse were deplorable and unfit for humans.

Rachel noticed Jacob was not beside her. She paused and turned to look at him. By his expression, she knew his attention was drawn to the Yankee soldiers being marched down the street by the guards, but couldn't understand his fascination with the event.

Jacob turned and approached Rachel saying, "I am sorry for making you wait."

"That's all right." Pausing and glancing at Jacob, she continued, "I wanted to thank you for watching out over Benjamin until I arrived. I know it means so much to him that you've been there by his side and offered your help."

"Benjamin is like a brother to me. Often I think of times when Luke, Benjamin, and I would fish along Piney Run or go hunting on Short Hill Mountain. I can still recall one time when we were deer hunting on the summit of the mountain above Derry's Tavern. It was in late November, there was about six inches of snow on the ground and it was still coming down quite heavy. On the rocky cliffs there was a buck, standing and gazing at the three of us. The animal was calm. He didn't try to escape, and probably knew what his destiny would be. I raised my musket and was going to shoot him, but when I got ready to pull the trigger, Benjamin pushed my gun to the side and said we shouldn't kill such a bold and noble animal. Instead, Luke discharged his gun in the air and the animal fled."

Jacob continued as they casually walked in the direction of the hotel, "After the deer ran away and I was frustrated with both of them for depriving me of an easy kill, Benjamin walked over to the cliff and gazed down at the snowy valley below. I must admit the view was quite majestic and picturesque. Suddenly, Benjamin slipped on one of the wet rocks and slid over the side of the cliff. Immediately, Luke and I raced to the cliff's edge. Benjamin was barely hanging on to the point of a rock. As I looked into his eyes, they didn't reveal a hint of fear, but only calm and determination. We didn't have any rope; there wasn't anything of use nearby. Instead, I took my musket and passed it to him. Once he grabbed the barrel of the weapon, Luke and I pulled him back to the top of the cliff. We all had a good laugh afterwards."

A smile appeared on Rachel's face. "As I remember, you boys came back to the house and sat shivering in front of the fireplace. I fixed you hot chocolate." Rachel's tone turned to somberness, "Those were the days when we thought we were so much in love."

"Yeah, I couldn't keep my eyes off you."

"Neither could I. When you looked at me and smiled, it sent a warm feeling over me. I felt blessed to have you as a part of my life. I never ever thought there could or would be someone else, even though I knew that Benjamin was interested in me."

Jacob paused and turned and looked at Rachel. Somberly, he said, "Running out on you was the worst thing I could have ever done. You only wanted what most every young lady who's in love desires and that is to be married and begin a family. And for the longest time, I really believed and prayed that would happen."

Rachel abruptly and loudly interrupted, "Stop it! Please! You don't have to explain to me, it's over with."

Jacob placed his hands on Rachel's shoulders and answered, "But I must."

"Why, to clear your conscience?"

"No because you deserve an explanation."

"Jacob, I am married to Benjamin now and I am carrying his baby. You and I should not even be having this conversation. It's pointless to go on with it because maybe you're feeling guilty and great condemnation over the way you treated me." Rachel replied loudly.

"I am sorry Rachel, so sorry."

"Jacob, let's just remember the good times and try to be civil and maintain a friendly relationship with each other. There is nothing we can do now about what might have been or what we might have accomplished. When you decided that you didn't want to marry me and disappeared, I was devastated. For a long time, I really believed there was something that I said or did that drove you away. The thought crossed my mind that there was someone else and you didn't have the heart to tell me. After all, you were gone for days at a time and you just said that it had to do with your father and you not being able to get along with each other. I accepted and trusted your words that you said to me, but you just shut me out of your life when it came to your relationship with him."

As she continued to speak, tears flowed freely down her cheeks because the hurt was still in her heart. "For days after you left no one in your family knew where you had disappeared. I stayed in my room struggling with my emotions and feelings for you. During that time, I didn't eat, I drank little, I didn't sleep, and I didn't have anything to do with anyone in my family or friends. And when you didn't return, it almost destroyed me. Finally, when I did make the attempt to begin living a normal life again, it was very difficult. Do you know why?"

"You were concerned about what people would think and how they would judge you."

"Yes, I was. Did they think I drove you off? Was there something wrong with me? I didn't know. You didn't stay around long enough to explain why you didn't love me, or why you didn't want to marry me."

"It had nothing to do with my love for you. Please believe me. Trust what I am saying."

"Oh Jacob," Rachel answered loudly and in an angry tone, "how can you ask me to trust you and believe you when you destroyed everything that we had worked so hard to accomplish in our relationship and life."

"If you'll let me explain."

"No Jacob, I won't. All that matters now is that Benjamin recovers from his wounds and I can persuade him to go home and help his father on the farm. My life now is with him and not you. He has earned my trust, my loyalty, and most of all my love. Yes, Benjamin has his faults, but we all do, right? From this conversation, I take it that you still have feelings for me, but I don't feel the same about you. Those feelings are dead and gone. Like me, you must move on with your life."

"Yes, I still love you. I won't lie about that. I'll always love you and think about everything that we could have had. But on the other hand, I know that you're married to the man that has always been there for me and has always regarded me with the same love as if we were brothers. There's nothing in life that I'll ever do that will compromise or destroy what he and I spent a lifetime of accomplishing. As for you, I'll always respect the truth that you are his now and not mine, no matter how difficult it will be. Maybe it's the just punishment that I deserve for the way I treated you and for the suffering that I caused by vanishing without a word of explanation. Again, I am sorry for all of the displeasure and misery I've caused you."

After seeing his humbleness and unwillingness to argue, Rachel sighed and said, "Thank you, I accept your apologies."

For the rest of the short journey to the hotel, Rachel and Jacob didn't speak to each other. He greatly desired to embrace her and bask in the smiling expressions that glowed from her face, to hear her words of comfort, especially the softness of her voice say, I love you. Jacob knew his love for Rachel was just as strong as when he left the valley right before the beginning of the war. Still, as difficult as it was, Jacob wouldn't do anything or make any attempt to come between Benjamin and Rachel.

*   *   *   *

After arriving at the hotel, Jacob escorted Rachel to her room, but didn't enter. He softly said, "When I first saw you this evening, I must admit for as long as I have known you, I felt quite awkward, as I am sure that you did also. But this situation we face as difficult as it may be, we will work out, not only for your sake and mine, but Benjamin's too. I don't want him lying over there and distrusting me nor do I want you to feel threatened by my presence. I don't want to jeopardize our friendship."

Rachel's eyes were on Jacob, as she answered softly, "I don't want you to stay away because we once were in love with each other. I don't want to be the one to come between you and Benjamin. I have always known that he meant quite a bit to you and if you did stay away because of me, I am afraid that it would devastate him. I don't want that to happen to him because I would feel like he was being punished for something that he didn't have a part in."

"Thank you. I appreciate that." Pausing and looking directly at Rachel, Jacob continued, "I will see you tomorrow."

Rachel watched as Jacob walked down the hallway and than she opened her door and slowly walked into the room. After closing the door, she leaned against it and began weeping. Looking up at the ceiling, she thought she had the opportunity to shut Jacob totally out of her life by asking that he stay away from Benjamin and her, but she knew she couldn't bring herself to such a drastic decision. Why, she thought? In many ways, it was good to see Jacob and to know he was alive and well, but she was concerned it might cause many problems somewhere in the future. When they were all growing up, Benjamin and Jacob were always competitive for her attention and love. Now that she was married to Benjamin, would he be able to trust her with Jacob? She would have to do everything within her ability to insure that Benjamin wouldn't have any reason to distrust her in their relationship.

Chapter Twenty-Three

It had been a restless night for Rachel. She tossed and turned and found her attempts at sleeping virtually impossible. The room was quiet, but her thoughts about the two men that had the greatest effect on her life continued. She found her life was full of challenges with being married to a man that almost lost his life as a soldier, and who again she knew would fight another day. Prior to the fight at Gaines' Mill, every time there had been some type of engagement or battle, her worst fears had tried to overtake her even though she attempted to keep her mind occupied with some meaningful chore or task. According to the newspapers and eyewitnesses, the battles were greater in numbers of participants and the fighting more savage in nature. Like Jacob, she knew the odds were against many of the men fighting for the Southern Cause and maybe they would never return home to their families. If Benjamin did, would he be an invalid or how would participation in a bloody war, seeing men dying and crying for help, affect him emotionally? Would his life ever be the same as it was prior to the war with the possibility he would relive battle scenes within his mind at night?

Another question constantly lingering within her mind was the reality that in a little over three months, she would give birth to either a baby boy or girl. The child would begin its life in a world that was plagued with unaccountable deaths, constant drama, and maybe if the Southern armies lost the war, the many uncertainties that would follow in the war's aftermath. What about her fears of raising a child alone? They were unthinkable. She couldn't imagine her life without Benjamin being a part of it, and sharing in her child's life.

Rachel tossed back the covers and walked over to the window overlooking Main Street. In the direction of the grassy hill, she gazed at the first yellow rays of dawn revealing its beauty upon the white-Roman edifice with its six Corinthian style columns that symbolized the power and strength of the new Confederacy. How would Thomas Jefferson feel now if he knew a rebel government was meeting and passing legislation for a disunion people in the building he designed many years ago before becoming the third President of the United States? Another question that surfaced within her mind was, would the lawmakers and President Davis be able to negotiate an end to this conflict before too many more lives were sacrificed? Would President Abraham Lincoln and the United States Govern-ment allow the Southern states to go their own way and live in peace? She really didn't believe this would happen. This was a war that would be fought to the bitter end and who knew the cost in lives it would require.

What about Jacob now that he has suddenly reappeared in her life? When she first saw him at the hospital, she was quite shocked and taken by his sudden appearance. Benjamin had not prepared her for Jacob's arrival. Usually something this dramatic wouldn't have escaped his thoughts, but she knew he was still weak and not always aware of his surroundings.

Out of all of the men she had known in her life, Jacob possessed the greatest impact on her. He was someone she always firmly believed would pour out his undying love for her, cherish their relationship every day they were together, and without hesitation protect and take care of her. Why he departed so hastily from her life, she wasn't sure nor did she really want to know. Fear gripped her heart at the thought of his denial even though earlier he was ready to tell her. She firmly believed their relationship was long over with even though she found it difficult throughout the night to purge her mind of their past life together and what might have been had they continued together.

Since her relationship ended with Jacob, she had become firm in her feelings about matters pertaining to her personal life and had battled many emotional obstacles to regain her self-esteem. The experience had taught her many characteristics of life such as the constructive application of wisdom and the proper use of its knowledge. She possessed no regrets in her heart about marrying Benjamin or the life they shared together. He was mature for his young age and knew the characteristics and priorities that mattered the most in his life. Not only these qualities did he possess, but wisdom had been his greatest teacher in handling the challenging responsibilities of operating the family's business. It was because of Benjamin, that his family had been so successful and prosperous in their financial affairs.

Within the hour, Rachel arrived at the hospital and noticed Benjamin was sitting up on his cot with his body leaning against the wall. There was a smile covering her face after noticing Benjamin's rapid improvement. She was optimistic and filled with enthusiasm. Rachel walked over and leaned down and kissed Benjamin on his lips. She sat next to him and taking his hands in hers, she joyfully said, "What an improvement in just a day?"

Benjamin smiled and replied, "I guess the best medicine for me was your arrival in town yesterday and being able to be with you."

"Have you eaten yet?"

"Yes, matter of fact, I have. Jacob stopped by earlier and brought me some country ham and eggs."

"Well that's good, I am so glad that he has helped you. I guess I'll always owe him for his generosity."

After noticing Benjamin's bandages were matted with blood, Rachel looked around and noticed there were some clean bandages and fresh water nearby. She rose from the cot and walked over and wet the bandages. She returned and quietly began to remove the soiled ones from his arm.

"Sometime today, I plan on looking for a boarding house room for us until you completely recover. I feel you'll do better there than in this oppressive atmosphere."

"Jacob has already taken care of finding one."

"He has?" Rachel replied with a tone of astonishment.

"Yeah, while I was eating, he informed me he needed to get us a place and get us out of here so I might benefit from being with you more than what is tolerable in this place. After all, this is not the best atmosphere for a lady such as you."

"I am no different than any of the other women I have seen in here tending to the needs of their husbands, but on the other hand, I do desire to be alone with you as much as possible."

Benjamin placed his hand on Rachel's abdomen and laughingly replied, "You mean you want to be with us as much as possible."

Rachel smiled, then she hugged and kissed Benjamin. "I hope you're home when our baby comes into this world. My greatest hope is that both of us can lay our eyes upon him or her at the same time. I don't want you to be off fighting a war when the baby is born. Its birth will be a time of rejoicing and celebrating with our family, not being separated from each other."

"I'll try and get a two-day furlough and be there with you."

The smile on Rachel's face had now vanished and was replaced with despair.

Benjamin noticed the rapid change in her expression. He said in a concerned manner, "I see your smile is gone and I know you have continued to hang onto the hope that I would resign my commission and stop fighting."

"I did, but somewhere in my heart I knew you wouldn't."

Benjamin looked away from Rachel and sighed. He remained silent as she looked at him for the next gesture or word. He turned again after pondering and said, "There are probably many wives that are here or at home trying to get their husbands to return. Just before the fighting at Gaines' Mill, I spoke with an officer in the 14th Alabama who had been receiving news from home. His wife said it was difficult trying to keep up their small farm of fifteen acres and trying to raise and take care of five young children. She was always up at four in the morning, seven days a week, milking the few cows they owned. She was giving it her best effort in tilling the ground to try and raise a crop so that they didn't go without food and would also have something to put away for the winter months. How do you think that soldier felt?"

"I can only imagine what was going on in his mind," Rachel answered somberly.

"He was thinking of deserting and going home."

"Well did he?"

"No. He was very depressed knowing emotionally what his wife and family were going through. He realized their hardship of sacrifice while he was away from home to lead his men in battle, and their difficulties and struggles of doing without, and the worry of his welfare. But he also knew it was his responsibility to lead his men into battle with the intentions of bringing as many of them back to their loved ones as soon as possible. We are fortunate we have the chance to see and be with each other. That officer informed me he hasn't been home to see his wife and kids since the war began. Living in that kind of separation must be pure hell to go through. And like many, he is fighting in this army."

"Than I guess I am being selfish in wanting you to return home with me?"

"No, you're really no different than any other woman that has a man fighting in this war. I am sure it is the same with the Yankee women."

"Well since you have your mind made up, I guess I will make the best of our time together. But somewhere in my heart my love, I have these very bad feelings about this war and your involvement if it continues to linger. I just don't know what it is, but I don't believe we will remain unscathed by it."

Benjamin's heart was troubled. He was silent, gazing continuously into Rachel's eyes, but he knew his pride and honor wouldn't allow him to surrender the quest for victory.

Chapter Twenty-Four

Five days after being wounded at the battle of Gaines' Mill, Rachel moved Benjamin to their temporary room at Miss Morgan's boardinghouse midway down Carey Street. The attending physician and Rachel were confident that with several weeks of rest, Benjamin would be able to return to the army. A little after noon, Rachel was feeding her husband some chicken soup when their attention was drawn to the loud knock at the door.

Rachel turned and placed the soup on the stand next to the bed and approached the door. When she opened it, there stood Jacob. She was lost for words.

"Rachel, who is calling?" Benjamin asked.

"Oh, it's Jacob," Rachel answered, softly continuing, "Please come in."

"How is my brother doing today?" Benjamin asked.

"You're looking much better. I went over to the hospital first to see if you were still there, but they told me you left this morning so I wanted to see how you were doing," Jacob replied, sitting in the chair next to Benjamin's bed.

"Ah, with Rachel here, I'm living like a king."

"The doctor said he needed to rest for awhile. They were confident the wounds were free of infection and I must keep them clean and his bandages changed as often as possible," Rachel said as she sat on the edge of the bed.

"Do you have plenty of supplies?" Jacob asked.

"I just have what little I was able to get from the nurses before leaving." Rachel replied as she glanced at Jacob.

"I will see you have everything that you need," Jacob answered confidently.

"How are things going for us? As I understand, McClellan's forces are retreating towards Harrison's Landing along the James?" Benjamin said looking at Jacob.

"That's true, but yesterday, Lee's soldiers paid a terrible price at Malvern's Hill in trying to crush McClellan before he could reach the security and shelter of the Yankee gunboats and their heavy artillery." Jacob handed Benjamin a copy of the Richmond Dispatch newspaper.

"How great were the casualties?" Benjamin asked looking at the front page of the newspaper.

"Five Thousand. Maybe more."

"What about the 8th, do you know anything?" Benjamin anxiously asked.

"I knew you would ask, so I inquired from Colonel Palmer before coming over here and he informed me they were not engaged, but held in reserve."

"Good, good." Benjamin whispered in a sigh of relief.

"The campaign was very costly to both sides. Many a good man died at the hands of the Yankee invaders while defending rights and freedoms that are our liberties."

"Benjamin, doesn't it bother you with everything you see happening in Richmond as a result of the seven days of hell that humanity has just been put through?" Jacob asked in a frustrating tone.

"Oh yeah, I saw and noticed the horrors and hell of battle, especially when I was lying on my back in the hospital. I saw what it did to men and their families. The cries of the suffering keep you from closing your eyes to rest at night, and the wails and weeping of young women hardly out of their teens grieving over a husband whose eyes are motionlessly gazing at them. Next to where I was lying, two darkie attendants were moving some men that had their limbs removed due to the injuries they received at the fighting around Gaines' Mill. The one soldier cried out 'what are you going to do with us'?

The one darkie answered, 'we want to make room for those coming in.'

The soldier cried out, 'can't you wait until we're dead'?

The attendant shouted, 'no.'"

Benjamin continued to speak with tears flowing down his cheeks. "I was so angry over the careless and inhumane treatment those men received after going out and getting badly wounded, and having injuries they might never recover from. To add to the insult, the darkies carried away the soldiers that were hopeless to what were called "dead houses" to die. As the darkies carried out their orders, many of us continued shouting retribution to show the authorities our displeasure over the way we were being abused and mistreated. Just think, I could have been one of those men."

"I wouldn't have allowed that to happen," Rachel swiftly said.

"Maybe it would still be for the best to get you out of this dismal city for the next few weeks." Jacob said.

"No Jacob, that won't do any good. I see the funeral processions go by for officers with their weeping widows quietly following, and the ordinary dead soldiers piled high in wagons with no ceremony at all. Just earlier this morning when Rachel stepped out and left the window open for me to get some fresh air, I heard several elderly gentlemen talking on the street below saying how the dead were being piled in mounds on the grass because the gravediggers couldn't keep up with the pace of burial. As I understand from their conversation, it's so continuous that many of the men don't even get a service. They just throw them in a pit as rapidly as possible because of the stench and offensive odor caused by the summer heat."

The room was quiet as Benjamin turned his attention out the window to hide the tears filling his eyes.

Jacob knew it was time to leave and allow Rachel the opportunity to settle Benjamin down from the emotional outburst.

"My friend, I must be going."

Benjamin stretched forth his hand and took Jacob's requesting, "Come and see me as often as possible. And please keep me abreast of what the 8th is doing."

Jacob quietly nodded and turned with Rachel escorting him to the door. After opening the door, Jacob turned and looked into her eyes and asked, "If you can, don't give up on trying to take him home."

"But his injuries are not severe enough to keep him out of the army."

"Well, I'll try and see if I can get him a transfer to the quartermaster's department. Colonel Palmer owes me a favor."

"What if he doesn't want to serve in that capacity? What if he wants to return to his regiment?"

"He can't do that. Not after the inhumane fighting that just took place."

Jacob put his hat on and walked down the stairway and out the front entrance onto the porch. Tears began to flow freely down his cheeks as he leaned against one of the white columns to hide his face. In his heart, he felt guilty knowing he was a spy for the Federal government and Benjamin, his best friend was in reality his enemy. Although he made a good show with words to Rachel, he knew as he looked into her worried and troubled eyes that Benjamin wouldn't accept another offer or transfer to another department. Benjamin, he was sure felt a bond and an allegiance to the men he had been serving with in the 8th Virginia Infantry. Benjamin's resolve was in all probability solidified by all that he had experienced and witnessed while here in Richmond and on the field of honor.

Chapter Twenty-Five

During the last week of July 1862, Jacob attended a meeting at Secretary Randolph's residence. When Jacob arrived, he was immediately escorted into the dining room, where he found Secretary Randolph, Colonel Palmer, and Captain Norris looking over a map of central Virginia spread out over the huge dining table. When they knew he was present, they turned and warmly greeted him.

"Jacob, I am glad you could join us," Colonel Palmer enthusiastically said.

"Thank you for having me, sir," Jacob courteously answered.

"Yes, Jacob, come over here and look at this map since we'll need to call upon your services once more," Secretary Randolph added, gesturing.

After Jacob approached, he glanced at the map. He knew Stonewall Jackson and the Army of Northern Virginia's II Corps was in the vicinity of Gordonsville, protecting the Virginia Central Railroad. He also knew the new Federal Army of Virginia under the command of Major-General John Pope was north of the Rapidan River near the vicinity of Culpepper Court House. Pope was of much concern to the Confederate authorities because of a possible thrust toward Richmond from the north. If McClellan decided to renew offensive operations on the peninsula, the Confederate army would be greatly outnumbered by these opposing forces and could be crushed as a result. It looked very bleak for the Confederacy, and if both Federal armies were successful, it could mean the end of the war. As Jacob looked at the map and listened to the conversation, he knew their suspicions and fears were just as he had perceived.

After discussing in some detail what possibilities Generals Lee and Jackson might undertake to eliminate the new threat, the men paused and congregated around the server where Secretary Randolph began pouring each a brandy.

"Yesterday at the bank, I was speaking with several officers and they told me Pope is fighting a new kind of warfare on innocent civilians," Jacob said after taking a sip of the liquor.

"Yes, in accordance with their new so called law, some of the Yankee generals are beginning to take a new approach to fighting the war under what is know as the Confiscation Act. And Pope is one," Captain Norris angrily replied as he sat down his empty glass on the stand.

"I pray to God we can get our hands on that Yankee scoundrel for all the horror he's doing to our people," Colonel Palmer added, shaking his head in frustration.

"Jacob, according to what we know from our spies, all kinds of atrocities against the citizens along the Blue Ridge Mountain area are occurring. Male residents were rounded up in such places as Luray in Page County and were being detained against their will. In Rappahannock County, the Federals arrested 150 men and brought them to General Milroy's headquarters at Sperryville where he demanded they take the Oath of Allegiance to the United States and recognize its laws and the presidency of Abe Lincoln. When some of them refused, they were banished from their homes and sent away. Their homesteads, and property such as cattle, horses, and possessions were seized for food for the army and for public use or as Pope chooses. It's just uncivilized what Pope is doing. They are trying to make our civilians feel the full effect of the war," Secretary Randolph answered in a frustrating tone.

"Not to say, the Federal soldiers and their officers feel this leniency in civilized warfare is giving them a free hand in treating our people anyway they choose," Colonel Palmer added in a fiery tone.

"This will only make the men in our army fight with greater determination and anger," Jacob swiftly and angrily replied.

"As citizens from the troubled area arrive in Richmond, the newspapers will begin to publish their accounts, but until we know for sure what McClellan's intentions are, we might have to fight at a disadvantage," Captain Norris said as he looked at Jacob.

"What do you mean?" Jacob asked.

"What I mean is simply this. According to our spies, Pope might have as many as 50,000 men in his army made up of mostly men that Jackson fought against in the Shenandoah Valley last spring," Captain Norris despairingly said.

Colonel Palmer abruptly interrupted, "What he is trying to say is this, under what circumstances and means do we fight against two different armies? Many of our men fell as casualties during the fighting around Richmond and haven't returned to the ranks yet."

"That's the reason that we've called you to this meeting," Secretary Randolph said as he approached Jacob.

"We want you to make another trip to Washington tonight and contact our agent, Amanda," Colonel Palmer said as he placed his hand on Jacob's shoulder.

"We need to find out as soon as possible what McClellan's intentions are so we can take that information and help General Lee decide what action to pursue in our defense," Secretary Randolph added, continuing, "and just in case you are captured, we will send another courier with you."

"I can travel faster alone," Jacob swiftly replied.

"I understand. This time, the message you'll deliver will be by word of mouth and not written in cipher. The other person traveling by another route will also have the same message. In this way one of you will be sure to get through," Captain Norris argued.

"That's how important this trip is," Secretary Randolph added.

"And who might the other person be?" Jacob curiously asked.

"You already know her as Miss Robins," Captain Norris swiftly answered as he sat on a chair near the dining table.

"But she was detained at Fairfax Court House when I escaped. When was she released?"

"First of all, it was you they were really after. As for Sarah, they thought she was harmless and knew little in the way of useful intelligence information. All of that sobbing and playing on their sympathy won her freedom. She was just warned what would happen if she was caught in aiding the Confederate government or its armies," Captain Norris confidently said, "They should have searched her, let's say in a more careful way."

"I don't understand," Jacob slowly replied.

"She was carrying additional dispatches of great importance to us and our agents in the north. She delivered them several days after you departed Washington City," Captain Norris laughingly replied, continuing, "The Yankees know nothing about secret activities."

"In other words, the Federals didn't believe she was really playing much of a role in spying."

"True. That was the Federals perception of things. Our women folk are more deadly at this game of spying than what the men are. The Federals only feel its sporadic here and there when in reality, any woman that has a husband, brother, or a sweetheart fighting for a noble cause such as ours, will do anything to help win the conflict so their loved ones can return home to them."

"So Miss Robins should be here at any moment," Colonel Palmer said as he lit a cigar.

As the other three men continued in conversation, Jacob turned away and walked over to the window and glanced out into the street. He was distressed with the knowledge that

Sarah was going to once again have a hand in this mission. He didn't know if Sarah would be angry with him for leaving her at Fairfax Court House, but as an agent, she should know the actions he took; he was compelled to do so in order to relay the intelligence to Washington City to Amanda. If anything, leaving her behind might have impressed her even more so than trying to secure her release from custody.

Sarah was sure to have questions about the escape and how Jacob entered Washington City. Jacob knew he would have to be careful with his words under Sarah's scrutiny and rehearse his story in his mind. Sarah was very shrewd and crafty at the game of espionage and she thrived on the risky challenges that were associated with such a dangerous profession. Jacob knew he would have to cover his every move. Once in Washington City, Sarah was sure to use some charade to intentionally extract information from Amanda with the intentions of determining his loyalty. He quickly discovered that spies didn't trust each other, especially when fighting for the same side, but this was how the game was played.

Chapter Twenty-Six

It seemed as though Jacob had been looking out the front window of Secretary Randolph's residence for an eternity when suddenly a black covered carriage arrived at the front entrance. This must be Sarah, he thought. Jacob noticed the coachman stepping down and opening the coach door. Jacob watched as Sarah stepped down from the coach.

With Sarah's arrival, Jacob turned and approached the other three men, who were still speculating on the strategies of the coming campaign. He walked over to the server and poured another drink. Without hesitation, he gulped it down. Jacob knew once he arrived in Washington City he could deal with Amanda, but Sarah was another question. As before, he had already determined in his mind that Sarah was far more lethal than Amanda and probably more than most men involved in this vocation.

Jacob turned and noticed Secretary Randolph walking over to greet Sarah as she walked through the door of the room. He was very cordially smiling when he kissed her on the hand and said, "Sarah, it's good to see you."

Secretary Randolph took Sarah by the hand. Jacob noticed she was looking with an astonished expression on her face. He remained calm and approached, "It's good to see you again, Sarah."

"We have a lot to talk about, don't we?" Sarah said, her eyes on Jacob.

"I guess we can learn from our experiences at Fairfax Court House."

"Yes, by all means."

"This is the main reason why both of you will be going by separate routes to get this information north to Washington City," Captain Norris said as he approached, continuing,

"Agents are already in motion and plans are already in effect. If both of you will please step over to the map, I'll lay all of this out to you."

Everyone quietly gathered around the map while Captain Norris continued to speak, "The last time when both of you went north, you took a roundabout way across the Rapidan to Culpepper Court House, then the Rappahannock to Fairfax Court House. Now, the area is too infested with the Yankee army. With their war on civilians, it makes it all too dangerous. Anyone that would be suspected or suspicious in any manner might be arrested and detained. Jacob, I want you to use the same route you did back in April on your return to Richmond. We have the most agents and operatives working this route. The only problem might be getting you across the Potomac. We have received word the Yankee Navy is more vigilant since several of our couriers have been captured along this route. So instead of you crossing at Pope's Creek, the usual way, we want you to follow the Potomac northwest for about three miles to where you'll be opposite an outlet across the river from Maryland. It will be on a bend in the river not far from Port Tobacco. You'll be met there by an individual by the name of Hughes. He's been watching the Yankee ships for days. He'll decide when it's practical and he will ferry you across the river where you'll again meet Mr. Jones."

Pointing with his finger, Captain Norris continued, "As for you Sarah, you will proceed as far as Port Royal. While you are crossing the Rappahannock River on the ferry, you'll come into contact with a gray-haired elderly lady."

"Won't that be too dangerous?" Jacob swiftly asked.

"Yeah, it will be very dangerous because Yankees will be in the area, but we have recently used this particular route and found it was quick and practical."

"What if she is captured this time? She will be sent to prison," Jacob answered, glancing at Captain Norris.

"I am a lot more experienced at this than what you think. Besides, traveling with an old woman lowers my risk of suspicion," Sarah replied as she smiled at Jacob.

"Will not the Federals be suspicious of you?"

"I'll have my papers and I have my ways of deceiving them if I am questioned."

"Yeah, look what happened at Fairfax Court House. We thought our passes and cover were authorized and look what happened. We got caught."

"That's part of the risk we take. We found out Thomas Mason's associate was a double agent. Today, he's dead. He'll never again work for the highest bidder," Sarah angrily replied.

"How do you know?" Jacob asked.

"Because I killed not only him, but also Doctor Mason. That's how I know, and that's how I work," Sarah replied in a cold-hearted manner.

"Why did you kill the physician?"

"Because the Yankees knew about him. I don't like to leave a trail where people can identify me. In this work, it is important no one knows the truth about me," Sarah fired back.

"I guess I am still too new and unskilled at this," Jacob quickly answered.

While everyone began to laugh at the verbal melee, Jacob looked into Sarah's cold eyes and knew all his suspicions had just been confirmed in those last statements.

"Now, if I may continue after you all stop bickering?" Captain Norris asked in a stern voice. "When you leave the Fredericksburg area, you're to continue by way of Burke Station. When you reach Alexandria, another agent will contact you. He'll escort you without any questions into the city."

"I am ready and can leave tonight," Sarah replied in a calmer tone.

"I'll write you out the necessary pass that's going to be required for travel on this route," Secretary Randolph said.

* * * *

The conversation ended. Secretary Randolph walked out of the room to his library to write out Sarah's pass. The others turned to have another drink. Sarah and Jacob remained and continued to stare at each other.

"I guess I am not the lady I portrayed to you." Sarah said breaking the silence.

"No, you are not. I didn't know that ladies, especially someone as charming and lady-like as you were so capable of committing such an act as killing another individual."

"What, killing the enemy? When you have as much hatred as I do for the Yankee scum, those emotions will compel and drive you to do what you have to do. Not only that, but the worst kind of Yankee scum is one who is also a spy for the other side. They deserve to die. They have no loyalties," Sarah replied, gazing coldly at Jacob.

"Maybe I got mixed up in the wrong kind of game."

"I am beginning to wonder if you really have the stomach for this. When you receive word about how the Yankees are tormenting and causing your family's life to be a living hell, or if one of them kills your pappy or mom, then you will bear the same hatred as the rest of us do that have already lost a loved one. I can't express or find the words that will adequately describe the animosity I feel against those brazen infidels," Sarah answered in a tone of anger as she walked over and gazed out the window.

"Do you have any family that's up north fighting for those brazen infidels as you call them?" Jacob asked as he followed.

"I have two uncles fighting for a Pennsylvania regiment, the 28th I believe. They may have been with McClellan. I don't know and I really don't care."

"How can you say that about family? You know you care."

"When my Uncle Andrew left Harpers Ferry after the armory was burned by the Yankees and then captured by the Virginia militia, he wrote my father one of the dirtiest and nastiest correspondences one could ever sit down and compose. He had the audacity to scold my father over his commitment and loyalty to his native state of Virginia and not the Union. He said that our rights to our property and liberties that we had won from the British in the War for Independence were all tied into a strong and prosperous Union. His correspondence had such a fighting tone to it. He informed my father he wouldn't think anything of his life if he had the opportunity to challenge him on the battlefield."

"There has to be more to it than what you're telling me. There are many family members fighting against each other in this war."

"Well, I guess it doesn't help when your father was elected as a delegate from his county to vote on whether Virginia stayed in the Union or not, does it?" Sarah slowly said, turning around and looking coldly into Jacob's eyes.

"No, I guess not," Jacob answered, sighing. "In Jefferson County, Alfred Barbour, the Superintendent of the United States Armory at Harpers Ferry had been chosen by the Unionist to vote and keep Virginia in the Union. When he betrayed that trust and voted for the secession of the state, he incited much anger and hatred among the gunsmiths and machinist at the government works, who were loyal to the Union."

"My Uncle Andrew and my father were once very close, as close as two brothers could possibly be. I can still remember when we would all enjoy barbecues and socials during the summer months when they would come and stay with us. We were all very close knit, happy smiles, and it appeared not a care in the world. And I really thought nothing could ever separate my family. But that all changed and I was so wrong about my perception of our life together. It was about 1858 when I noticed the excuses were given for not attending a social and the correspondences slowed to a halt. I knew something was terribly wrong, but I was always given some sort of an excuse by my mother why my uncle and his family wouldn't come around to see us," Sarah said in a calmer tone.

Tears began to fill Sarah's eyes as she continued, "The hurt and anguishing pain that filled my father's heart was obvious. Day and night I know, he punished and blamed himself over their separation, but he held firmly to his convictions until the day he died, a hero for our cause. That's why if need be, I'll avenge his blood in anyway necessary to hold onto those convictions and beliefs that he gave his precious life to preserve."

"How will you get into Washington City?" Jacob asked, changing the subject and to gain information on the new route.

"I don't know. The old lady has all of the details I need."

"Would you also kill her if she betrayed you?"

Sarah didn't answer Jacob's question, but just gazed at him. Somewhere within her heart, she began to question if Jacob really had the heart for such a dangerous and ruthless game that sometimes required the most drastic and heartless actions to be taken in order to achieve its success. On the other hand, Jacob's last question began to raise some suspicion and questions within her own heart and mind over his loyalty to the cause and the bloody cost that was required for total victory. Sarah hoped the feelings surfacing within her heart were unfounded and untrue because she found herself attracted to him. In many of his actions and words there was something about his personality and character that was drawing her closer to him.

Chapter Twenty-Seven

Within the hour, Sarah departed by carriage from Richmond to Port Royal. Under the cover of darkness, the journey had been slow because of rain showers and had taken nearly four hours to complete. In accordance with Captain Norris' instructions, she met Miss Bessie Carleton at Fox's Tavern and spent the night at her residence, an old plantation from the 1700's that was near the river and once very productive in the tobacco agriculture.

The next morning at dawn, Sarah arrived to take the first ferry across the Rappahannock River in accordance with her orders. It was sunny and the river in the area was wide and calm. As she boarded the vessel, she looked around her surroundings to see if there was an elderly lady that was to be her contact and guide for the duration of her journey. She noticed there were three ladies fitting that particular description and they were escorted by males. There was nothing said to her by Captain Norris about this and she became concerned something might have happened to her contact.

As the ferry departed the riverbank, Sarah glanced back at the town. Sarah opened her parasol and shaded her eyes from the bright sunlight. She thought of the hazards of this journey and how she might penetrate and pass safely through Federal lines into Washington. There were many thoughts concerning various scenarios that might challenge her mission. This new route was one where there would be agents she wasn't familiar with. Nor were there individuals she could trust such as she had with some of the other routes to the north she had taken in the past. This mission, she thought, would be one with great risk, but as always, she was ready for such a challenge.

When the ferry was three-quarters of the way across the Rappahannock, a female's voice said, "Hello young lady. The weather is sure nice out here today, ain't it?"

Sarah turned and looked at the smiling lady and answered softly, "Yes, the weather is nice today, but unfortunately, these are perilous times that we live in."

"My child, the times will improve, the war will pass and we can live as free people once more."

"It must be soon," Sarah somberly answered, playing the game as an innocent civilian until she heard the key words in the introduction that were previously given to her by Captain Norris.

"And to what color should we look to?" the elderly lady asked.

"To the butternut and gray," Sarah replied confidently, knowing those were the key words.

"Do ya have your pass?"

"Yes, I do."

The elderly lady smiled. She softly said, "You're on time. Once we arrive on the other side, ya can get into my buggy."

"Who is the gentleman with you?" Sarah cautiously asked.

"Oh my dear girl, that old fool is my honey, Tom. He's as harmless as a dang fly. You mustin' feel threatened by him."

"I just like to know who I am associated with, that's all," Sarah swiftly snapped.

"Ya don't like surprises?" the elderly lady said laughingly, continuing, "Well so ya know who yall's a travelin' with, my name is Maude, and your's?"

"My name is Molly," Sarah replied, using once again her assumed name.

"Well Molly, were gonna get ya to where ya need to go, and we are gonna do it my way. Does ya understand?" Maude answered in a stern tone.

"Do you know most of these people on the ferry?" Sarah asked as she looked around.

"Yeah...sure do. These folks live around here. They catch the early ferry so they can go about their business," Maude replied as she looked around to see if there were any strange faces among the people.

When the ferry arrived on the opposite shore from Port Royal, Sarah stepped up into the buggy, and Maude did likewise. Maude turned and said as Tom began moving the horse-drawn buggy, "If anyone says anything to ya, ya is my niece from Richmond." Pausing and looking inconspicuously at the people leaving the ferry, she continued, "Once we arrive at the homestead, I want to see ya pass. If ya don't have it, then I'm a gonna have old Tom here deal with ya, understand?"

"But I gave you the phrase to the riddle, that is supposed to be sufficient to travel this route."

"Young lady, ya can't be too over cautious when ya life is involved."

As Sarah looked at Maude, she felt some pressure against her side. She glanced down and noticed Maude had a small derringer against her ribs.

"I thought we were on the same side! Are you a Unionist! Why the weapon?" Sarah anxiously asked.

"Now just ya quiet down young lady. We are on the same side once ya show me the pass. But until then, I'm a not a trustin' anyone," Maude calmly replied, as she continued to hold the weapon against Sarah's body.

Sarah was very uncomfortable with the situation because at the moment, she didn't know for sure who she was dealing with and what harm they might try to inflict on her. Until they arrived at the old lady's homestead, she would have to play the game and see where it would lead and then make her escape should it come to that action.

Sarah and the elderly couple hadn't traveled far when they came to a white weather-board house, surrounded by trees along the road leading to Fredericksburg. When Tom brought the horses to a halt at the rear of the house near a dwelling that might have been where a servant or slave had lived at one time, Sarah stepped down from the buggy. Maude took the lead toward the house and Tom quietly gestured for Sarah to follow.

Once on the inside of the dwelling, Maude turned and kept the small weapon pointed at Sarah.

"All right Molly, let's see the pass that ya's suppose to be carrying?" Maude demanded.

"If I may freely move my hands, I will show you," Sarah replied as she kept her eyes on Maude and the weapon.

Sarah removed her blue bonnet and laid it on the table. As she continued to look at Maude, she unwrapped her hair that was made up in a bun, removing a small piece of paper. She took and handed the paper to Maude.

Maude unraveled the paper and read its contents with caution. She looked up at Sarah and said, "I am sorry for taking such action, but I am quite careful of everyone I deal with."

"Why does someone like Tom and you get involved in something you could get killed for?"

"Because we has a son that's fightin' with General Lee against those dang Yankees near Richmond. And if he's a gonna put his precious life on the line to protect us why should we not do our best to help him," Tom swiftly and angrily answered.

"I guess maybe we wanted to give something back to the boys that are fightin' from this area with our son," Maude said as she looked intently on Sarah.

"As I understand, you know the next move in this route and will help me to get past the Yankees at Fredericksburg and Aquia Creek."

"That's right and your next guide should be here soon," Tom answered as he walked over and glanced out the window.

"Sit down while I fix us some coffee," Maude said as she walked over and opened the lid on the pot. She continued, "Tom, could ya go and draw me some water from the well?"

"But who is coming and what am I to do next?" Sarah impatiently asked.

"I don't know. We are only given our part of the mission. We never know what the next agent will do. This way if one of us is caught by the Yankees or one of their detectives, the rest of the route is protected because we have no idea what the other hand is going to do. So, don't be so dang nosey." Pausing and looking at Sarah, Maude continued, "This route is quite different than what ya are used to travelin'. I can tell by your actions and expressions that you are a little uneasy. I am sure the route that ya are used to takin', ya knows mostly all of the agents that help out, but it's not that way with this one. As I understand, only the most trusted and best will use this one. I guess we didn't expect a lady. The only one to come through was a man and we don't know if he ever made it or not. So do as I ask and sit for a spell."

Sarah did as she was asked, but even though she was out of immediate danger, she still felt quite uneasy about this venture. Her thoughts were interrupted when Tom walked through the door with a pail of water.

"There is a rider coming down the road," Tom said.

"Do you know who it is?" Sarah asked.

"No, but were surely gonna find out," Tom said in a rough tone.

Sarah stood and quickly approached the window. She stood to the side of the window and far enough away so she could see who was approaching but not be seen by anyone passing the front of the house. Even though she still felt uneasy about everything that had happened and the uncertainty as to the challenges and risks ahead, she knew she didn't have any other choice in the matter but to continue to play out the role.

The sound of horse hooves slowed until the mysterious rider brought his horse to a halt and looked toward the house. Sarah watched as the rider, dressed in farmer's clothing removed his hat and wiped the brow of his forehead. He was looking at the house. He spurred his horse and rode to the back of the dwelling. Sarah remained calm and quietly repressed the sudden fears and emotions that were attempting to overtake her. She quickly glanced at Tom, then Maude. They appeared to be calm, but expressions of concern covered their features. Apparently, Sarah thought, neither Tom nor Maude had ever worked with this agent. Sarah calmly moved to the table where she saw a butcher's knife lying on a wooden board. There she waited and would make her move should this individual be someone who might cause harm to her accomplices or jeopardize her mission to Washington City.

Chapter Twenty-Eight

Sarah's eyes were continuously on the stranger as he dismounted his mare. The mysterious individual again looked around the outbuildings and then the house before approaching. Sarah tried to determine by his actions if he was carrying a weapon. Her heart continued to race. As she glanced at Tom and Maude, they too were silently gazing at the individual. She was sure Maude still possessed the small derringer.

Once satisfied with his surroundings, the mysterious individual approached the doorway to the rear of the house and knocked several times.

Tom looked at Maude for some indication for proceeding with the situation. He noticed Sarah was gesturing for him to slowly open the door. He slowly pulled up the door latch and asked the stranger, "What do you want?"

"I have traveled far and I am hungry and thirsty. Can you please open the door?" the graveled voice middle-aged man asked.

"How do I know that I'm speakin' to friend or foe?" Tom slowly asked.

"You have to trust me."

With the nod of Maude's approval, Tom cautiously opened the door and allowed the stranger to enter.

As the stranger removed his hat and gazed at Maude and Sarah, he quietly nodded his head in a friendly gesture while Sarah continued to stand near the table where she could grab the butcher knife and use it if necessary.

"I don't believe I've ever seen ya in these parts before." Tom said as he closed the door.

"No you probably haven't. I am from north of Fredericksburg."

"What brings ya to these parts?" Maude asked as she removed the coffee pot from the stove.

"That young girl standing over there," the stranger said, pointing at Sarah.

"These are my folks. Why would you come after me?" Sarah defensively asked.

"Because I am the only person from here who knows this route and can get you into Washington City, and these people are not your folks."

"How do I know I can trust you? That you're not some Yankee in disguise?" Sarah swiftly asked.

"If I may?"

The mysterious individual sat on a chair near the table and removed his boot. He looked at Sarah and asked, "Give me that knife that you're hiding for a moment."

Sarah was surprised and her expression revealed this man's perception. Cautiously, she slowly began to comply with his request.

When the stranger noticed her caution, he stood and opened his duster and said, "See, I am not carrying a weapon. Now hurry, we don't have much time."

Sarah handed the stranger the knife and watched him rip the heel off his boot, and asked, "What is your name?"

"Edward. Edward Murdock. But most people I know call me Ed."

"Well, Ed, how do I know you're not going to double cross me?" Sarah asked.

"This is why." Edward said as he handed Sarah a piece of paper.

Sarah quickly glanced at the paper that only said, "To Virginia and the Gray." It was signed by Secretary of War George Randolph.

"How do we get pass the Federal lines near Fredericksburg?" Sarah asked as she rolled up the paper and returned it to Edward.

"I have my ways, but I am not obliged to reveal them at this time."

"I understand."

"We must leave immediately. I would like to be beyond the Federal lines as soon as possible," Edward commanded.

"I must change into something more comfortable so I can ride the horse," Sarah anxiously said.

"We don't have time for that."

Sarah nodded as she put on her bonnet and grabbed her parasol. She turned and glanced at Maude, whose features were still covered with concern.

Edward said to Maude, "That coffee sure smells good. Could I have some?"

Maude poured Edward a cup and he gulped its hot contents down and wiped his mouth. He turned his attention to Sarah and said, "Let's go."

Shortly, Tom and Maude watched as Edward and Sarah departed their house. They walked over and continued to gaze at the two as Edward assisted Sarah onto her horse. As Edward mounted his mare, Maude said to Tom, "That young girl is takin' such a big risk."

"There's nothin' that we can do about it now."

*   *   *   *

Since they were alone on the road, Edward and Sarah rode at a gallop west toward Fredericksburg. Once they were several miles from Tom and Maude's homestead, Edward slowed the pace.

"You are so mysterious. I would like to know more about you?" Sarah asked as she looked at Edward.

"There isn't much to tell."

"I would like to know something about the man I am trusting my life with," Sarah said as she rode closer to his horse.

"All right. Some years ago, I was a scout with the 1st Cavalry fighting Indians in Kansas. Once the war broke out, like many I guess, I resigned from the army and pledged my service to the Confederacy. Rather than accept a field command with the cavalry, I offered my services in doing what I do best and that is taking a risk to gain intelligence. That is until this opportunity came about," Edward replied with a smile.

"Do you have anyone else in your family fighting for the Cause?" Sarah asked.

"Yes, I have a younger brother, Jim, with the Alexandria Light Artillery. I haven't heard from him in sometime, but then, we are not as close as family should be," Edward replied as he turned, his blue eyes on Sarah.

"Where was he last?" Sarah asked gazing around her surroundings.

"He was with General Lee on the peninsula."

"Did he also resign from the Regular army?" Sarah asked as she once more returned her full attention to Edward.

"No, I was the only one, but I did serve with a group of soldiers that were just like brothers. There was that kind of respect, trust, and loyalty among us."

"Who did they cast their allegiance to?"

"Most of them stayed to fight with the Union. But there was a very gallant young officer I'll never forget that led our company that really stood out during those days when we were fighting the Indians. He was an officer we all respected because he was always in the front of the fighting and never asked anything of another man that he wasn't willing to do himself. Matter of fact, he was seriously wounded one afternoon while covering me during some fighting with the savages along Solomon's Creek. We became the best of friends, so much so that one might have thought we were brothers. Now this miserable conflict has divided all of us and who knows how many are still left, including 2nd Lieutenant Martin," Edward somberly replied as he removed his hat and wiped his forehead.

Sarah immediately brought her horse to a pause and shouted, "Martin! What was his first name!"

"Jacob. Jacob Martin."

"Are you sure of that?"

"You don't forget someone who has saved your life and at one time was just like family."

"What did he look like?"

"He had the thickest wavy brown hair I ever saw on a man, clean shaven, vivid blue eyes that were very sensitive in nature and his feelings about matters were always reflected through them." Pausing and pondering, Edward continued, "I'd say he was medium in height and weight. The thing I remember the most is that the ladies at Fort Leavenworth considered him very handsome and he could have had his pick of the lot, but for some reason, he didn't. All the men from our company so envied him."

"That's the same man I am working with, only now he has a full dark beard. At that time, how strong were his sentiments for the Union?"

"The absolute! He was very much a Unionist. It was the one thing that separated us from each other. Sometimes we would get into very heated arguments over the sovereignty, and rights of states to secede from the Union. At one time, he advocated that men who were disloyal to the Union should be court-martialed. But for some unknown reason, he left the army a little over a year before the war began. We all figured when he suddenly disappeared that he had been asked to resign his commission from the army for his over-opinionated views. I haven't seen or heard from him since. He just disappeared from off the face of the earth. It just wasn't like him to act this way."

"Are you very sure he was that loyal to the Union and its fight against us?" Sarah asked in an angry tone.

"The Jacob Martin I knew would have had you shot for treason if he could have for saying anything disloyal about the Union. He is over there with the Yankees, I am sure of that," Edward confidently said.

"We have problems," Sarah said in a frustrating tone, continuing, "Back in April, the man I know and you just described traveled the same route with me under the pretense of being a banker in Richmond. At Fairfax Court House we were both captured by the Federals, but only he escaped. The same man that fits your description is traveling the other route as we speak to Washington City with the same message. Now I fear my suspicions of him are more evident. I fear he might be a Federal spy. And he has earned the trust of government officials at the highest level within the Confederacy."

"Then I am sure that he'll make contact with someone in Washington City before he delivers the message."

"We have to get there first and deal with him."

Edward gazed at the fiery glare beaming from Sarah's eyes, knowing the determination to carry out the threat. He knew this war had caused individuals to bear a hate and animosity that would be unquenchable except with the shedding of blood. Human life that was once considered priceless was now meaningless while playing this game. What if it was really the same Jacob Martin riding courier across the Potomac that he knew? Was he really a spy? What would happen once they arrived in Washington City?

Chapter Twenty-Nine

Edward remained silent after Sarah expressed her desire to hastily deal with Jacob once he was discovered. Edward knew the Jacob Martin he had served with in the United States Army wasn't going to change his views concerning his loyalty to the Union for anyone. The only conclusion he could arrive at was that Jacob was working undercover for the United States Government, as a spy. Not only did Jacob know the important contents of the message he was carrying to Washington, but he also knew the agents to contact and possibly other agents working within the spy ring. Another important factor was he might also know how deeply planted they were in the various government agencies in the nation's capital. Jacob having the knowledge of how they operated and the methods they used to deceive their victims and relay messages back to Richmond would be damaging. All this would be disastrous to the Confederate covert activities that were functioning within the Lincoln government. Another matter of great importance is that he knows this particular route. This might be the only time it could be used if Jacob wasn't stopped. In the future, many Southern lives might depend on the operation of this route for covert activities. Edward knew he would have to stop his friend from carrying out his scheme, even if it meant killing him.

As Sarah and Edward continued in the direction of the Stafford County line they noticed the road ahead passed through a heavily wooded area.

"Look, down the road," Sarah said as she pointed.

"Yeah, I see. It's a buggy. Just be normal and let me do all of the talking," Edward cautioned.

"I've been through this many times," Sarah answered in a defensive tone.

Once the buggy was closer, Edward brought his horse to a halt and waved for the individual in the buggy to do likewise. He noticed the buggy was slowing and when it was near, the male individual brought his horse to a halt.

"Howdy," Edward said, continuing, "I am lost, can you tell me what is ahead?"

"Go directly west and this road will take you to Fredericksburg. But Sir, I caution you going that way."

"Why?"

"About four miles back, there was a Federal cavalry patrol watering their horses along the river."

"I will do that. Thank you sir, and have a good day," Edward swiftly replied.

As the buggy with the gentleman began moving, Edward quietly watched until it was a short distance away. Edward turned and said to Sarah, "There is another road ahead, we can take that one."

"But what if we run into the Yankees?" Sarah asked.

"It's a chance we'll have to take."

After riding another mile and a half, Sarah and Edward came to a small white-weatherboard church, surrounded by maple and oak trees with a cemetery in the rear of the dwelling. Edward and Sarah paused and looked ahead.

"Dust clouds beyond those trees over there," Edward said as he pointed.

"It must be the Yankee patrol," Sarah affirmed.

"I wanted to go beyond the woods, but that's going to be impossible now. We are sure to be stopped and questioned." Quickly looking around, Edward noticed a farmer's lane heading toward a homestead near a wooded ridge. He shouted, "This way!"

Sarah and Edward smacked their horses and galloped at full speed toward the farm. Once they came near the farmhouse, several mounted Yankee cavalrymen emerged from one of the outbuildings with their pistols at the ready, yelling for them to stop. Edward pulled his revolver from his bedroll near the pommel of the saddle and cocked the hammer.

Sarah broke off from Edward and headed out across a field near the house. One of the Yankee cavalrymen dashed after Sarah. Immediately, Edward discharged his firearm, dropping the soldier from his saddle. The second Yankee cavalryman made a mad dash toward Edward. The soldier fired several times at Edward, but missed. Edward had ducked down alongside the horse's neck to give him some shelter from the flying missiles. Once Edward was alongside, he took the butt of his gun and struck the Yankee cavalryman across his forehead, dropping him from his saddle. Edward grabbed the reins of the soldier's horse and fled, following Sarah into the wooded slope.

Along the tree line, Sarah and Edward paused under the shade. Off in the distance, they watched as the twenty-man Yankee patrol paused near the little church. Some of the soldiers dismounted while others looked around the immediate area of the building. Once convinced the patrol would not pursue them, Sarah and Edward continued slowly westward toward Fredericksburg, using the shelter of the wooded tree line.

*   *   *   *

Within the hour, Sarah and Edward arrived at a homestead that was quite quaint in appearance, and possessed a homey atmosphere. Sarah noticed the double-veranda, the well-kept white fence surrounding the stone dwelling, and the multitude of various flowers covering the front and side of the house. It reminded her of the days when she was growing up in Chesterfield County. It was a time when family gathered around the dinner table laughing over some foolish incident and sharing the prospects of the future. During those days, who was to know of the horrors and tragedies of war. They were so far away. She knew those special times were in the past and were never to be experienced again because death had enshrouded its wings over her friends and family and had given her the image of an uncertain future.

When Sarah and Edward brought their horses to a halt at the front gate, a little girl ran onto the porch and asked, "Who are you?"

The little girl reminded Sarah of the days of her youth when she anxiously and recklessly ran into the front yard to see who was arriving. Sarah dismounted and smiled saying as she approached the child, "My name is Molly. What is yours?"

"I'm Gracie," the child replied in a shy manner.

"How old are you, Gracie?" Sarah asked as she knelt down near the child.

"I just had a birthday yesterday," Gracie replied she held up six fingers for Sarah to see.

"Is there anyone home with you?" Sarah asked.

"Just my mother. My mother is out back and I don't know where my Papa is. What do you want with them?"

As Sarah answered, "we are friends," Gracie's mother began to call for her.

"Out here Mother with some people," Gracie shouted loudly.

Suddenly, a young tall lady walked through the door. At first the expression on her face revealed an uncertainty, but when she recognized Edward her features revealed relief. She sighed and said, "Edward, it's you."

"Yes Maggie, it's me," Edward replied as he approached and took Maggie by the hand.

"If I may ask, who is this lovely friend of yours?"

"This is Molly," Edward replied not knowing her last name.

"Molly Gibson," Sarah said finishing the sentence.

"Well come on in, you must be hungry. I have some fresh bread that I baked and it will go good with the stew I have been cooking."

After Sarah and Edward entered the house, they both cleaned up and sat at the table where they were served by Maggie and Gracie.

"Where is Kendall?" Edward asked as he buttered his bread.

"He will be here shortly. He had an errand to run and should be back soon Maggie said as she poured the coffee.

"We ran across some Yankees. Were they here?"

"Yes, earlier this morning. Several of them stopped by and wanted something to eat. So I obliged them and they were on their way," Maggie said as she wiped her hand on her apron.

Neither Edward nor Sarah said anything, but knew it was probably the two cavalrymen they killed several miles away at the other homestead.

Suddenly, Edward heard the gallop of a horse approaching. He wiped his mouth and walked to the back of the house and looked out the rear window. There was a single rider leisurely approaching. He assumed that it was Kendall.

When Kendall walked through the back door, he recognized Edward and said, "I see you made it."

"We arrived not too long ago and had some of Maggie's cooking," Edward jovially replied.

"Well, you can't stay. The Yankees are looking for you," Kendall said in a concerned tone.

"What do you mean they are looking for me?"

"I was stopped about two miles back and a Captain Birnny asked if I had passed anyone on the road. I told him only a gentleman in a buggy. He told me two of his scouts had been killed and he was informed by Mr. Bradley that a man and woman, fitting your alls description had killed them in a firefight on his property. Birnny warned me if anyone harbored them and gave them shelter, they would be punished and their homes and barns would be destroyed."

"Those people were Unionist. That's probably why the Yankees were there, to obtain information. They were spies," Sarah angrily said.

"Come with me. We must hurry. I fear for my family," Kendall cried as he glanced at Gracie.

Edward gestured for Sarah to go and get the horses while he followed Kendall to the barn. Once on the inside of the structure, Sarah and Edward followed Kendall to one of the back stalls. They watched with interest as Kendall knelt down and began to remove by hand the straw covering the flooring. Once it was cleared away, Kendall took a spade and pried open some boards that were actually part of a trap door. Kendall leaned over and pulled from under the flooring, a small wooden box. When he opened it, there were several Yankee uniforms neatly placed. Kendall rose to his feet and handed one set each to Sarah and Edward.

"What is this?" Sarah abruptly asked.

"What's it look like," Edward said as he looked at Sarah.

"Oh no, I am not putting on no Yankee uniform," Sarah angrily shouted.

"If you're traveling with me, you'll do as I say, understand? Now go into that stall over there and change so we can get going," Edward angrily replied.

There was a frustrated and humiliating expression that covered Sarah's face as she complied with Edward's demand.

As Edward watched Sarah walk away, Kendall asked as he once more covered the areas with straw, "Where in the world are you taking that girl?"

"You know you are not to ask me my business. The little you know the better it will be for Maggie and you and especially little Gracie," Edward answered in a stern tone.

For a moment, the two men just stared at each other without saying another word.

When Sarah was ready, she walked out and asked, "Will I pass if the Yankees see me?"

Edward still noticing an expression of dissatisfaction on Sarah's face nodded quietly in the affirmative.

"What do you know about Federal forces near Fredericksburg?" Edward asked as he turned his attention to Kendall.

"I heard rumor through the underground that some of Burnside's men of the IX Corp are to arrive within the next couple of days near Aquia Creek. I feel it might be a good word because just yesterday, I was in the area helping Maggie's father on the farm and I noticed there was quite a bit of activity taking place near the landing."

"They're apparently going to reinforce Pope," Sarah added.

Without another word, Sarah and Edward mounted their horses and said their farewells to Kendall. Kendall watched as the two rode quickly across the rolling green meadows of the farm in the direction of Fredericksburg.

Chapter Thirty

Jacob slipped into Washington City un-noticed around 9 o'clock the next evening, under the cover of darkness, and proceeded directly to the residence of Secretary Stanton with the information that was in his possession. Again Lieutenant Stanley was on duty and escorted Jacob into the parlor where Secretary Stanton would receive him.

When Jacob entered the room, Secretary Stanton was standing and looking out the window at the gas lighted street rubbing his gray beard. Jacob knew he must be in thought because the Secretary didn't notice his presence.

Lieutenant Stanley cleared his throat and Secretary Stanton softly said, "Stanley, I know you're there. What is it?"

"Captain Martin is here from Richmond."

"What do you have for me, Captain?" Secretary Stanton asked as he continued to gaze out onto K Street.

"I am once more carrying a message for Miss Wilson."

"And do you know what it says?"

"Yes sir, I do. The information wasn't written in code, but given to me verbally by Captain Norris himself. The Confederate authorities want to know if General McClellan is planning to reinforce General Pope's army and move against Richmond from the north."

"I see. Let me ask you, what do you feel the Rebels' intentions are?"

"Already as you must know, Stonewall Jackson's II Corps has been moving into the Piedmont region to intercept some of General Pope's forces. I believe if they feel General McClellan is no longer a threat to Richmond from the Virginia Peninsula, than the rest of Lee's army might move to reinforce Jackson."

"All General McClellan can do is talk a big talk of what he could do if he had more reinforcements, a larger army. A few weeks ago, General Halleck returned from seeing General McClellan at Harrison's Landing, trying to determine his intentions for once again commencing operations against Richmond, but General McClellan would only commit himself to battle if he were reinforced." Secretary Stanton turned and faced Lieutenant Stanley and Jacob. He continued, erupting into an angry tone, "Unfortunately, we don't have the men to meet his demands! Once more if he would only begin operations, we could strike Richmond a blow from the north as well, destroying Lee's army while divided and end the war! But no, General McClellan plays politics with the army! He plays politics with the war! The man is not fit to command an army!"

"Sir, I must caution, I am not the only courier on this mission. There is another," Jacob added.

"Do you know who?" Lieutenant Stanley asked.

"Yes, a female, Miss Sarah Robins. She is the young lady I was traveling with back in April when captured at Fairfax Court House. She was detained and later released, but it would have served us better if she hadn't been set free."

"Why, she is just a woman," Lieutenant Stanley replied in an unconcerned tone.

"She isn't some charismatic chivalrous female like Belle Boyd, she is as deadly as a copperhead. She killed a double agent and the physician that ran a safe house on the outskirts of Culpepper Court House. If we capture her while she is in the city, we must keep her imprisoned until the war is over," Jacob answered in a serious tone.

"It will be done," Secretary Stanton ordered, continuing, "But for now you must hurry along and see that Amanda receives her instructions. Unfortunately, we still don't have any knowledge of who her associates are within the city that she's been working with. I don't know that we can continue to honor your request of not arresting her."

"Yes sir, I agree. I just thought if we watched her for awhile that somewhere she would slip up and reveal her accomplices."

"That hasn't happen even though she was constantly watched," Lieutenant Stanley replied.

"Her servants must be more loyal to her than I assumed. I almost blundered and had one of them deliver my message to you back in April. Thank God I didn't. But I have one question," Jacob said.

"What is it?" Secretary Stanton asked.

"Is she still seeing Senator Putman?"

"Unfortunately yes, but we have been careful with the information he has been entrusted with. And fortunately for us, his wife has been staying with him in the city, so between her presence and some of the social functions they have been attending, I doubt that he's had much time to see Miss Wilson," Lieutenant Stanley replied.

"Before I return to Richmond, Amanda Wilson will be in custody," Jacob promised.

As Jacob turned to leave with Lieutenant Stanley, Secretary Stanton said, "Somehow, you must find out who else is working with her so we can destroy this whole nest of Rebel activity."

"I suggest that Captain Martin meet me tomorrow morning at 10:00 o'clock at Harvey's Oyster Saloon. Do you know where it is located?" Lieutenant Stanley asked as he looked at Jacob.

"Yes, it's down in the area of the city where all the bars, brothels, and slums are located. No one with any sense of mind would want to go into that part of the city."

"Well the President did and if it is good enough for him then it will be good enough for you," Secretary Stanton swiftly answered in a scolding tone.

"I would like to meet with you there because we won't be noticed in that area of the city. I will be wearing civilian clothing. If everything works accordingly, tomorrow will be the day we will arrest Miss Wilson," Lieutenant Stanley added.

Jacob looked and remained silent, only nodding in agreement. Jacob quietly turned and was escorted to the rear entrance of the house by Lieutenant Stanley.

*　　*　　*　　*

After leaving Secretary Stanton's residence, Jacob headed to Amanda's, knowing he must conclude his business before Sarah's arrival. When Jacob arrived at the rear entrance to Amanda's home, he noticed a light was still burning in the drawing room. He knocked several times before Malachi opened the door. It was almost like Jacob was expected. After Malachi escorted him to the parlor, Jacob patiently waited for Amanda's arrival. He glanced around the room and noticed some of the photographs covering her fireplace mantel. He walked closer and gazed carefully at one photograph in particular. Amanda was with a gentleman of wealth and several young ladies and a young gentleman who were well dressed. They stood before a double veranda mansion surrounded by trees. The only conclusion Jacob could assume from the photograph was that at one time, Amanda must have possessed great wealth. The figure that continued to draw his attention and scrutiny was the young lady standing beside Amanda. After closer observation, Jacob recognized her as Sarah. He was greatly surprised by this revelation. In reality, he concluded that Amanda was Sarah's mother.

Jacob's attention was interrupted when Amanda entered the room and said, "I see you're interested in my photographs?"

"I am sorry, I guess I was being nosey while waiting on you."

"That's quite all right. The photograph was taken five years ago while I was living near Chesterfield, Virginia with my husband Roger and my family."

"I see. If I may ask, what happened to him?"

"He passed away with the consumption not too long after that photograph was taken," Amanda replied in a somber tone.

Jacob knew she was lying because of his conversation with Sarah on their journey to Washington City back in April. He was determined to play along with Amanda, but wouldn't ask any questions regarding her relationship with Sarah.

Amanda continued in a more jovial tone, "Jacob, you must have something of importance for me to be here at this late hour of the evening."

"Yes, I do. Captain Norris wants you to find out as soon as possible the intentions of what will transpire with General McClellan's forces. They need to know if he will resume offensive operations against Richmond, especially since Pope's Federals are threatening from the north."

"I know, I've been following events from reading the newspapers. I don't have any information as of yet."

"How long will it take?"

"I don't know. They must be patient," Amanda swiftly replied in an irritable tone.

"What will you have me do?"

"Stay out of sight in the carriage house."

As Amanda departed the parlor, Jacob followed her to the library. He waited at the entranceway while she jotted down a few lines on a piece of paper. When finished, she hastily sealed it in an envelope and rang the bell for a servant. Malachi answered the call.

"Deliver this immediately!" Amanda commanded in a tone of urgency.

"Yes'um," Malachi softly replied.

"And don't return until you have an answer, understand!"

Both Amanda and Jacob quietly watched as the servant departed by the rear entrance to the house for his destination.

Chapter Thirty-One

Once Malachi had departed, Amanda turned and quietly looked at Jacob for the longest time. She walked past Jacob. He gazed at her. Amanda turned once more and said, "You must be exhausted from your travels. Why don't you come and sit down and tell me what's going on in Richmond."

Jacob followed Amanda into the drawing room across the hallway from the library. When he entered the room, he sat in a chair near the rosewood harpsichord. Amanda smiled and asked, "Why don't you pour us a drink."

Jacob quietly walked to the server and complied with the request. When he finished, he turned around and approached Amanda with the liquor.

Amanda quietly gazed at Jacob and placed her hand on the sofa as a gesture for him to be seated near her. When he complied with her invitation, she softly said, "My servant Francy will be up before sunrise in the morning and I don't want her disturbed by us talking. Besides, I can't retire for the evening until Malachi returns so why don't you keep me company."

Jacob quietly nodded in agreement and asked, "Why did a Southern lady such as yourself move to Washington City?"

"Washington City is a Southern community," Amanda said laughingly, continuing, "I didn't want to operate a large tobacco plantation by myself. As you know, many women don't have much of a say in local or state political affairs or even their business matters."

"What about your son? They would have respected him on your behalf?" Jacob asked taking a sip of the liquor.

"That's true and would have been the traditional thing to do, but I guess I am different," Amanda replied in a soft tone.

"In what way?"

"I have always wanted to do something adventurous and challenging. I guess that's the real reason why I sold the place. As for my son, he wanted to study the arts abroad in France and he got his wish."

Jacob knew she was lying to some degree, but he let her continue her tale.

"So to fulfill the desire for adventure, you became a spy?" Jacob asked looking into her eyes.

Amanda was silent, but a bright smile beamed the width of her face. She said, "It has its challenges and risks that have been very beneficial to me."

"It does have its challenges and risks and it is a game of intrigue, but unlike us men, you are let's say smacked on the hand and we are hanged."

Amanda laughed and took a sip of the liquor. She placed the glass on the stand next to the sofa, turned and said, "I do what I have to do to obtain the information that we need to bring this conflict to an end. The war has financially cost us a great amount of money and many of our noble and bravest men will never return home to their families because of the Yankee oppression in their attempts to exert their will upon us Southerners."

"I agree with your feelings."

"Do you have a brother or someone in your family that's fighting for the Cause?"

"My good friend, Benjamin Hart from Loudoun County. I've been able to spend sometime with him after he was wounded at Gaines' Mill."

"I hope he wasn't seriously injured," Amanda said in a sympathetic tone.

"His arm was all shot up, but he'll recover and he is determined to return to the army. His wife Rachel has been in Richmond taking care of him and I expect soon, she'll return home."

"Benjamin is a real patriot. It's men like him that I am willing to do whatever I have to in order to contribute to the Cause. If I am ever captured, the cost that I'll pay will be very little in comparison to men like him who have sacrificed so much for all that we believe in."

Jacob remained silent as he looked into Amanda's eyes. She was silent and moved her hand and touched his.

"As I told you before you left for Richmond back in April, I said I was fond of you."

"I remember you saying something to that effect."

Amanda's eyes were fixed on Jacob. She remained silent as she leaned forward and kissed Jacob several times gently on his lips. She was quiet and began to caress his cheeks, when suddenly she passionately kissed him again. When she broke their embrace, she smiled and said, "You must feel the same as I do or you would have refused my aggressiveness."

"That would be difficult seeing I wanted it to happen as much as you," Jacob replied with the intentions of deceiving Amanda.

Again, Amanda embraced and kissed Jacob passionately. When finished, she smiled and stood to her feet. She took him by the hand and softly said, "I want you to stay with me tonight rather than in carriage house."

Jacob looked into her eyes and softly answered, "All right." .

"Give me a few minutes and then come up to my bed-chamber," Amanda said with a smile.

Once Amanda disappeared to the second floor of the house, Jacob looked around and walked over to the library. He thought maybe she kept some of the names and addresses of individuals she was associated with in the spy ring concealed in the room. It was very quiet in the house and he didn't want to make any noise to arouse anyone's suspicions concerning his treachery.

Jacob looked on the top surface of Amanda's desk and carefully shuffled through some of the papers. There wasn't anything of value that would implicate her complicity with other associates. Again, he looked around, knowing he didn't have much time before she would be looking for him. Without a sound, Jacob opened some desk drawers, but came up with nothing of use. Time had passed and he knew he must give up the search. He proceeded to the upstairs bedchamber where Amanda was waiting.

When Jacob entered the room, Amanda was lying under the quilt smiling at him. He sat alongside the bed. He gazed into her eyes for the longest time and then he began to caress her long hair. Jacob noticed she too was gazing into his eyes, revealing her vulnerability. He knelt over her body and kissed her passionately.

The sound of the door opening downstairs interrupted Jacob and Amanda. Both knew Malachi was returning with valuable information.

After coming down to the lower level of the house, Amanda asked Jacob to wait for her in the parlor. She proceeded to the library to speak with her servant.

Once Amanda entered the room, she asked, "What information do you bring to me?"

"Mr. Harry will meet ya at da park tomorrow at 2:00 o'clock."

"Is that all?" Amanda anxiously asked.

"Yes'um."

Amanda nodded as the Malachi turned and walked away.

When Jacob knew Malachi was gone, he entered the room. He looked at Amanda who was standing near the desk in great thought. For some unknown reason, she appeared mystified.

"You look bewildered? What did your servant say?" Jacob asked approaching Amanda.

"I am to meet someone tomorrow afternoon."

"Why do you appear so surprised?"

"Because Harry always finds some reason to come here. Maybe, the Federal authorities or the Pinkerton's know about us. It's not like Harry to want to be seen with me in public." Amanda began to pace the room in thought. She turned and looked at Jacob, continuing, "Maybe, he knows about me and it's a trap. I might be arrested."

"It's a chance you'll have to take."

Amanda sighed and said, "I must be alone and think about this for awhile. I will see you first thing in the morning."

Without another word, Amanda departed the room and headed back to her bedchamber.

When Jacob began to walk toward the back entrance to the house, he looked into the kitchen area and noticed there wasn't a wood box near the stove. This caught his attention. He thought this was strange because wood was always kept somewhere handy near a stove. Walking over to the stove, Jacob held his hand over the top of it and the stove's surface appeared to be cool. He opened a door on the front of the stove that was used for baking. His eyes glanced along the flooring; there were no loose boards.

Jacob noticed there was a small closet built into the wall near a table. Opening the doors, he looked around. It was well stocked, but there were several bags of flour leaning against one side of the closet wall. Moving them to the side, he found what appeared to be a crack in the seam of the wall. Removing his knife from his trousers, he pried the board loose only to discover that it was part of a small opening that had been constructed in the wall. After removing the board, Jacob found an old leather folder. Immediately, he removed and opened it to see what was in it. There scribbled on a piece of paper were initials of the names of individuals with notes of interest on military troop movements in the city and local area. He was sure some of Amanda's informants worked in the government agencies, maybe even the War Department, which was the heart of military activity for the Union. On some of the other papers he found a description of various signals used in case of danger. But there was nothing in writing that would indicate Senator Putman's complicity.

Jacob returned to the library where he began looking through some of the vast selections of books on Amanda's shelves. After several minutes, he turned up nothing and was rapidly becoming frustrated until he came to one that was on the bottom shelf in the corner. The book was large, but it was so old the title wasn't legible any longer. Jacob removed it and opened several pages. Nothing out of the ordinary appeared until he came to an area of the book where there were numerous letters of the alphabet. All twenty-six letters of the alphabet were written across the top and down the page with various alphabetic letters written within the text. This configuration of numbers was known as the Vigenere alphabetic square used by Confederate intelligence to send their coded messages. Jacob knew this was Amanda's code.

Even though Jacob still didn't know the identities of the individuals working with Amanda, he did know where her cipher was located and important information that could be investigated by the Pinkerton's once she was arrested.

With this knowledge, Jacob departed by the rear entrance to the carriage house to await tomorrow's outcome.

Chapter Thirty-Two

Early the next afternoon Sarah and Edward arrived at a tavern on Duke Street in Alexandria. When she walked into the establishment, she found the dimly lit tavern was unfit for a lady. The men that crowded around the smoke-filled bar were obscene in their manner and liberal in their oaths. She noticed some of the men wore the Federal uniform such as she was dressed in.

Edward glanced at Sarah and said, "I must apologize, but this is where we will meet the next agent. Like the others, we will act normal, sit in that corner over there and have a drink and wait for his arrival."

"How long will that be?" Sarah asked as she looked around the dwelling.

"I don't know," Edward answered.

"Do you know him?"

"No, I don't, but he'll find us," Edward replied in an irritable tone.

For the past hour Sarah and Edward waited patiently while drinking a beer. During this time, the men in the establishment had become livelier in spirit and a fight had taken place between two individuals. Edward remained silent, giving the appearance of being somewhat nervous and concerned. Sarah didn't understand.

"Will you be going into the city with me?" Sarah asked after taking a sip of beer.

"No, once you are with the other agent, I'll be heading home."

"I didn't ask, but do you have a family?"

"No, I really didn't feel the life of a soldier was appropriate for a family."

"Really? Why did you feel that way?"

"It's a dangerous life that one undertakes, and you never know if you're coming back to them. Why should a wife and child live in that kind of uncertainty and fear." Pausing and continuing in a tone of humor, "Besides just look around at what they might be exposed to. I wouldn't want my family around a bunch of drunks."

"Maybe, our contact won't show," Sarah said looking in the direction of the entrance to the establishment.

"He is here. Edward reassuringly replied.

"How do you know?" Sarah asked quickly glancing around the room.

"I just know. I can feel it."

At about this time, a tall, middle-aged officer that Edward had been watching, standing at the bar approached the couple. For a moment, he was silent and took a long look at Sarah and then Edward. Sarah tried to determine his intentions. The officer commanded, "Calmly stand up and follow me."

"Why should we follow you?" Edward swiftly asked as he lit a cigar.

"Because we still have some unfinished business to attend to, that's why."

Sarah looked at Edward, knowing there must be some type of coded identification within the officer's statement because he appeared much more relaxed in his manner. Without hesitation, Edward and Sarah complied with the officer's command.

Once Sarah, Edward, and the officer departed the tavern, they walked several blocks to Smith's dry goods store not far from the Potomac River. Instead of entering the building through the store entrance, they instead walked to a side entrance and entered the building. They quietly followed the officer to the second floor.

Standing at the top of the stairway entrance was a middle-aged woman. She softly said, "I am Mrs. Taylor and whom might I have the pleasure of meeting?"

"I am Edward Murdock and this young lady is Molly Gibson."

"I have been expecting you. But you are late."

Once everyone entered the small room, Edward looked at his surroundings and said, "We were briefly held up near Aquia Creek. Federals were beginning to arrive from North Carolina."

"Burnside's IX Corps. Actually some of those troops are coming from Newport News," the officer confidently replied.

"You haven't introduced yourself. What is your name?" Edward asked as he gazed at the officer.

"I am Major Ronald Archer of the Washington City District Marshall's office."

"You are a Yankee?" Sarah shouted.

"Yes madam. Let's just say that I am a Southern Yankee and leave it at that."

"If you'll come with me, you can clean up and I will get you some lady's clothing to put on before you go with Major Archer into the city," Mrs. Taylor suggested as she took Sarah by the hand and headed for another room.

"But he is a Yankee! I am not going anywhere with that scoundrel," Sarah loudly insisted.

"Madam, respectfully, you are to do as you are told." Major Archer authoritatively demanded.

"I don't understand. Why would you fight for the Confederacy instead of the Union?" Edward swiftly asked as he approached the officer.

"Originally at the beginning of the war, I wanted to obtain a commission with a field command in the Confederate service, but that all dramatically changed when I met Mr. James Howard. At that time, Mr. Howard was working for Rose Greenhow gaining whatever information he could garnish from the District Marshall's office for the Southern war effort. But just being a clerk didn't entitle Mr. Howard to the entire inside knowledge that was needed concerning military matters and troop movements, and particularly those individuals that were suspected and arrested for possibly spying. At the time of our acquaintance, he was looking for more information on troop movements because Federal forces were moving into Arlington, Virginia."

"How did he recruit you?" Edward asked.

"In short what everyone else desires in this life…money."

"So your services are supplied by the one with the most money? You bribed him."

"You might say that, but then too, you might look at it in another way."

"Such as?"

"I provide a very valuable service for Jeff Davis's government, but with a very substantial cost to him. But whether you believe it or not, my loyalties are with the Confederacy," Major Archer replied with a smile on his face.

Edward remained silent, but was greatly concerned because he didn't know these individuals or if they could be trusted. In the past, he knew the other agents involved in the schemes, but this was all new to him. Maybe they were double agents, but for now, he would have to play the game.

Chapter Thirty-Three

It was 10:00 o'clock in the morning when Jacob arrived at Harvey's located on 11th and C Streets. From first appearances, the buildings in this area of the city were dingy and greatly tarnished with neglect. He knew beforehand one must take precaution because it was considered one of the most dangerous areas of the city. This was largely due to the notorious gang activity, which considered robbery and murder as its main occupation. Under his coat, he carried a pistol for protection. The region was known as the slums of Washington City. He noticed trash and debris of all kind being tossed by the wind over the streets. There was a smell that was very offensive to him. It was coming from the Washington Canal that flowed through the city from the Potomac River to the Anacostia River. He knew the canal was notorious for being littered with rotted fish from the markets and dead livestock.

When Jacob walked into the former blacksmith shop, he immediately looked around and noticed Lieutenant Stanley standing by a bar gazing at him. Jacob approached and said, "Stanley, you arrived before me."

"Sir, I am always on time. What do you have for Mr. Stanton?"

"I discovered late last evening Miss Wilson's cipher in a large black book on the bottom shelf in her library. Also in the kitchen in a closet near the stove is a secret opening that I opened with my knife. There is proof of her complicity of traitorous activity found in a leather folder. And Miss Wilson is to meet Senator Putman this afternoon around two at Lafayette Park."

"We will be there and arrest her once she leaves the company of Senator Putman and returns home."

"I am sure because of the Senator's prominent position, the Secretary wishes to eliminate any kind of embarrassment to him." Jacob replied looking around the saloon once more.

"Yes, he does. It is unfortunate for us that the Southerners use their ladies in this manner to deceive and take advantage of men that possess great wealth and influence in our government. But these are unfamiliar times."

"Yes they are. I must also inform you Miss Wilson is the mother of the second agent, Miss Robins. I just discovered this information yesterday when I arrived at Miss Wilson's home."

"Interesting."

"I must return before Miss Wilson discovers I am missing."

Jacob turned and began to walk away. Lieutenant Stanley asked, "Has Miss Robins arrived yet?"

"No, but she is the one you must fear the most. If she arrives before Miss Wilson is arrested, I'll be the one to deal with her, understood?"

"Yes sir, I do."

As Jacob departed Lieutenant Stanley's company, there was a gentleman also dressed in civilian attire standing nearby where the oysters were being prepared. He had been inconspicuous in his nature during Jacob and Stanley's conversation, and unable to overhear the exchange between the two men. He was skilled at his profession and knew by all he observed that there was valuable intelligence information being shared. This individual also knew their identities and their function within the United States Government. He decided it would be feasible to follow Jacob and learn his intentions.

*   *   *   *

When Jacob returned to Amanda's residence, he immediately went to the house to see her. Once Amanda's servant answered the rear door, he entered and asked, "Is Miss Wilson at home?"

"Yes'um. If ya's will jist follow me."

Once Jacob entered the parlor, he noticed Amanda sitting on the sofa. At first she didn't look at him, but instead continued to gaze aimlessly at the floor. Finally when she did glance at Jacob, there was a sense of betrayal covering her somber expression. He pondered within his mind if she thought someone close might have betrayed her.

As Jacob quietly approached, Amanda softly asked, "I haven't seen you this morning. Where have you been?"

"Since we were up late last evening, I was tired from my journey from Richmond and slept in later than usual," Jacob calmly answered.

"I understand. Are you hungry?"

"No ma'am."

Amanda laughed and said, "Please do without the formalities. After all, we were very affectionate and passionate in our emotions toward each other last evening and matters as you know were becoming very intimate."

"I must apologize for allowing things to get out of hand. After all, we both had too much to drink."

"By all means, no. It was my hope that Malachi would have taken longer to return with an answer to my correspondence. Like I have said all along, I am very fond of you."

"Then why do you look so somber and appear so distressed?"

Amanda stood and walked over to the fireplace and looked at the photograph. For a moment, she gazed at the picture, turned once more and looked at Jacob. She sighed and said, "For over a year, I haven't seen or heard from my oldest daughter, Sarah. Actually, I don't even know where she is. It's almost like she disappeared from off of the face of the earth. With the fury of this war and the atrocities I have heard against civilians, I don't even know if she is dead or alive."

Jacob noticed the tears begin to flow down Amanda's cheeks. Somewhere in his heart, he believed she was sincere and not trying to play the game of espionage. He knew if Sarah showed up in Washington City before he departed there would be questions. Questions regarding his honesty as to why Amanda wasn't informed that he already knew Sarah and that she was the other agent working on this mission. The question was did Amanda already know her daughter was the other courier or did she know another courier existed with the same information? He decided to prove to Amanda that he was honest and dependable and not give her the slightest idea that he was an agent for the Federal authorities. It was imperative that he keep his identity and purpose as an agent secret for as long as possible and not be compromised so he could return to Richmond and continue his art of spying.

"I know her," Jacob softly said approaching Amanda.

"You do? How?" Amanda surprisingly asked.

"Such as I, she also is a courier and an agent for the Confederate War Department. Last April when I was captured at Fairfax Court House, unfortunately, she was the agent that I had to leave behind."

"Sarah was with you, coming here?" Amanda asked.

"Yes, she was. And now, she is the other agent carrying the same message as I, but taking another route. We did this just in case one of us was captured the other would get through to you. That's how important this mission was to the Confederate authorities."

"Something must have happened to her!" Amanda replied in an anxious tone as she embraced Jacob.

"I don't know the route. Maybe it takes longer and there might have been some delays. After all, when Sarah and I traveled this way back in April, we came by another way that was going to take longer than the ordinary and preferred route that agents used."

"It gives me great relief after all of these months wondering about her and her welfare. She was always such a mysterious young lady and not like my son. Sarah always preferred to keep us guessing about her life and what direction she would pursue."

The clock chimed once. Amanda glanced at the timepiece and said, "You must excuse me. I have to change my dress and get ready to meet with Harry. I want you to remain out of sight until I return and then you'll be contacted. I'll give you what information I am able to get from him, but before you leave this afternoon, I want to speak to you."

Amanda looked into Jacob's eyes and leaned up and kissed him. When she broke the embrace; she had a glimmer of a smile on her face.

Jacob quietly watched as Amanda slowly released his hand while her eyes were gazing at him. Once Amanda departed from the room, Jacob knew he was buying time. Eventually, Sarah would arrive and there would be many questions to answer. Maybe by some great fate, he could escape from Washington City and not have to encounter her.

Chapter Thirty-Four

The afternoon was sunny when Malachi and Amanda rode the short distance from her home to the entrance of Lafayette Park along Vermont Avenue. After Malachi assisted Amanda from the carriage, she glanced at the white edifice known as the Executive Mansion where President Abraham Lincoln resided. Amanda possessed a great contempt for Lincoln and believed as most Southerners that he should have refused to be engulfed into state affairs and leave the fiery social issue to the state governments to resolve. If it hadn't been for his election maybe this nation wouldn't be in the turmoil and struggling with the winds of war such as was ravaging the country.

Amanda walked a short distance through the park and paused, gazing at the beautiful Magnolia trees. Her attention was focused on the bronze equestrian statue of Andrew Jackson. It was a monument by Clark Mills that didn't impress her. As she continued to look around, within her view were the homes of some of the most prominent individuals within the United States Government. Residing near the park were the homes of Secretary of State William Seward, the abolitionist Massachusetts Senator Charles Sumner, Speaker of the House Schuyler Colfax, and General George B. McClellan, who was still waging war on the peninsula with his Army of the Potomac.

Her blood boiled at the thought of these men leading a nation to war against an innocent civilization and society and these thoughts continued to solidify her resolve for the Southern Cause. The only atmosphere that gave her comfort were the birds in the trees filling the air with song.

Amanda walked over to a bench and sat down. She glanced toward the park entrance and noticed Malachi was still standing obediently by the carriage. After a few minutes had passed, she noticed Harry Putman slowly approaching alone through the park entrance.

When Harry was nearby, he said, "Amanda, how are you doing?"

"Well considering I haven't hardly seen you in some time, I guess I would say I am doing good," Amanda softly answered.

"May I be seated?"

"By all means."

"I must apologize for neglecting you my love the way I have, but I've been very busy with affairs."

"You mean your wife don't you?" Amanda snapped.

"As difficult as it is to see and be with you because of Abigail being in the city, I don't want you to feel for a moment my dearest affections, have died for you. It's just I am in a very prominent and highly respected position in the Senate and I can't have my work and position compromised by the scandal of infidelity. She will be returning to Boston next month and we'll have all of the time in the world to be together," Harry said in a pleading tone.

Harry noticed the distressful expression covering Amanda's features. He took her by the hand and continued in a calm tone, "I am sorry, but there is a great deal happening with military movements, trying to destroy the Rebel army and capture Jeff Davis and Richmond at the moment. I am having to spend long evenings at my work." Pausing and looking at Amanda, he expected a response, a word of understanding, but she remained silent. Harry continued, "Even now, I am under a great deal of emotional stress. For now my love, you must be patient with me and I believe you will if you have the highest affection for me."

"It's just I have missed your companionship and it's been very lonely in the evenings without you," Amanda replied as tears filled her eyes.

"When matters have been resolved, I will come to you," Harry softly replied taking her by the hand.

"What is so important that could keep you away from me? Please Harry tell me so that I'll understand," Amanda cried in order to deceive him into telling her all that he knew of military matters.

"I shouldn't, but I will only because I want you to know I am sincere with you and that you must try to arrive at some understanding of all that I am going through at this time. For sometime now, General Halleck has been prodding General McClellan to once more take the offensive against Richmond and Lee's army, but he refuses to do so until he is reinforced. Therefore, since he isn't willing to move as hoped for, it is most likely with the President's permission that General McClellan's forces will be withdrawn from the Virginia peninsula and join with General Pope along the Rappahannock."

"I see." Amanda said as she softly stroked Harry's hand. "I do understand, but please come to me soon."

"I trust what I have said you will not repeat. Not even around your servants, whom I know you trust," Harry said gazing at Amanda.

"Your secret is my secret my love. I will not betray your trust," Amanda reassuringly replied.

"I know you wouldn't do anything to place me in a harmful way, but if it were to be repeated, someone such as a spy might pass the information on to Richmond and just as bad, that someone might know about us and attempt to blackmail me," Harry said in an excited tone.

Amanda leaned forward and kissed Harry on the cheek. She stood and smiled knowing she had received more information on military movements than what she had expected with her visit.

When Amanda boarded her carriage, she glanced at the wooden bench where Harry was still sitting. He appeared to be gazing at the ugly statue of Jackson. She knew he was in great emotional anguish and struggling with the reality of missing her companionship.

*   *   *   *

When Amanda returned to her residence, she immediately sent Malachi to the carriage house for Jacob. She quietly paced the floor of the library where she patiently waited for him to enter.

Once Jacob arrived, Amanda said, "You must leave immediately for Richmond. McClellan's army is going to be pulled away from the peninsula and join Pope's army against Richmond. There probably isn't much time. I don't know if this is beginning to take place as we speak or if it will occur within the next couple of days."

"I will get my things together and leave within the hour," Jacob swiftly replied.

As Jacob turned to leave the room, Amanda called, "Wait!"

Jacob turned and looked at Amanda as she approached. There was a serious expression on her face and in her manner. He knew from earlier she wanted to speak to him, but he wanted to leave the city before Sarah arrived, which could be at anytime.

"Jacob, don't leave yet," Amanda said as she placed her hands on his arms, softly continuing, "I need briefly to speak to you. I won't hold you up, but there has been something on my mind I need to say."

"What is it?"

"Most of last night, I couldn't sleep because I was thinking about you. We both know we share a strong bond and affection for each other. Yes, I am a little older than you, but I find myself in love with you. That I can't deny."

"Amanda, there is a war going on out there. There is no time for that sort of thing."

"But there is," Amanda cried.

Jacob attempted to interrupt, but Amanda touched his lips and swiftly asked, "Please, Jacob, let me finish." Speaking in a softer tone, Amanda continued, "I don't want to be spying and deceiving people in any way or means to get information out of them anymore, such as Harry Putman. I just want to enjoy some type of normal life with someone I can love. We both know it's only a matter of time before we get caught. The risk is high and the game is too dangerous. I don't want to give up something I have spent many years looking for."

Jacob walked away from Amanda toward the window near the desk. He silently looked out onto the street, knowing when he departed from her house that she would be arrested and imprisoned.

Amanda swiftly approached, continuing to speak, "When you finish delivering this message to Richmond, I could be waiting for you and we could leave for England and stay there until after the war. I have money, plenty of it. We could live comfortably for many years."

Jacob heard the clock in the hallway chime three times, knowing he must quickly leave. He calmly turned, faced Amanda and reluctantly said, "All right, I will come back to you as soon as I can. War is not a desirable occupation and true, if I am caught, I'll be hung, especially since we hung Timothy Webster. The Unionist would be looking to get even."

"Please be safe and return to me soon," Amanda said as she looked into Jacob's eyes.

Jacob was silent, but he held Amanda close to him and kissed her farewell. When he broke their embrace, he walked to the entrance of the library and turned and looked at her. There was a fearful expression on her features, almost like she was expecting something terrible to happen. He was quiet. Once more, Jacob turned and walked away knowing he might never see her again.

Chapter Thirty-Five

Less than an hour had passed since Jacob departed from Amanda's residence when a carriage with three men and a lady dressed in civilian clothing arrived at the front entrance to her home. Several of the men and the lady approached the entrance and rapidly knocked several times in succession while the third individual watched the back of the dwelling.

Malachi opened the door and asked, "Yes'um, may I'se help ya?"

"I am Lieutenant Stanley from the War Department. With me is detectives John Donaldson and Katherine Patterson. Is Miss Wilson at home?"

"Yes'um. She's in da upstairs."

"Come on! Hurry!" Lieutenant Stanley shouted to the other two detectives as he shoved Malachi to the side.

Once in the house, Lieutenant Stanley and Detective Patterson raced to the upper floor of Amanda's house while Detective Donaldson dashed toward the rear of the house on the bottom level.

At the top of the stairway, Lieutenant Stanley and Detective Patterson rushed to the front where Amanda's bedchamber was located. When they entered, Amanda was sitting at a desk and scribbling something on a piece of paper.

"What is the meaning of this?" Amanda shouted standing to her feet.

"We are here to ask you a few questions," Detective Patterson fired back as Lieutenant Stanley grabbed for the paper.

"About what!" Amanda shouted.

"About collecting information on military matters and passing it south to Rebel authorities," Detective Patterson snapped as she approached Amanda.

"What! How dare you to accuse me of such disloyalty to my country," Amanda screamed. Continuing in a loud voice, "By whose authority do you have the right to invade the privacy of my home!"

"By Secretary Stanton's," Detective Patterson shouted.

"Who is Betty Jo Wiles?" Lieutenant Stanley asked as he continued to glance over the paper.

Amanda turned and looked into Lieutenant Stanley's eyes. She calmly said, "A friend. I had sometime to spare before going out, so I thought I would drop her a few lines before going."

"I see."

"Do you know Senator Putman?" Detective Patterson asked as she began to look through Amanda's armoire and her wardrobe.

"Yes, I do. But only socially. Nothing more," Amanda replied after regaining her composure.

"No, it's more than social," Lieutenant Stanley fired back.

While the questioning was taking place, Detective Donaldson came to the upstairs and said, "Detective Green has arrived and is searching the kitchen area as you previously ordered."

"Start searching the upstairs. Tear this house to shreds if you have to, leave nothing unturned, understand?" Detective Patterson said as she approached Detective Donaldson.

Detective Donaldson nodded his head in agreement. He began carrying out all that was ordered. He searched dresser drawers, tossing Amanda's undergarments in a pile on the floor. When satisfied, he looked under the bed and bedding. He turned around and entered the closet where he emptied all of the hatboxes on the floor and searched Amanda's various colored hats inside and out.

"Please don't destroy my home," Amanda cried as tears flowed from her eyes.

"I am sorry madam, but I must do as ordered," Lieutenant Stanley commanded.

Another detective entered the room and said, "Detective Patterson, some of the Pinkerton's have arrived. I found this leather folder in the closet in the kitchen and the cipher code in this book. The other detectives have Miss Wilson's servants in the parlor awaiting questioning and some of them are continuing our search of the downstairs area of the house."

"Thank you," Detective Patterson said as she took the folder and the book with the cipher.

Detective Patterson knew this was the envelope and the book with the cipher that Jacob had spoken about earlier to Lieutenant Stanley. When she opened the book, her eyes rapidly looked over the contents until she came to the page containing the cipher. She walked over to Amanda and asked, "Is this book with this cipher in it yours?"

Amanda sighed and nodded her head in agreement, knowing there wasn't any use in resistance any longer.

After escorting Amanda to the library where she remained with Detective Patterson, Lieutenant Stanley and the other detectives began the interrogation of the servants of the house.

As Amanda watched Detective Patterson look through her desk, she pondered on the individual that might have betrayed her loyalty. Could it have been Harry Putnam? Was he afraid of being blackmailed? She quickly dismissed him as a possible suspect because he was too concerned and fearful about his position within the government and the damage it could do to tarnish his reputation and marriage. Senator Putnam knew any complicity with her and he would be ruined for life. Was it Jacob? After all, her acquaintance with him had been short in its duration, but their emotions for each other had been passionate and sincere. It was a devastating thought that caused enormous anguish and pain at such speculation. She continued to ponder on the reasons and complicity of other individuals she had association with in the spy ring and those individuals she had attempted to use for information.

Chapter Thirty-Six

As Sarah and Major Archer approached Amanda's residence, they noticed a large crowd of spectators had assembled around the house. What could have happened, Sarah thought? Was there a shooting or did the unthinkable happen? When they came near the crowd, Major Archer asked the coachman to bring the horses to a halt.

"I wonder why all these people are in front of Miss Wilson's house?" Major Wilson asked Sarah.

"I don't know, but we best find out before we go any further."

Major Wilson noticed an elderly man standing near the curve of the street speaking to another gentleman. He called out, "Hey old man." When the elderly gentleman turned, Major Archer gestured, "Yes, you. Come here."

The old gentleman finished speaking with the other individual and then he complied with the request and slowly approached the carriage.

"Why are all these people gathered in front of that house over there? What's going on?" Major Archer calmly asked.

"There are detectives in that lady's house." the gentleman replied pointing in that direction, continuing, "Someone said she has been accused of operating some kind of a spy ring in the city. The detectives have arrested everyone in the house including the darkies."

"I see. Thank you, Sir."

Major Archer turned and looked at Sarah. He could tell by the angry expression on her face that the whole operation had been jeopardized and most likely someone within the spy ring had been the one that betrayed Miss Wilson's trust.

"We must leave immediately before a detective or someone begins asking questions," Major Archer said.

"Take me to the National Hotel," Sarah snapped as the coach began moving away from the crowd.

"Is there some other way you can obtain the information that is needed?" Major Archer asked.

"No. The mission is over with," Sarah replied as she continued to look ahead.

Shortly, the carriage came to a halt in front of the National Hotel on Pennsylvania Avenue. Major Archer assisted Sarah from the carriage and called for a porter to help her with her bag. He asked, "May I escort you to your room?"

"No, Major that won't be necessary."

"All right then, I guess I will try and find out what I can about Miss Wilson and where she will be detained. I suspect the Old Capitol. When I know something, I'll come and inform you."

"Thank you. I need to know everything you can possibly find out, so my superiors in Richmond may access the damage done by her arrest. And I need it by morning."

"Are you sure I can't help you in anything else?"

"I am a big girl, Major," Sarah replied smiling as she walked away.

It was 8:00 o'clock in the evening according to the clock on the fireplace mantel. Sarah knew the return journey to Richmond in the morning would be long and tedious. She wasn't sure of the route she would take to Richmond, but she was sure she'd have to take the most practical and report all that had taken place today.

As Sarah prepared for bed, there was a soft knock at the door. She wondered who might be calling this late in the evening. She wasn't expecting anyone unless it was Major Archer returning with some news concerning Amanda.

"Who is it?" Sarah asked approaching the door.

"A friend of Miss Wilson's."

Sarah cracked the door and glanced at the individual. She asked, "What is your name?"

The individual whispered, "Truman Berry. I have information pertaining to the reason why Miss Wilson was detained."

Sarah cautiously opened the door and allowed Truman to enter her room. When she closed the door, Sarah carefully chose her words not knowing if she was dealing with a Federal or Pinkerton agent. "How do you know Miss Wilson?"

"Through Major Archer," Truman replied as he looked around the room.

"Are you his friend?" Sarah asked as her eyes followed him to the window overlooking the avenue.

"Just professionally. I am a Union soldier, but my loyalties are with my native state of Virginia."

"Why are you not fighting with General Lee?"

"For the same reasons that Major Archer does," Truman replied turning and looking at Sarah.

"Of course, the money," Sarah swiftly replied.

"The Major and I take bigger risks than most people can appreciate. We would definitely be shot or hanged if we were captured."

"I guess you are right about that," Sarah replied with a half-forced smile.

"Well what do you have for me?"

"Oh how soon you forget. To have the information I possess, it comes with a price," Truman confidently replied approaching Sarah.

"I thought you said you were a friend of Miss Wilson?"

"Yes, I am."

"Did she also pay for information?"

"Sometimes."

"I won't pay a penny for it. Where are your loyalties you just proclaimed to have for the Confederacy?" Sarah asked in an angry tone.

"Madam, I have no idea how much longer I am going to be able to work at this trade. But, if I am going to risk getting caught and possibly dying then I want to make sure that my wife and two little girls are taken care of," Truman answered in a calm tone.

"How much?"

"Fifty dollars."

As Sarah walked over to the stand next to her bed where her purse was, she was angry at the thought of paying for information. If she had a gun, she thought, she would have killed him after obtaining the valuable information he claims to possess. After quietly and swiftly removing the money from her purse, she approached Truman.

"Greenbacks, I hope," Truman demanded looking at Sarah's hand.

"By all means," Sarah sneered placing the money with force into his hand.

As Truman began counting the money, Sarah reassured, "It's all there."

"Yes it is," Truman answered looking again at Sarah.

"Now, what do you have for me?"

"Miss Wilson was betrayed by an officer that is actually an agent for Secretary Stanton and the War Department. Someone that's been to her home before."

"What's the scoundrel's name? Tell me!" Sarah angrily demanded.

"Captain Jacob Martin of the United States Army."

Sarah silently turned from Truman in a rage of anger. She turned once more facing him and asked, "Are you sure? There isn't some mistake?"

"No. He is the one."

"How do you know?" Sarah asked in a whisper.

"Late one evening in early April, Captain Martin arrived at Secretary Stanton's residence and showed the proper identification for an officer of his rank, even though he was dressed as a civilian. I didn't hear any of the information he had in his possession that evening because I was on the outside of the Secretary's home on guard duty. But as is my usual practice, I follow or sometimes obtain indirectly information from Lieutenant Stanley and pass it on to Miss Wilson. Just this morning, I followed Lieutenant Stanley to Harvey's on 11th Street and observed Captain Martin and him together. When they were finished, I followed Captain Martin to Miss Wilson's residence where she departed alone for about an hour. When she returned, I watched Captain Martin leave the carriage house and enter her residence. He was in there for about thirty minutes at which time, he departed by horse and I am sure left the city."

"Very good Mr. Berry," Sarah said in a sigh. "Your information was worth the money. Now if you'll excuse me."

Sarah opened the door and Truman departed. After closing the door, Sarah leaned her back against it and thought of how she would have to make an expeditious effort to get the message to Richmond. The individual that the Richmond authorities trusted the most was an agent for the United States Government. For a moment, Sarah thought of how Jacob had fooled everyone in Richmond and even her with his purity, sincerity, and naïveté in the world of counter intelligence and espionage. The first matter of business after getting a message to Richmond would be to contact Edward and have Jacob eliminated.

Chapter Thirty-Seven

It was after midnight when Jacob passed the Confederate sentries on the outskirts of Richmond. He was exhausted and hungry from his swift return journey from Washington City. As Jacob rode along the streets of Richmond to the boardinghouse where he was living, he pondered on his next move. With Amanda in custody, Sarah was sure to return to the safety of the city with many questions when she saw him. Jacob knew he needed to come up with a believable alibi that not only she would accept, but also Secretary Randolph and Captain Norris. It was his intentions to continue to be used by Federal authorities in the trade of espionage and spying against the Confederacy.

When Jacob brought his horse to a halt in front of his residence, he dismounted and looked around the lifeless surroundings, but didn't recognize the shadowy figure standing near the tree on the opposite side of the street. As Jacob entered the dwelling, everyone with the exception of one of the servants was sleeping. After giving him charge of his horse, Jacob quietly walked to the top of the stairway, turned and headed to the back of the house where his room was located. Jacob slowly opened the door and walked through and laid his bags on the stand next to the bed. Jacob began to remove his coat when suddenly the clicking sound of the hammer of a pistol broke the silence.

"Who is there?" Jacob asked looking into the darkness, thinking it might be Sarah.

"Light the candle," the male voice commanded.

Jacob lit the candle and turned to recognize the identity of the intruder. Jacob was greatly surprised. "Edward! Edward Murdock, what are you doing here?"

"It's been a long time Jacob," Edward replied. Edward gestured with the pistol and commanded, "Sit, we'll talk for a spell before I take you to General Winder's headquarters."

"Talk about what, old military days before the war?" Jacob asked.

"I wish it were that simple, but it's far more complicated and serious than that."

"What do you mean?" Jacob asked trying to determine how much information Edward knew.

"Like, why did you betray Amanda Wilson? Why did you cut off the best source of information we had in Washington City?"

"I think that is probably obvious by now, especially if you're going to take me to the Provost Marshal's office to be arrested." Jacob paused and lit a cigar. He looked at Edward and calmly asked, "How did you find out I was the one."

"Yesterday morning, another agent saw you speaking to Lieutenant Stanley. Later after speaking to Miss Wilson, you departed her residence and she was arrested."

"It still doesn't answer my question," Jacob replied taking a puff from his cigar.

"Molly. Molly Gibson."

Jacob smiled and replied, "No, you mean Sarah Robins, or in reality, Sarah Wilson, Amanda's daughter."

Jacob noticed the astonishment covering Edward's face. He continued, "Molly as you call her or Sarah as I know her is just as dangerous as any man or soldier I have known in this war."

"What do you mean? She is just a woman," Edward snapped in a defensive tone.

"Woman or not, she will kill you in a moment if it will serve her purpose or if you cross her. I guess she would like to get her hands on me right now."

Jacob began to stand when Edward commanded, "Stay seated."

"But I've been in the saddle for the last twenty-one hours," Jacob replied.

Again, Edward quietly gestured with the weapon in his hand and Jacob complied. "This will all come as a serious blow to Secretary Randolph when he receives the news. It will be embarrassing to him and the Confederate government. It will present grave consequences for you since you were trusted with so much information and intelligence concerning the way and manner that we act and carry out our plans."

"Edward, it was my duty to my country and government."

"And I am doing my duty to my country and government, even though we were like brothers after you saved my life."

"No one could have seen this happen. But this war and the issues that have divided us have placed my father against me, my brother against me, and now you my friend against me. This war is ugly and it will get uglier before it is over with. It makes no difference if you or I survive, it will continue to consume many lives before it is concluded. And once it is, then what happens?"

"I don't know, I guess that will be up to the politicians."

"Are they not the ones that started this war? But we are the ones that are expected to fight it, and that I'll do such as you until it is finished," Jacob said in a serious tone.

"Then I guess that finishes our conversation. There is nothing left to say between us," Edward replied as he raised his weapon and pointed it at Jacob. Edward continued, "Let's go."

When Jacob walked to the door with Edward following, he knew he had nothing to lose by making an escape attempt. If taken to General Winder's headquarter, he would be found guilty of spying for the Union and his fate might be death or imprisonment at Libby.

Jacob opened the door and quickly turned around, catching Edward off guard and striking him in the face. Stunned by Jacob's aggressiveness, the gun fell out of Edward's hand as he fell back against the floor. Jacob jumped on top of Edward and hit him several times in the face, but Edward, who was much larger and more muscular in size pushed him away. Both men noticed the weapon lying nearby on the floor and jumped for it. Jacob was the first to grab the weapon. Edward was unwilling to give up the struggle. He wrestled with Jacob for control of the pistol that was against his body. Suddenly, the weapon fired and Edward gasped and fell to one side.

Jacob tried to catch his breath as he looked at Edward's lifeless expression. He examined Edward's body, noticing the bullet had entered his chest to the left of the heart. There was a sickening feeling that consumed him. Jacob listened and looked around to see if Mr. Anderson in the next room or any of the other six occupants living in the house had been disturbed.

With haste, Jacob dashed to the window. Jacob looked around before opening it. Once satisfied no one was nearby, he climbed through onto a porch and then down the stairway to the ground. Looking back at the house, he noticed there were now lights burning. Soon Edward's body would be found in his room and the authorities would be notified.

Before Jacob reached the street, he heard the familiar voice of Hezekiah, "Jacob!"

Jacob paused and answered, "Hezekiah?"

As Hezekiah stepped from behind a tree, Jacob anxiously continued, "What are you doing here this late at night and how did you know I was back?"

"Cause I'se been a watchin' dis place for some days now and da Provost detail was here earlier dis evenin' lookin' for ya. I'se knew dat ya mus' be on ya ways back here."

"Well, I have to get out of Richmond. I just killed another Confederate agent. If they weren't sure before, they will be now that I am guilty of spying."

"I'se has a friend around da corner from here," Hezekiah swiftly answered.

"Let's get out of here," Jacob said.

Once Hezekiah and Jacob moved onto the street, they came to the corner of Broad and 13th Street. Both men turned and looked in the direction of Jacob's boardinghouse. Arriving at the front entrance were six cavalrymen. Hezekiah and Jacob watched the cavalrymen dismount and approach the front of the dwelling. Hezekiah and Jacob turned and rapidly crossed 13th Street near the Powhatan Hotel where there was Hezekiah's friend waiting with a wagon full of straw. Hezekiah looked around and quickly commanded, "Ya git under da straw and stay put until old Amos tells ya to come out from under. Ya understand?"

"Yes, and thank you for everything."

"Amos gonna take ya to a safe place until ya can 'scape from here."

Once Hezekiah covered Jacob with the straw, he quietly gestured for his friend to leave while he disappeared into the nearby alleyway.

Chapter Thirty-Eight

Rain was falling heavily as Benjamin Kelly dismounted his horse at the front entrance to Secretary Randolph's office at Mechanics' Hall located on 9th Street. There was the lingering question why such an important official of the Confederate government was requesting him to report with haste to his office. When he entered the dwelling, he proceeded to the secretary's office located on the first floor. After walking up to the door, the guard saluted and allowed him to pass.

Once Benjamin entered, he walked over to the clerk and said, "I have been requested to report to this office as soon as possible."

"Are you Lieutenant Kelly?" the clerk asked.

"Yes, I am."

"Please Sir, wait here while I announce your arrival to Secretary Randolph."

While the clerk was announcing Benjamin's presence to the secretary of war, he walked over and looked out the window in the direction of the capitol building. As he gazed at the rain beating forcefully against the window, he thought of Rachel and what she might be doing today. He greatly missed her. It had only been several days since she departed for Loudoun County, but it seemed like an eternity and his heart was full of anguish over her absence. In another month, she would give birth to a new generation of Kelly's. It still didn't make any difference to him if the child was a boy or girl as long as he lived to see the child's face and smile.

Benjamin's thoughts were interrupted when the army clerk reappeared and said, "Lieutenant Kelly, Secretary Randolph will see you now. Follow me."

Benjamin quietly did as requested. Once through the door, he removed his brim hat. He noticed an army colonel standing near the edge of the desk. Benjamin said, "Lieutenant Kelly reporting as ordered, Sir."

"Lieutenant Kelly, have a seat," Secretary Randolph insisted as he gestured with his hand, continuing while Benjamin was complying with the request, "this is Colonel Palmer."

Stretching forth to shake his hand, Colonel Palmer cordially said, "Thank you Lieutenant for acting so expeditiously to our request."

"I'll come right to the point Lieutenant, what do you know about Jacob Martin," Secretary Randolph asked.

"He is probably the dearest friend I have in this whole world. We grew up together and are just like brothers. Just recently after I was wounded at Gaines' Mill, he saw that I had food and was cared for until my wife Rachel arrived from Loudoun County." Pausing and looking at the grim expression covering the secretary's and colonel's expressions, Benjamin asked, "What is all of this about? What has he done?"

"For over a year," Colonel Palmer said, "I have been his friend and have expressed the greatest amount of trust and confidence for him, but…"

"He has betrayed us!" Secretary Randolph shouted, "His atrocities are unforgivable. He has defied and used our confidence in him to pass information to Washington City, and is responsible for the capture of one of our best sources of information in that city since Rose Greenhow."

Benjamin was stunned by the secretary's accusations and request. He looked at Colonel Palmer and asked, "Could there be some mistake?"

"Hardly."

"I don't believe it for a moment," replied Benjamin.

Secretary Randolph turned and looked, gesturing to Colonel Palmer. The officer quietly walked to another door and opened it saying, "You can come in now."

Immediately, a young woman, lavishly dressed walked through the door to the chair opposite of Benjamin. "Lieutenant Benjamin Kelly, this is Miss Sarah Robins, a former associate of your friend Jacob Martin," Colonel Palmer said.

"Miss Robins, it's a pleasure to make your acquaintance."

"Lieutenant, the pleasure is mine," Sarah replied in a cordial tone.

"Miss Robins is an agent working with this War Department on counter-intelligence for our noble cause. On occasions, she has worked with Jacob Martin and did so just recently. Fortunately, she wasn't arrested and imprisoned such as our other agent in Washington City, but instead arrived too late to be of assistance to that agent."

"Respectfully sir, this doesn't mean Jacob is guilty of any complicity in some scheme," Benjamin swiftly replied in a defensive tone.

"But it does," Sarah insisted.

"In what way?" Benjamin demanded as he turned and looked at her.

"On the day that our spymaster in Washington City was arrested, one of our agents witnessed Jacob speaking with a Federal agent that's very close to Secretary Stanton. Matter of fact, our agent confronted and witnessed Jacob Martin's presence on the evening of April 10 at the secretary's residence on K Street in Washington City. Afterward, he returned to our agent's residence until she met with her source where she obtained very valuable information to pass on to us. Once she delivered this information intended for us to Jacob at her home that same afternoon, he departed and within the hour agents from the Federal War Department arrested her. And just several days ago, he shot and killed an agent of ours who was at one time a soldier in the Regular army. That agent had served with Jacob while fighting with the Cheyenne's. During that time, Captain Martin as he is known now in the Yankee army, saved this individual who he considered just the same as his flesh and blood. He deliberately killed him because this one-time friend of his was going to take him to the Provost office and turn the traitor in. This so-called friend of yours will do anything to anyone. Loyalties mean nothing to him. He is a scoundrel that needs to be severely dealt with."

Benjamin was silent as he looked at Sarah. The words penetrated deep within his heart. His thoughts returned to several weeks ago when he was in the hospital suffering from his battle wounds before Rachel arrived. Jacob and he had freely spoken of the ongoing campaign. He felt betrayed and wondered if their friendship had possibly been used for the benefit of gaining information such as troop strength and design since the fighting around Richmond was still continuing at that time. It was unimaginable Jacob would be fighting for the Northern cause and betray his friends and the native soil where he was born. Benjamin stood and walked over to the window.

Sarah looked at Colonel Palmer, stood and followed Benjamin. She noticed the distressful expression on his face. She softly said so the others couldn't hear her words, "I sympathize with you. I know the emotions you are feeling. It was also a shock to me because he was someone I had learned to trust."

"I still have a difficult time believing Jacob is a Yankee spy," Benjamin said turning and looking at Sarah.

"Rest assuredly, he is. We wouldn't be putting you through this if it wasn't necessary," Sarah replied in a convincing tone.

"What do you mean?"

"We want you to find Jacob and bring him here to Richmond where we can question him and determine the damage he has done to our efforts," Sarah said in an assertive tone.

"I see. And you just think he is going to come just like that," Benjamin angrily answered as he turned once more and looked out the window, continuing, "I really don't want any part of it."

"You're the only one who can carry out this mission. Our other agents don't know nor will they be able to identify him. That's why we chose you. Besides, he won't be so suspicious of you returning home, especially after being wounded."

"He knew I was returning to the army as soon as I was fit for duty."

"Tell him there was a change of plans. You are having difficulty using your arm. You can convince him you have returned home for this reason. He'll believe you."

"I don't know. It sounds too easy. Jacob is too smart to accept such a scheme."

"He'll trust you. You're his friend. Now, we believe he has escaped from the city and will go home before he heads north," Sarah pleaded as she touched his arm.

"Why home?"

"Because he wants to see your wife, Rachel."

"How do you know about Rachel?" Benjamin swiftly asked turning and facing Sarah.

Sarah knew she had touched a sensitive subject with Benjamin. Now she wanted to drive the point home and use her greatest asset, deception to enlist his help in capturing Jacob. She said in a convincing tone, "He spoke enough about Rachel on the first mission north. He even wanted to delay our arrival in Washington City so he could see her, especially knowing you were busy fighting the Yanks on the peninsula. We didn't want to tell you any of this because we didn't want to run the risk you would kill him instead of bringing him back here. But now you know, it might help to convince you that we need your assistance and also it would give you the opportunity to return home."

Benjamin silently nodded and than replied, "Yes, I would like to return home and make sure Rachel is all right."

"Remember, we want Jacob alive. Understand? But if there is no other alternative, then kill him," Sarah whispered in a serious tone as she turned away from him and walked back to where Secretary Randolph and Colonel Palmer were waiting.

Now Benjamin knew the reason why Jacob never knew about Rachel and him. It was because Jacob was serving the Union and was an undercover agent for the United States Government. This explains why Jacob and his family never kept in contact with each other. His father was a secessionist and most likely banished him from the family and refused to maintain communications with him. He would leave for home today.

Chapter Thirty-Nine

As Jacob rode through the eastern entrance to Vestal's Gap, he looked across the valley that had always been known as Between the Hills. It was a narrow, long valley with rolling green hills, small streams, and agriculturally rich farms. The valley extended from the outskirts of Hillsborough to the Potomac River.

Jacob was apprehensive about the reception he would receive once he arrived at his family's farm, about six miles north of Vestal's Gap. His departure from home wasn't under the best of circumstances, but out of concern and love, he wanted to know his family's welfare.

When Jacob was only about a mile from the family's farm, he paused and headed along the William Graham Road, taking him to the base of Short Hill Mountain. After riding for about 1,000 yards, he paused once more and looked at the two-level stone Ebenezer Methodist Church. It was surrounded by oak and cedar trees giving it the perfect setting for serenity. When services began in 1834, his family was one of the first to attend. It was a place of worship where he was baptized and learned to appreciate family values.

Several individuals Jacob knew, Charles and Annie Virts, were emerging from the church's entrance. They owned the farm to the west along the base of the Blue Ridge Mountain.

"Good afternoon, Mrs. Virts," Jacob said cordially tipping his hat in a friendly gesture, and looking at her husband, "Sir."

"Jacob Martin. Where in the world have you been boy?" Charles asked as he approached.

"I have been working in Richmond and decided to return home. How is my family?"

"Your father was taken with some kind of a spell several days ago. He's been laid up unable to keep up the farm."

"Ya ma has done the best she can. Pastor Luke has been helpin' them with some of the chores."

"Is Luke here?" Jacob asked looking toward the church.

"He's in there praying," Charles said.

"I must see him," Jacob said dismounting his horse, continuing, "How is Michael?"

When the couple didn't answer, and there appeared a solemn expression on their faces, Jacob knew what had happen. He somberly said, "I am sorry. When did it happen?"

"He was serving with the 2nd Virginia at a place in the Shenandoah called Port Republic," Charles replied wiping the tears from his eyes.

"This war has been difficult on everyone. It will greatly change all our lives."

"He was my only son. I have nothing else to give to the effort."

Jacob said his farewells to the Virts and walked through the cemetery to the entrance of the church. When he entered the dwelling, he noticed Luke on his knees praying before the altar. Jacob was still listening to his friend cry out to God to bring this dreadful conflict to an end and restore peace to the families of his parish because many had been divided over their loyalties.

When Luke was finished, he stood and turned and noticed Jacob. He was surprised, but relieved to see Jacob unharmed. He rushed to the back of the church and embraced Jacob, asking, "Where have you been? What happened to you?"

"I have been in Richmond."

"You are staying out of the war, I hope?" Luke asked as his hazel eyes were on Jacob.

"It's difficult, but to answer your question, yes."

"I guess you've returned knowing about your father?" Luke asked in his compassionate tone.

"I want to thank you for helping them. But now, I'll be home for awhile."

"Earlier this morning, I was there and your father was sitting up in bed. Of course, he wanted to help me with milking the cows, but I wouldn't have anything to do with it."

"He was always too proud to ask for help or to take charity."

"As for your mother and Lily, they are doing fine." Pausing and sitting on one of the wooden pews, Luke asked, "You know about Rachel and Benjamin?"

"Yes, I do. Back in April, I saw Benjamin and his regiment as they passed through Richmond on their way to the Peninsula. He wanted to be the first to tell me since I hadn't heard from the family. I guess they didn't want to tell me. As I am sure, they were very angry with me because I didn't marry Rachel."

"Jacob, listen to me, Benjamin loves Rachel. Next month, she will give birth to a child. I would only hope that you're..."

"I am not here behind Benjamin's back to cause trouble or to woo Rachel back into my arms. What we had together is long over and I only want the best for both of them."

"You know, when you mysteriously disappeared, she was quite upset," Luke said in a serious tone.

"I know and I want to apologize for hurting her. That's why I must see her."

"No Jacob, that wouldn't be a good idea," Luke insisted as he stood.

"But I must. I owe it to her. When she was in Richmond last month to take care of Benjamin, I wanted to tell her then, but she wouldn't listen."

"No Jacob. I really don't feel you should see her."

"I have to," Jacob snapped.

Luke swiftly followed Jacob from the church. Luke grabbed Jacob by the arm. "Please, I don't want Rachel hurt. She has suffered enough. We all have in some way."

Jacob turned, removing Luke's hand and looking coldly at him walked from the church. He mounted his horse and rode off at a gallop.

A strong breeze began to blow. Luke brushed aside his curly blonde hair. He knew no matter how hard he had pleaded with Jacob, he would find Rachel. Jacob was always stubborn and believed he knew best concerning matters. He prayed Jacob wouldn't make the attempt to come between Rachel and Benjamin in an effort to renew his love and affection for her. It was all up to Rachel at this point because he didn't trust Jacob's intentions and motives.

Chapter Forty

Jacob continued the short distance on the Harpers Ferry Road until he came to the little one-room schoolhouse seated on a ridge overlooking the road. He could hear the sounds of children playing and jubilant shouts after turning up the path leading to the stone building. Although Benjamin's and Jacob's fathers voted for the Virginia's withdrawal, many in the area had voted to keep the state in the Union.

When Jacob arrived near the entrance, he noticed the few children that were under Rachel's guidance playing games. He gazed at them. He knew some of them had fathers and uncles fighting for the Southern cause that might not come home. Rachel was standing quietly nearby. He stood and gazed at the children and then at Rachel. As Jacob approached Rachel, she didn't turn around and look at him, but instead, kept her eyes on the children playing.

Jacob paused and said, "You always did have a gift for teaching children."

Rachel recognized Jacob's voice, but still refused to turn. She softly said, "Somewhere in my heart, I knew you would return. I guess your father being ill gave you the reason to come home."

Jacob approached a little closer and replied, "I didn't know about my father until I spoke with Mr. Virts at the church."

"I see. I guess you also saw Luke?"

"Yes, we spoke," Jacob said looking at the children playing.

"About what, may I ask?"

"About me not seeing you."

"Why didn't you just take his advice?"

"Because I had to see you and explain why I walked out on you. That's why."

"Our life together is over. You don't have to feel guilty on my part any longer."

"But I do. I want you to listen and hear me out and then, I'll be on my way and I will never interfere in your life again. I promise."

Rachel turned around and looked at Jacob. She said in a frustrating tone, "Then go ahead if it will make you feel better."

"About a month before the war and three weeks before you and I were to be married, I received a telegram from the War Department. In it, I was requested to come to Washington City and meet with General Scott and Secretary of War Simon Cameron."

"For what?" Rachel angrily asked.

"Everyone knew with the Southern states seceding and with Lincoln taking office in March that it was only a matter of time before the fighting would begin. Since I had been an officer in the army and previously served my country well scouting Indians in the Midwest, and knew how to obtain information, I was called upon to serve the Union in some meaningful capacity. I was asked to move to Richmond and use my skills to obtain information that would be useful to the Union cause. I found a job at the bank and did exactly all that was expected of me. Matter of fact, things worked out better than expected when Richmond became the capital of the Confederacy. That's why I was there when I first saw Benjamin in April and then again when you came to take care of him."

Rachel quietly walked to the edge of the embankment with Jacob quietly following. As the breeze became more intense, she turned and asked, "You mean to tell me you couldn't marry me because you wanted to run off again and play soldier? Once before when you were in Kansas, I waited for you to return home to me. And when you did, I thought we would be married and live happily ever after, but I was so wrong. You did it to me again.

Gesturing with his hands, Jacob pleaded, "With war coming, I couldn't marry you. It would have been unfair of me to do that not knowing what my fate might be."

Rachel turned, crying and screaming, "I should have been the judge of that. Not you!" Rachel quickly walked over to the entrance of the schoolhouse. She turned and angrily said, "You were not honest with me then and how do you expect me to believe you now. And as far as that goes, I am sure you have probably used Benjamin for information for your precious cause. Just think for a moment how he would feel, knowing his best friend was a Yankee spy. You've betrayed him and now he is your enemy."

"Do you think I am proud of what I do and have done to others since this war began? Well the answer is no. This war sickens me. I have pleaded with Benjamin to get out while he can. He is too stubborn and as always, he won't listen. The odds are against the Confederacy that they'll win this war. We have more machinery, factories, and men to fight a prolonged conflict while the South only has cotton."

"I do not agree with this war, but as long as my husband is in the field fighting, I will support him and stand by his side until it ends."

"Well Rachel, hopefully he'll come home to you and your baby in one piece when it ends. If you see him, tell him to get out while he still can."

"Are you finished?" Rachel angrily shouted with tears flowing down her cheeks.

"Yes, I am finished," Jacob angrily snapped.

"As far as I am concerned, our acquaintance and relationship is over with. You have said what you came here to say, now please leave me alone. Please!" Rachel said as she called for the children and entered the building.

Once within the security of the schoolhouse and the children were being seated, Rachel walked over and looked out the window before beginning class and noticed Jacob leaving. Her feelings were mixed. Her heart was torn. The wounds were still deep and prevalent, sometimes dominating her life even though she continuously made the vigorous effort to repress them. The revelation and reality that he had neglected, taken advantage, and wasted her love to serve the Union caused the pain to penetrate its knife deeper into her heart. Being a spy for the Union made him an enemy against her husband, Benjamin, which would cause great difficulties now and in the future once the war ended. Rachel knew she had acted in the right manner and felt no guilt for expressing her emotions. As Jacob disappeared beyond the ridge, she turned to resume class, but there was a sorrowful feeling and nudging within her heart that she couldn't repress or explain.

Once on the other side of the ridge, Jacob paused and looked back in the direction of the schoolhouse. He had taken a risk and accepted the challenge and had failed. At least his conscience was clear, but he knew he may have reopened old wounds and unintentionally injured Rachel.

Chapter Forty-One

Once Jacob passed the Harrison homestead along the base of Short Hill Mountain, he came to the crest of a ridge overlooking his family's farm. Off in the distance, surrounded by oak trees, he recognized the two-story stone house that he had called home since his birth. As Jacob looked at his family's property, he could see they had suffered a drought by the appearance of the corn and wheat growing in the field and the diminutive size of the peaches in the orchard. Jacob spurred his horse and galloped a little faster until he came to the lane that led to home.

Jacob arrived at the front entrance, dismounted, and removed his hat and wiped his forehead. As he approached the door, his mother appeared.

"Jacob, Jacob my son," Mother said dashing forward and embracing him.

As Jacob's mother brushed the hair from his face, he noticed her long brown hair was beginning to reveal streaks of gray. Her green eyes revealed the strain and lack of sleep she had been suffering from over the last several days.

"How is father doing?" Jacob asked.

"Oh, that man, he is as stubborn as a mule."

"What happened to him? I just saw Mr. Virts at the church and he said father had some kind of a spell."

"We don't know what it was. He just had these feelings of weakness come over him and he fell to the ground and hit his head. Today, he shows some signs of improving, but I am still trying to keep him down for a while longer, at least until he gets his strength up again."

"I would like to see him and then I'll get busy with the chores."

Jacob's mother quietly nodded in agreement, but he noticed her worried expression. Jacob remained silent and walked into the house and up to the second floor. It was quiet and he didn't know if his father was sleeping. Once at the entrance to his parent's bedroom, he noticed his father coldly looking at him with his beady brown eyes.

"What are you doing here?" Jacob's father angrily asked using his hands to sit upright on the bed.

"I've come home. The war is over for me. I want to help out for awhile, at least until you're able to manage things again."

"We don't need your help. We've run this farm for the last two years without you and we'll run it another two years without you," Father said after taking a drink of water.

Jacob walked into the room. He noticed how his father's tall muscular frame had begun to deteriorate. One time of day, his father could do the work that it would have taken several men to accomplish, but whatever he had been suffering from was beginning to physically take its toll on him.

"Then what I'll do, I'll do for Mother and Lily. They can not manage a two hundred-acre farm."

"No boy, we don't need your help. Get out," Father shouted.

Jacob's mother came running into the room, shouting, "No John, this is his home and we need his help."

A flush expression appeared on Father's face as he angrily shouted again, "Now look Mary, I'll make the decisions around here."

Jacob's mother took him by the arm and commanded, "Jacob, you come with me now."

Jacob and his mother left the room while his father swore every oath imaginable. The words pierced Jacob deeply. Once Jacob was alone in the kitchen with his mother, he asked, "Does Father hate me that badly for leaving home?"

"Here, sit a spell while I fetch you some of my deer stew. You must be hungry," Jacob's mother said dipping the meal onto a plate from the pot.

"Mother, you didn't answer my question," Jacob demanded as she walked back to the stove.

Mary paused and refused to speak or turn and look at her son. Her heart was racing with anxiety. What would she say? She placed the pot on the stove, turned and smiled. "You know that your father has always been a proud man who never showed much in the way of feelings. And since he is down, it's hard for him to admit that he needs help."

"No Mother. You can't protect him any longer." Jacob said standing and approaching. "It's obvious how he feels about me. The trouble is that everyone lives in another world and has ignored the hard truths and realities that have confronted this family. Father is mad because I went against his wishes and pledged my loyalties to the Union. I followed the convictions of my heart because I don't believe we have the right as a people and state to withdraw from the Union. In the long run, it will hurt the people I love and care for the most. This war is very much a conflict where father is against son, brother against brother, and best friends fighting against each other, such as Benjamin and I. When men stand in a line of battle at two hundred yards from each other and fire their weapons, they don't know if the bullet they have shot is going to kill or maim someone that is a family member or friend. War is a serious matter. Many individuals such as Father and you don't know what it is like. Men scream like demons when they have been seriously inflicted with a mortal wound while others quietly accept their fate."

Jacob placed his hands on his mother's shoulders and continued, "War is ugly. I wish the fighting would just stop and everyone could come home and try to pick up the pieces of their lives, but I am afraid we have a long and winding road ahead before it all comes to an end. Just before leaving Richmond, I pleaded with Benjamin to get out of the fighting and return home while he was still alive. The odds are against him that he'll come out of this thing in one piece. He was shot up pretty bad, but he'll survive to fight another day because he is too bullheaded to come home to Rachel."

"Well, you're home now and safe and you can begin to put it all behind you," Mary said as she wrapped her arms around Jacob and cried.

"No Mother. It won't end until the last rebel dies or they give up. And it doesn't appear the rebels are anywhere ready for that to happen."

"Well, you can stay a spell, or as long as you need to."

Jacob looked at his mother and replied, "Mother, you've always shown your humility toward others, loyalty to this family, even when you've had to constantly deny yourself of the desires of your heart. You've always been loyal to me because I have taken a different stand on issues from my father, but I am still a soldier in the United States Army and that's not going to change."

"When you were a little boy, I always knew there was something special about you. When your father was trying to make a farmer out of you, you tried to please him I know, but your heart wasn't in it. I could tell. Mother's intuition I guess. Instead, you wanted to play soldier. Even though you pursued this vocation against your father's will, it was a proud day for me when you left for the United States Military Academy and became an officer. More than your father, I understand and appreciate your loyalty to your country and convictions for what you believe. And as far as I am concerned, this will always be your home, and I'll always be your mother and love you. No war or social issues will ever come between us, as surely as there is a God in heaven, I promise.

Jacob took a long look at her peaceful expression and than quietly departed to do the farm's chores.

Chapter Forty-Two

Early the next morning after sunrise, Jacob was in the barnyard, kneeling and examining one of the horse's hooves. The birds were singing and the morning sun promised to be another scorcher. He looked up from his labor and noticed in the distance a short petite young lady walking along the lane. Immediately, he recognized his younger sister, Lily. Gazing at her as she approached, Jacob thought of the many conversations in front of the fireplace on cold snowy winter nights when they opened the family Bible and looked at the front pages where everyone's birth was recorded and spoke of their rich family ancestry. Their great uncle endured the bitter-cold winter at Valley Forge in 1776 with General George Washington during the Revolutionary War and their great grandfather witnessed the surrender during that same war of British troops in a field several miles on the outskirts of Yorktown in 1781. Their grandfather, James Martin was the first to settle in this area in 1806 and then turned the property over to their father John.

Jacob remembered Lily being supportive and possessing a loving humbleness in her nature. Like their mother, she was calm, patient and persistent in her characteristics, and by her natural beauty had already at the age of twenty, broken many young bachelors' hearts. Lily had thick auburn hair with the biggest brown eyes he had ever seen. She was returning after spending the previous night taking care of the elderly Widow Williams who lost her husband the previous week.

Jacob stood and walked to meet his sister. When near, he knew by the bright smile covering her face that she recognized him. Jacob dashed forward and embraced her, saying, "Lily, it's been too long."

"Why didn't you write?" Lily asked breaking the embrace.

"I apologize, but I couldn't."

"Why? Why couldn't you write a few lines to let us know where you were and what you were doing?" Lily asked.

"I was in Richmond working undercover for our government," Jacob replied, waiting for her reaction.

"You mean spying."

"Yes, spying."

"Why did you come home?"

"I didn't tell mother because I didn't want her to worry, but I almost got caught. I escaped when confronted with the reality of being arrested."

Lily and Jacob turned and began walking back to the house. Lily said, "Everyone thought this war was going to be short in duration and the boys would be home before they knew it, but it just drags on and there doesn't seem to be an end to it. Quite often since the Yankees have occupied Harpers Ferry, their cavalry patrols this road. Most are friendly and cordial, and the thought of one of them dying sickens me, but it also does when I think of men like Benjamin Kelly who's fighting for the Southern cause."

"Is that why you never married Thomas James?" Jacob jokingly asked, waiting for a reaction to the question.

"No: Maybe, I just haven't found the right gentleman yet. And until this war is over, I don't intend on getting married to anyone," Lily swiftly replied as she smiled at Jacob.

"It makes good sense."

Lily paused and looked at her brother. She softly asked in a serious tone, "I assume you know about Rachel and Benjamin?"

"Yes." Jacob nodded and sadly answered. "I was very surprised, but then too, the way I treated her by running out on her, I am not surprised."

"How will this affect you now that you have returned home?"

"I have to live with it even though I still love her. In no way will I attempt to come between Rachel and Benjamin. I saw her yesterday before coming here," Jacob replied as they began walking once more.

Lily quickly paused and turned, scolding, "No Jacob, please tell me you didn't."

Jacob held his hands up in defense before Lily and smiled. "I just felt she needed an explanation why I did what I was compelled to do. I didn't want her going through life thinking she did something wrong and was to blame for some act that in reality I committed. It was only with the intentions of clearing things up. That's all."

"Somewhere in my heart, I don't believe you," Lily replied in a serious tone.

When Lily and Jacob were near the house, he asked, "I am concerned about Father. He can't do the work around here, no one is sure what is wrong with him, and he is still very angry with me for returning home."

"Jacob, you have to understand he believes you betrayed him. You went against his wishes."

"No, I disagree. I have a right to my beliefs even if it is in disagreement with his." Jacob replied in an angry tone, continuing, "I stood firm for my convictions with my father just the same as when I was in the army fighting Indians in Kansas alongside men from some of the Southern states. In some cases the men under my command did not accept my views. The Southern patriots in my company voiced their opinions concerning the goodness and righteousness of slavery, the liberty in states' rights, and the justification of secession. But like them, Father refuses to see the evils of holding another man in bondage against his will and deprived of his rights as an individual."

Lily quickly interrupted, "Is that why you are fighting this war?"

"Yes, partially, but more so to preserve the Union and to keep the Negro disarmed. If the Negro could, he would rise up and be more vicious than the white man in getting his freedom and revenge. Isn't that what old John Brown was trying to do, and what about Nat Turner? Not only those two examples, but also Father doesn't understand the south cannot win this war. Too many good men have already gotten killed defending their beliefs. I respect the thought that every man is entitled to his opinion. That's what this country is all about, but not to take such drastic action as secession and forming another so-called country."

"I had hoped and prayed that maybe our family wouldn't take sides and stay out of this fight, but that all changed when you left home."

"Are you saying I am the blame for our family being divided?" Jacob asked in a defensive tone.

"No, I am not saying that, but if you would have stayed home and out of the war than maybe things would be different today between you and Father," Lily replied.

Jacob noticed the fearful expression on her face. He placed his hands on his sister's shoulders and softly replied, "We all want this war to be over, maybe now for me, it is. I don't want to go back."

"I know mother doesn't nor do I want you to return. We will need your help around here for awhile until Father gets back on his feet again."

Jacob nodded in agreement and entered the house with Lily, but as he gazed at her, he pondered on when the whirlpool of death would draw him back into the conflict once more.

* * * *

During the late evening, Rachel was sitting by the fireplace looking aimlessly into the flickering flames. She was holding the latest correspondence that she had received this afternoon from Benjamin. Her thoughts were on him and what he might be doing this late in the evening and why his pride overruled the possibility of coming home and being with her. She took consolation in his letter that he hadn't reported back to duty yet with the 8th Virginia. Instead, he had remained in Richmond waiting for orders, but still she was fearful for his safety. She saw the family Bible and took the Good Book into her hands and turned to the 4th Chapter of Philippians in the New Testament where it said in verse 7, "And the peace of God, which passeth all understanding, shall keep your hearts and minds through Christ Jesus." It was a verse of scripture her brother Luke had preached on or referred to quite often since the beginning of the war.

Rachel's thoughts were interrupted when her father-in-law approached from behind and placed his hands on her shoulders, saying, "Rachel, honey this whole thing will be over soon and Benjamin will be home with you before you know it."

"Father Robert, I just wish he would have come home with me when he had the chance to. I would feel more comfortable having him here with me than where he is," Rachel replied in a saddened tone.

"The boy is too proud. He's too much like me. Takes great pride in what he is doing. That boy of mine, he's a scrapper, he'll come through this war, you just wait and see, and so will his little brother, James."

"I was just looking at this verse of scripture and I am trying to do what it says, but sometimes it is so difficult."

Robert walked around and faced Rachel. He knelt on his knees and took her by the hand and said, "Rachel, you must always trust the Lord and know that he'll work everything out to the good. Now I'm going to bed and sleep soundly knowing my boy wherever he may be is in the Lord's hands. Goodnight."

Rachel acknowledged Robert with a nod of agreement and a smile. When he departed the room, she gazed back into the flames and attempted to accept the words of comfort he had spoken.

After some meditation and thought, Rachel stood and looked at the clock. It chimed twelve times. Walking over to the table and blowing out the candle, she heard the sound of a horse approaching over the roaring noise of an approaching thunderstorm. Who could it be this late at night, she thought? She walked over and looked out the window, but was unable to recognize the mysterious rider. She patiently waited. When the rider dressed in civilian clothing paused in front of the house and dismounted, she recognized him as Benjamin. Her heart was overwhelmed with joy as she rushed out into the nighttime darkness to greet him.

"Benjamin, Benjamin," Rachel cried embracing and kissing him.

Once Rachel and Benjamin broke their embrace, Rachel noticed the cold expression on his weary face. She asked in a concerned tone, "Benjamin, what's wrong? Why are you so cold towards me?"

Benjamin was silent as he looked into Rachel's eyes. He turned away from her and began to tie his horse to the hitch.

"Please tell me! Just don't turn away from me!" Rachel pleaded grabbing his arm.

Benjamin turned and took a deep swallow. He softly said, "I am home on business. What I have to tell you will trouble you as much as it troubles me."

Both Benjamin and Rachel silently stared at each other in the darkness. The manner of business that Benjamin had returned home to address would have a profound effect on both of them.

Chapter Forty-Three

Rachel was mystified as she followed Benjamin through the door. She waited until Benjamin put his saddlebags near the fireplace and removed his hat. Again Rachel approached and asked, "Benjamin, do you want some coffee or something to eat?"

Benjamin nodded his head and replied, "I'd like some coffee."

Rachel turned around and walked over to the stove and began to dip some water from a wooden bucket into the coffee pot. She turned and looked over her shoulder and glanced at her troubled husband sitting in a chair near the fireplace. What kind of business would bring him home? How would she approach the situation or would she just wait and give him time. She kept quiet and pondered on these thoughts until the coffee had boiled. Once ready, she poured a cup and walked over to the fireplace where Benjamin was lost in his thoughts.

"You're very exhausted," Rachel said handing him the cup of coffee.

"I have been riding almost constantly around the armies for the last three days trying to get here."

"Why? What is so important you won't tell me?" Rachel asked kneeling down on the floor before Benjamin, taking his hand in hers.

After sipping the coffee and putting it to the side, Benjamin sighed as he looked at Rachel. He softly said in a cold tone, "The business I came home for is to capture or kill Jacob, my best friend."

"What? What are you talking about?" Rachel surprisingly asked with great astonishment.

"Jacob is a spy for Federal authorities. He's been living all this time in Richmond under a lie so he could pass information back to Washington City," Benjamin said, taking another sip of the coffee.

Rachel stood and remembered when Jacob confronted her at the schoolhouse and confessed his covert activities. The question that surfaced in her mind was should she tell Benjamin she already knew of Jacob's confession and loyalties to the Union or should she remain silent?

"I don't believe it for one moment. How do you know these accusations to be true?" Rachel asked standing and walking to the fireplace.

"Several days ago, I was ready to report back with the 8th, but I received a message by courier to report to Secretary Randolph's office." Benjamin somberly said looking at the flames. "So I complied as ordered. At the meeting was Colonel Palmer, who oversees the intelligence received at the telegraph office in Richmond. Jacob knew all our military designs and intentions, and many of the messages that President Davis received. Palmer was also a good friend and I might add an intentionally good source of information for Jacob."

"How did Jacob get involved with him?" Rachel asked in a whisper looking at Benjamin.

"He wrote out and delivered drafts for covert operations to Secretary Randolph. He used the opportunity to earn their confidence," Benjamin said looking up from the flames.

"Jacob was always good at persuasion," Rachel said walking over and looking out the window, continuing, "What else did Jacob do that warrants his death?"

"One of the best spies we had in Washington City was a very good and reliable source of information. Jacob was instrumental in her capture."

"Who was she?"

"Amanda Wilson."

"That still doesn't prove anything," Rachel replied turning and facing Benjamin.

"I have more. Once Jacob returned to Richmond, another one of our agents was waiting in his room at his boarding-house. That agent, Edward Murdock, was once a good friend of Jacob's. Jacob had saved his life while fighting Indians in Kansas. And just recently, Murdock escorted a female agent to Washington City, one that Jacob knew and had worked with back in April while carrying a request for information to Mrs. Wilson. Once Murdock and the other female agent that Jacob was associated with arrived in Washington City, they were informed by another one of our spies of Mrs. Wilson's arrest and Jacob's involvement in the whole affair. When Jacob arrived in Richmond from Washington City last week, Murdock was waiting on Jacob to arrest him. Jacob must have gotten the upper hand in the struggle because he killed Murdock, the man who saved him."

"So what will you do when you find Jacob? Kill him," Rachel coldly asked.

"No, no, I don't want to kill Jacob, but even if I take him back to Richmond, it will only be a matter of time before they hang him," Benjamin said as he stood.

"I see. And you can do that to your best friend and then live with it through the rest of your life?"

"Have you seen him in the last several days?" Benjamin asked looking into Rachel's eyes.

Should she be honest or should she lie to protect Jacob, Rachel thought. As Rachel looked at Benjamin, she chose the latter and calmly said, "No, why should I want to see him."

"It's not you I am worried about, but according to this other female agent, traveling with Jacob to Washington City back in April, he continued to confess his love for you."

Rachel smiled and replied, "Now, I don't believe that to be true. If Jacob really loved me then I guess I'd be married to him today instead of you. Now wouldn't I?"

"Yes, I am sorry. I guess I just don't trust him. When I saw him back in April after my brigade arrived in Richmond, I asked him about serving. His answer was, fighting the Indians in Kansas and being wounded had taken the fight out of him. I really believed him. And then in the hospital in Richmond after being wounded at Gaines' Mill, he appeared so sincere. I wouldn't for one moment think I was looking into the eyes of a traitor. A spy."

Benjamin began pacing. His tone turned to anger. "Now I know he is someone who was out to do me harm, steal from my family and maybe our future. How many of my good men have died in battle as a result of him passing information to that tyrant government in Washington City."

"Benjamin, you must calm down," Rachel softly replied touching his arm.

When Benjamin turned and faced Rachel, she caressed his face. She gently kissed him. She whispered, "You're tired, we'll continue this in the morning, all right."

A smile was on Benjamin's face as he silently nodded in agreement.

Rachel knew she didn't have to ask any more questions. She had it all figured out. She knew Benjamin would go to the Martin homestead first light in the morning and confront Jacob. That's why he was here. She didn't desire to see either of the two men harmed in anyway. It would be difficult, but she would have to warn Jacob, somehow that Benjamin was here to apprehend and take him back to Richmond.

Chapter Forty-Four

It was a restless night for Rachel. She found it difficult to sleep, knowing Benjamin was here to arrest Jacob and maybe get injured in the process. Her thoughts revolved around an idea of communicating to Jacob his immediate danger, and that he must take refuge in the mountains or escape north. The latter was desired. Turning and looking, she gazed at Benjamin soundly sleeping by her side. She thought of all of the overwhelming hardships he had endured, the difficulties of sacrifice, and the traumatic war experiences engraved in his mind. These things had changed Benjamin because he was a different person than when he left home fourteen months ago. Now he was home, would it be to possibly shed more blood? It had to be prevented.

Rachel looked out the window. She noticed the candle-light burning in Easter's cabin window. Easter was the family's servant. If she could get a message unnoticed to Easter, than maybe she could be successful in delivering it to Jacob. If she was caught, then Benjamin would believe she was betraying not only him, but also his trust. If successful, the risk would be worth it.

Again looking at Benjamin, Rachel was confident he was so exhausted he wouldn't miss her, but she was concerned about disturbing the rest of the family. She sat up in bed without disturbing Benjamin and pulled back the quilt. She grabbed her robe and put it on. Walking over to the door, she gently cracked it open and peered out into the room. All was quiet. Rachel emerged quickly from her bedroom and went to the desk nearby. Quickly scribbling a note on paper she folded it tightly. She looked around and dashed toward the door. After opening it, Rachel slipped through and without hesitation headed for Easter's cabin.

Once at her servant's cabin, Rachel swiftly knocked several times. When Easter opened the door, Rachel noticed the surprised expression on Easter's face.

"Come in here girl. What's wrong with ya to be out dis late in de night," Easter scolding Rachel as she took her arm.

"I am all right. But I do have a problem and I need your help," Rachel anxiously insisted.

"Tell me Misse Rachel what can I'se do for ya?"

"I have to hurry. Late this evening, Benjamin unexpectedly came home. He is here to capture Jacob Martin and take him back to Richmond for spying for the Yankees. He'll be up soon and will go to the Martin farm. I am afraid that something is going to happen to him if he tries to arrest Jacob."

"What yose want me to do?"

Rachel reached for Easter's hand and said placing the paper in her hand, "I want you to go to the Martin homestead and deliver this to Jacob. Tell him this is from me. He'll understand."

"That won't be necessary," Benjamin calmly said, standing at the open door.

Rachel swiftly turned to look at Benjamin. She knew by the cold expression on his face that he was angry and felt betrayed.

Benjamin walked into the cabin and looked at Easter and quietly held out his hand. After Easter dropped the note into his hands, Benjamin opened and looked at its contents. He turned and asked, "Rachel, why? Why did you do this to me?"

Rachel remained silent. Easter compulsively said, "Cause she's a tryin'to…"

"Woman, keep quiet." Benjamin shouted. Turning toward Rachel once more, Benjamin again asked, "Why Rachel? Why!"

Tears began to flow from Rachel's eyes. She screamed, "I just wanted to protect you! I don't want you and Jacob harming each other, that's all."

"Well apparently you didn't take to heart anything I told you earlier. Because of him, some of my men might have died. And if he isn't stopped what will he do next? If given the opportunity, he might just come up with the silly notion of being a Confederate soldier if it means he can keep on spying. I know him too well and know he will accept the most extreme challenges, take the gravest risk, and gain the greatest advantage from it all. He must be stopped, and stopped now!" Benjamin shouted turning and leaving the cabin.

Rachel fell into Easter's arms and uncontrollably cried, "Oh no! No! Please God no."

*   *   *   *

When the first rays of the sun began to peer over Short Hill Mountain, Jacob was in the field looking at the dry corn stalks. Already, he could tell by the sultry humidity that it was going to be another hot and oppressive day. He knelt and picked up some of the dirt clods, knowing the ground was extremely dry. When he rose to his feet, he looked off toward the house and noticed his father slowly approaching. Jacob gazed and waited until he was near before speaking. "Father, you shouldn't be out here yet. You need to stay in bed and try to rest."

"Boy, don't tell me what to do," John said in a low tone of anger.

"I can handle our farm on my own," Jacob replied taking the hoe and beginning to till the cloddy soil.

"It's not your property. As far as I am concerned, I have no boy," John angrily retorted.

Jacob dropped the hoe and walked over to where his Father was standing. "Why are you angry with me? What have I done that deserves this type of treatment?"

"I'll tell you. You've betrayed everything this family stands for. It's not enough you gave up a lovely and dedicated woman that any man would have been proud to have had, but no you had to run off to fight for that dang blasted Yankee government against your state, your most loyal friends and worse yet, your family. You have embarrassed me and dishonored this family. You are a disgrace to every one of us and I am ashamed beyond words to ever say I ever called you my own. You don't even have a lick of pride about you!" When Jacob didn't respond, his father continued his angry rage, "I always taught you to honor your state and its values. This was the patriotic thing to do. That's why I finally accepted your going to the Military Academy, so you could defend Virginia in her time of need from the Yankee invaders."

"No Father, I didn't go to the academy to just defend Virginia, but to defend all the people. That's what a soldier does. I am sorry I disappointed you and didn't live up to your expectations," Jacob angrily replied.

"I knew some of those scoundrels from up north would confuse and twist your mind. I tried to prepare you for it before you left, but it didn't sink in deep enough. Now you're just like one of them. My son is dead. I don't know who you are anymore."

"It's not the way you think or believe. Your mind is so full of hatred that it has blinded you," Jacob pleaded.

"Get out of my sight and off my property before I take my shotgun and shoot you. Now boy!" Jacob's father shouted pointing toward the Harpers Ferry Road that paralleled the property.

Jacob silently took a long look at his Father's cold expression. He didn't have the words to say that might convince him that he was wrong. His father's heart was solidified and firm in his belief that the Southern cause was the right way in life. Over the last two years, it appeared the animosity had grown deeper with a rage of wrath that seemed unquenchable. Jacob wondered how he could escape such treachery and hostility. Could he travel far enough north, west, or anywhere to escape it all.

Jacob began walking toward the house. He paused and looked over his shoulder at his father coughing, but didn't return to his side to comfort him. Jacob's emotions were bruised. The close relationship he once enjoyed with his father had vanished like a cold vapor on a winter night. The remarkable wisdom, enduring patience, and the abiding love had disappeared. The bitterness over the fiery social issues between Northern and Southern factions had changed many families and friends. Could it ever be the same again, Jacob wondered?

Chapter Forty-Five

Without hesitation, Jacob went to the house and to his bedroom where he began packing a few articles of clothing into a carpetbag. It was not his original intentioned to do so, but now he wanted to leave as soon as possible and return to Washington City where possibly he would receive a field command in the army. His thoughts concerning his disagreement with his father were continually on his mind and also how his family would manage the farm without his help. Once Jacob finished, he closed the bag and turned to leave. Waiting quietly at the door to his room was Lily.

"Did you and Papa have a fight?" Lily asked entering the room.

"Yes, and a pretty serious one at that," Jacob said reaching for his hat lying on the bed.

"I know. I was watching out the front window. He hasn't been right since you left home."

"It's all of that hatred built up inside I guess," Jacob replied taking his bag in hand.

"No family is safe from this war. Everyone only thinks about their beliefs in what is right and what is wrong, and willing to kill the other to prove their point. When this conflict ends, I hope Papa and you can straighten out your differences and we can live in peace as a family once more."

"If the South loses the war, that might be difficult for him and some of the others living in this valley to do. Life may never be the same again, least not for some time," Jacob answered approaching Lily.

"I am concerned for Papa's health. He is still so sick. He can't manage this farm," Lily said as tears filled her eyes.

Jacob dropped his bag and embraced his sister. He softly assured her, "Before I leave, I'll speak with Luke and see if he can manage to help out a little longer until Father is on his feet again." Jacob broke their embrace and continued, "I really don't want to go. I've had enough of this war, but I can't stay where I am not wanted and where my family is going to be divided by it. Once Father is back on his feet, matters around here will improve. As for me, I might not be back until the war is finished, but I promise this time I'll stay in touch with you."

After Jacob kissed Lily on the cheek, he tearfully gazed at her and walked slowly down the stairway. They had always been close. She feared for his safety. The war was becoming increasingly costly in money, emotional strain, and the sacrifice of lives. The farm was too large for her family to manage without Jacob's help. She sadly witnessed day after day her father and mother willingly laboring in the fields to make the farm profitable, but the war was still taking its toll on the finances they received for their efforts.

Once Jacob's horse was saddled, he walked the animal over to the house to gather his baggage and say farewells to his grieving mother. When he arrived, she was tearfully waiting.

"Somewhere in my heart, I was afraid this day would come," Jacob's mother said as she approached.

"Even though I didn't plan it this way, I guess I did too. Now knowing the hatred Father feels for me, the sooner I leave the better it will be for you and Lily. Who knows, maybe he'll recover a lot quicker?"

"It's not hatred he feels for you, but it's bitterness over feelings of betrayal."

"No Mother, it's hatred. And if he continues to feel this way, then it's going to kill him. That's why I have to get out of his sight as soon as possible."

As Lily walked out the door, Jacob's mother answered in a whisper, "I know, I understand."

Jacob turned and looked toward the front yard, noticing his father watching. Jacob walked the horse in that direction with his mother and sister following. When he paused before his father, he said, "Father, I'm leaving. But before I do, I will practice something you and mother always taught me while growing up and that is, I forgive you. I hold no bitterness or animosity toward you for what has happened between us. I just wish things had been different. It was wrong of me to run out on Rachel. It's a mistake I'll regret for the rest of my life, but fighting to preserve the Union was the right thing to do. I don't expect you to understand or accept my views.

Jacob waited for a reaction to come from his Father, but he remained silent and cold. He mounted his horse and took his bag from Lily.

"Who's coming?" Lily asked stepping back and looking toward the mountain.

Jacob turned away from his father, and paused to see if he could recognize the rider. Once closer, he knew his identity. It was Benjamin. Immediately, Jacob assumed Benjamin had taken his advice and quit the war to return home and be with Rachel, especially since she was ready to give birth to a child.

"It's Benjamin! He's returned home like I hoped," Jacob said as he continued to observe his friend approaching.

When Benjamin rode alongside of Jacob, he tipped his hat in a gesture and said, "Mr. and Mrs. Martin and Lily, how are you all doing this morning?"

"We are doing good. How is Rachel?" Mary asked walking near her husband.

"She's coming along, but I am not a father yet," Benjamin answered.

"Well you tell her I'm coming over later on this afternoon when all of the chores are done," Lily replied turning and walking toward the house.

"She'll be glad to see you," Benjamin turned and replied, waving.

"I guess you two have something to talk about, so if you'll excuse John and me, we'll go about our business," Mary said as she too departed with her husband.

Once everyone had departed, Jacob turned and looked at Benjamin. By his friend's expression, he knew something was wrong. At first, he thought it might have something to do with him speaking to Rachel several days ago. He knew Benjamin's jealously and temper was easily aroused.

"Somewhere I don't feel this is a friendly call," Jacob said looking at Benjamin.

"I want to know why you did it?" Benjamin asked leaning forth in the saddle.

"For sometime it's been bothering me that I never gave Rachel..."

Benjamin interrupted, "I am not talking about Rachel."

"Then what are you talking about?" Jacob asked not understanding the nature of Benjamin's behavior.

"Why you betrayed us? Why you were spying for the Yankees. Why you used Amanda Wilson and then had her arrested? And most of all why did you betray me, your best friend and more so your Ma and Pa? Why, Why, Jacob!" Benjamin asked in an angry tone.

"So that's what this is all about," Jacob calmly replied.

"Yes, that's what this is all about!" Benjamin loudly answered.

"Yes, while living in Richmond, I spied for the Union. I made very important acquaintances and cultured loyalties to achieve my purpose. But just as you, I have my convictions. I've paid the price for them by my father completely disowning me and I guess you also feel the same knowing the truth about me."

"Yes, I do disown you as a friend. I have been sent here to arrest and return you to Richmond," Benjamin replied pulling a gun from under his coat.

"You know they'll hang me once I am returned to them," Jacob answered looking at the weapon, knowing he wasn't carrying one.

"Yes Jacob, I know. It's something I struggled with on the trip back here. But soldiers must do their duty no matter how difficult it is. They taught you that I am sure at the Military Academy."

When Jacob knew he had Benjamin's full attention, he swung his carpetbag around and stunned his friend with the blow, knocking the pistol from his hand to the ground. Immediately, Jacob placed spurs to his horse's hindquarter racing across the front yard toward the Harpers Ferry Road. When Jacob was near the edge of the property, he heard several shots fired. Jacob looked back after hearing a sound strike a tree. He noticed Benjamin standing near his horse and his revolver in his hand. Quickly glancing at his animal's body, Jacob noticed some blood near the animal's back hip. The horse was still moving at a good gait. Apparently, Benjamin was shooting to injure his horse and guaranteeing his capture.

Jacob knew Benjamin would quickly follow. How would he escape being captured? As he neared the bend overlooking Piney Run, he turned and glanced over his shoulder to see if Benjamin was following. He was just entering the road about 1,000 yards behind him. Jacob knew he had a good lead on him.

Jacob came to Piney Run, he slowed the animal to cross the shallow waters and then again laid spurs to the animal's hindquarter until he came near Nisewarner's Cemetery in the little hamlet of Turneysville, which was not far from the stream. Jacob briefly paused and his eyes followed Benjamin's progress. He had gained ground on him.

Looking back and examining the horse's wound, Jacob knew he had to hurry to the Potomac River before the animal succumbed to its injuries. Again, he hurried along the Harpers Ferry Road over a ridge and down toward the river.

About 500 yards from the river, Jacob noticed little Bud Butts near their mountainside home, watching his father working at his specialty of making iron gates. As Jacob rode pass them, he warned them to flee for safety.

Again, Jacob looked over his shoulder and noticed Benjamin rapidly gaining ground. His horse was beginning to give out from being injured and he pressed vigorously on. Jacob knew once near the river, Harpers Ferry would be in sight and he would only be about a mile away from crossing the river. Garrisoned at Harpers Ferry were approximately 11,000 Federal soldiers under the command of Colonel Dixon S. Miles of the United States Army. He could seek refuge in town.

When near Harpers Ferry, Benjamin was less than 100 yards behind. He began to rapidly fire off several shots. This time, Jacob's horse shrieked and dropped to the ground, throwing him down over the steep embankment along the river shore. Quickly, Jacob got to his feet and raced for the water. As he began wading the river, he looked back and noticed Benjamin had dismounted and was racing down the slope after him. Jacob determined Benjamin would have to kill him in order to prevent his escape. Several more times, Benjamin discharged his pistol. One bullet skimmed the surface of the water nearby and the other hit a rock where the water rushed over. Jacob continued his escape not knowing if the next bullet would strike him.

When Benjamin fired again, the bullet lifted Jacob's hat from his head, but he kept up the race. He noticed while nearing the Harpers Ferry shore that Benjamin had entered the water and was following. On the Harpers Ferry riverbank, five Federal soldiers appeared with weapons in hand. Once they knew that Jacob was the intended target, they began to fire at Benjamin. When Jacob paused and turned to see Benjamin's fate, he saw him turning and running for the opposite shore from where they began the race.

Jacob was relieved Benjamin was all right, but he didn't know if he would try again. Once on the other side, he knew he would be arrested and questioned over this affair because the town of Harpers Ferry would surely be under martial law. He didn't have a pass in his possession to prove his innocence. But at least he was alive.

Chapter Forty-Six

Nestled between the Shenandoah and Potomac Rivers is the picturesque town of Harpers Ferry. It was founded in 1747 by Robert Harper. The town eventually grew to become one of the largest and most productive weapons facilities in the south. From 1801 to 1860, over 600,000 various weapons were manufactured at the twenty-two building United States Armory.

Prior to the war, residents from both the North and South equally divided the town's population of 3,400 citizens. Over half of the town's male inhabitants worked in the weapons industry even though there were other industries to choose from. Within six months after the outbreak of hostilities, the town's population had diminished dramatically to about one hundred citizens. The town was no more than a military encampment for thousands of Federal soldiers. One of those soldiers was Jacob Martin.

After Colonel Dixon S. Miles, the commanding officer of the Harpers Ferry garrison interviewed Jacob, and a telegram dispatched to Lieutenant Stanley at the War Department in Washington City, his identity was verified. Jacob was ordered by the War Department to remain in town. His identity had been compromised and since the nation's capital was full of spies, he would be of little use in covert operations and his life would be in peril. During the past month in Harpers Ferry, Jacob made a new and close acquaintance from Adams County, Pennsylvania by the name of Sergeant William Edwards from C Company of the 1st Maryland Potomac Home Brigade Cavalry. They were known also as Cole's Battalion after their commanding officer, Major Henry Cole from Frederick, Maryland. Since

Jacob was familiar with the surrounding area as were Cole's men, he was attached as a scout to Cole's command.

Late in the afternoon of September 4, 1862, Jacob was scouting along with several other men from Cole's battalion. They were riding along Piney Run in Loudoun County where he used to spend countless hours fishing and swimming on hot summer afternoons. They turned onto a trail that led over the Short Hill Mountain. Once on a slight ridge above the creek, Jacob knew he was near his family's farm. Jacob rode alone onto another ridge and looked through a spyglass in the direction of his family's farm. When he didn't see anyone working on the property, he directed his men to follow him. Once the cavalry patrol arrived, Jacob's sister slowly emerged from the entrance to the house and approached.

Jacob dismounted while his men watched. He removed his hat and noticed the sad expression on Lily's face. He knew something was wrong.

"I know, it's father," Jacob said in a broken tone embracing his weeping sister.

"When Father heard the gunshots, he rushed to the window. He watched Benjamin chasing you and he fell dead. It must have been his heart or whatever he had been suffering from. We didn't know where you had gone and besides, with Benjamin shooting at you, we knew it wouldn't be safe for you to return."

"You and Mother did the right thing. There's nothing to feel guilty about," Jacob said in a reassuring tone breaking their embrace. He wiped her eyes with his handkerchief and asked, "Where is Mother?"

"She is sleeping. I will awaken her and let her know you are here."

"No. Don't. With everything she has been through lately, she is probably exhausted. Let her sleep,"

What will you do?" Lily asked in a soft tone.

"I want to visit Father's grave. Where is he buried?"

Lily pointed in the direction of a grove of peach trees on a ridge, a short distances west of the house. Jacob took the reins of his horse and walked over to the area alone. Once there, he viewed the freshly covered grave. His future expectations of redemption with his father and a relationship had vanished. Too many misunderstandings and not enough rationale had inflamed their emotions and caused their division. While standing over the grave, feelings of guilt and condemnation were more than Jacob could endure while uncontrollably weeping. Once composed, he mounted his horse and returned to where Lily and his soldiers were waiting.

"Are you and your men hungry?" Lily asked.

"No, we must continue on," Jacob softly answered.

"I see."

"Is Benjamin still around?"

"No. He left several days after his disagreement with you."

"Than I guess he has returned to Lee's army."

"He wouldn't tell Rachel where he was going, but that's what she believes. She hasn't heard from him since, and with the fighting that took place four days ago at Manassas, she fears even more for his welfare."

"Have you seen any rebels along this road?"

"No, but keep a watch out for bushwhackers. They come down out of the hills, "Lily cautioned as she took Jacob's hand.

"If you need me, I'll be in Harpers Ferry."

Once the cavalry patrol and Jacob departed, they came next to Benjamin's farm. When they arrived, William and Jacob dismounted while the rest of the men stayed mounted. He knocked on the door, but there wasn't any answer. He cautiously opened and entered with William following. Inside, Jacob heard the sound of a baby crying. Immediately, he knew Rachel had given birth. He walked over alone to the bedroom and slowly opened the door. When Jacob entered, he noticed Rachel lying in bed, holding the baby in her arms.

"You are safe and have returned," Rachel said in a soft tone.

"Yes, I am on patrol and thought I would see how you were doing."

"My son was born this morning. Come near and look at him," Rachel said pulling the blanket back that covered the baby.

Jacob walked to Rachel's bedside. He softly asked, "What did you name him?"

"Benjamin, after his father," Rachel replied smiling while looking at her son.

"I am sure Benjamin will be honored when he receives word of his son's birth."

"I am sorry to hear about your father. He was a good man and will be missed by the folks in this valley," Rachel said as she looked up at Jacob's somber expression.

"Thank you. I just found out myself."

"I didn't know until the day before yesterday that your father and you were having serious differences. And I know now that it's part of the reason why you left home when the war started."

"The war has affected everyone, every family, and friends such as Benjamin and me. I never thought the day would come when my best friend would take a weapon and try to harm me. I don't know the reasoning for such hostilities. What could I have done to him?"

"He hasn't been the same person since the war begun. He wasn't the same person when he returned home."

"War affects a soldier's mind when he witnesses and experiences the death and carnage of battle. When he hears the cries of the wounded pleading for death to relieve them of their suffering, it's almost unbearable, and I know that Benjamin has seen plenty to change him. It will always leave scars on his mind. But knowing him as I do he won't give up until the last gun is silenced. He is too determined to win because he firmly believes the Southern Cause is the right one."

As Jacob turned to leave, Rachel emotionally asked, "I haven't heard from him. It's not like him not to write after there has been a fight. Maybe he was captured at Manassas, I don't know, but if you see him will you tell him he has a son and everyone is doing fine."

Jacob turned and said jokingly, "I'll send him home to you."

Jacob turned and walked out the door. He feared Benjamin might have been killed in the fight at Manassas. Thousands on both sides had died during the two-day battle. At the moment, he also knew his love for Rachel had surfaced once more after seeing her. It began to torment him as it so often had over the last two years. Jacob didn't show his emotions when he saw William standing by the front door, but silently walked by.

*   *   *   *

It was 8:00 o'clock in the evening, just before sunset when both William and Jacob were standing at the corner of High and Shenandoah Street watching some aides and staff officers rushing in and out of Colonel Miles's headquarters at the Master Armorer's House.

"Headquarters has been busy all evening. Jacob, I wonder what is going on?" William asked taking a puff from his pipe."

"I don't know, but we need to find out," Jacob replied crossing the street with William following.

Once near Colonel Miles's headquarters, he noticed an officer rushing from the building's entrance.

"Lieutenant, what's all of the activity about?" Jacob asked.

"Rebels sir. Rebels are crossing in great strength at Noland's Ferry along the Potomac."

"How many?"

"Maybe as many as thirty thousand," the officer said in an excited tone.

"Lee's army. Now they have defeated us again at Manassas, they must be headed toward Frederick City," Jacob replied looking at the officer.

"But we didn't see any of them today when we were scouting across the mountain," William said.

"No, we didn't, but apparently, the rebels are taking the war north. The days ahead will bring more fighting and killing. When will it all end?"

Jacob looked at both the officer and William and knew another great campaign was underway. What would be its outcome? Was Benjamin still alive and will he fight another day?

Chapter Forty-Seven

Ten days had passed since the Confederate Army of Northern Virginia crossed the Potomac and entered Maryland. Since that time, General Lee divided his army and sent the Second Corps under General Stonewall Jackson to capture Martinsburg, which was located seventeen miles west of Harpers Ferry. With Jackson's approach, Brigadier-General Julius White and his 3,000 Federal soldiers garrisoned at Martinsburg evacuated the town and arrived at Harpers Ferry. Jackson wasn't content with capturing Martinsburg only, but looked to the bigger prize of Harpers Ferry. As Jackson's Confederates moved on Harpers Ferry there were two additional Confederate divisions that appeared in Pleasant Valley.

Pleasant Valley in Maryland was located about three miles east of Harpers Ferry between South Mountain and Elk Ridge Mountain where Maryland Heights rested at the southern end. On Maryland Heights, there were 2,000 inexperienced Federal soldiers sheltered by natural fortifications. A great battle had been fought on September 13th, but the battle-hardened rebels had driven the Federals from the mountain. Now during the early afternoon hours of the 14th, the beleaguered town was under siege by Confederate forces.

When Jacob arrived at Colonel Miles's headquarters along Shenandoah Street, he dismounted and pulled his timepiece from his pocket. It was 1:45 in the afternoon. As he returned the timepiece to his pocket, he noticed Captain Samuel Means of the Loudoun Rangers leaving the building's entrance. Jacob waited until Captain Means was nearby.

"Captain Means," Jacob addressed the officer in accordance with military etiquette.

"Captain Martin, sir, are you going in to see Colonel Miles?"

"Yes sir, I am. I've just returned from scouting along the Shenandoah with about a dozen men from the 12th Illinois Cavalry."

"And what did you find?" Captain Means excitingly asked Jacob.

"We didn't go far when we came upon rebel pickets. And not only are they along the banks of the Shenandoah near Keyes Ferry, but also I noticed them on Loudoun Heights. It might only be a signal station to pass information from Jackson to the rebels on Maryland Heights.

"Just giving up that mountain yesterday makes me so mad. It was the worst thing that could have happened to us. It has to be the most prized possession for the rebels thus far in this fight," Captain Means answered in an exasperating tone.

"I agree. Maryland Heights should have been held at all cost. It was the most important area to the capture of the town. Now there is a sense of hopelessness among the men. It's written all over their expressions."

"If the Johnnies are on Loudoun Mountain, then that means Old Jack must have us penned in. Trapped like a bunch of helpless lambs!" Shaking his head in frustration, Captain Means continued to pour out his concern and frustrations, "I have to get out of this town as soon as possible because there is a price on my head by Jeff Davis. They'll take me back to Richmond and surely hang me after they make a mockery of me."

"Captain, you're not alone."

"Son, you don't have anything to worry about such as I."

"But I do. I was in Richmond up until the first of August when I barely escaped with my life. After returning home, which is across the Loudoun Mountain, someone who was once my best friend chased me into town. He was sent from Richmond to capture me, an enemy agent. So I am in the same predicament that you are."

"Spying! That would be the only reason they would send someone after you. They must have been desperate for you. But son, it's good to have someone from Loudoun County that's on the right side of this war."

"Thank you sir."

"But as for me, I am leaving sometime after dark with or without Miles's permission."

Jacob quietly departed, but his last statement had left a dramatic impact on his thoughts. As an officer of the United States Army, Jacob was always taught orders were orders and must be obeyed regardless of the sacrifice, but would he be serving his country by needlessly dying or being captured?

After Jacob gave his report to Colonel Miles, he mounted and headed toward the Hall's factory where his battalion and Companies H and I of the 1st Maryland, and Captain Means' Loudoun Rangers were resting and taking care of their horses.

When Jacob arrived near what was once the barrel-drilling and finishing shop, he dismounted and began to un-strap the saddle from his horse. He was exhausted and hungry from scouting for hours. Like Captain Means, Jacob knew he had to find some way of escaping before the garrison of soldiers at Harpers Ferry were forced to surrender to the rebels.

William approached Jacob and anxiously asked, "have you heard the news?"

"What news?" Jacob asked lifting the saddle from his horse's back.

"As I am sure you know, the loss of those heights yester-day was a serious blow. Something interesting did happen last night. While I was on courier duty at Colonel Miles's headquarters, Colonel Davis of the 8th New York and several cavalry officers from other regiments confronted Colonel Miles about escaping."

"What happened?" Jacob asked as he turned and looked at William.

"At first, Colonel Miles agreed, but just as quickly, he changed his mind saying the Shenandoah was too full of holes and would be impassable. Instead, he sent Captain Russell with nine men to make an effort to get a message to General McClellan."

The conversation between William and Jacob was interrupted by the sound of artillery fire coming from the direction of Bolivar Heights. Jacob looked toward Loudoun Heights where he heard another cannon firing from the mountain. As the smoke from the artillery piece lifted above the mountain's treetops, William and Jacob took shelter, not knowing where the shell would land. Soon, artillery fire commenced from Loudoun Heights, and also the sound of cannon came from the direction of Maryland Heights and the muffled sound of the weapons could be heard further west of town. Federal forces in Harpers Ferry were completely surrounded. Would it mean surrender?

*　　*　　*　　*

The artillery duel continued throughout the afternoon. Most of the men from the Maryland and Loudoun cavalry units knew they were in a helpless position. Unable to maneuver or fight, Jacob knew they had to wait it out. The shells continued to thud and shriek overhead. Apparently, the forces on Bolivar Heights and Camp Hill were the Confederate artillery's main objective. He looked around and thought about their dilemma. The horses and cavalry equipment would be of great benefit to the Confederates. When there was a lull in the shelling, preparations for the proposed escape from the Ferry such as issuing ammunition and food supplies, were carried out. When darkness settled in over Harpers Ferry, Colonel Miles called his cavalry officers to his headquarters. After a serious confrontation on the part of Miles and his cavalry officers, Miles relented and gave his permission for the cavalry's attempted escape. It was decided that 1,500 cavalrymen would use the pontoon bridge across the Potomac.

It was drizzling when the forces began assembling along Shenandoah Street near the ruins of the small arsenal building; Lieutenant Green from the 1st Maryland Potomac Home Brigade Cavalry rode up to Jacob saluting "Captain Martin, sir, Colonel Voss sends his compliments. Colonel Voss has requested that you would do us the honor and ride at the head of the column. As I understand you know the area very well and might be of good use to us."

"Tell Colonel Voss, I send my compliments and would consider it an honor to ride at the front of the column."

"I feel the Johnnies are waiting on the other side of the river for us. They'll cut us to pieces if they have the chance," William said.

"That might be true, but it's better than just staying here and allowing them to take us prisoner. Nothing would be more disgraceful and bring more dishonor than to stay in this place and surrender. We must make the attempt. At least some of us might make it." Pausing and looking at the fearful expression on William's face, Jacob calmly continued, "I know you're concerned you won't see Lydia Rose or your family again. As for myself, I have continuously thought of my fate throughout the day, and not having or seeing my mother or sister. Times such as this really makes you think of your mortality."

"Well as you said, we are soldiers and it would be a dishonor and a disgrace to surrender to the Johnnies."

The order was given to the cavalry to proceed. It was Miles's request that the cavalry would depart the Ferry as inconspicuously as possible. Miles's reasoning for such action was that the infantrymen and artillerymen wouldn't know of the escape attempt. If they did, it might cause a panic among them with everyone at once dashing for the pontoon bridge. The commotion would arouse the rebels and great casualties among the Federal soldiers might be the end results.

The Federal cavalry began to move slowly in the direction of the entrance to the old armory grounds. William and Jacob were riding side by side toward the front of the lead column along with several companies of the 1st Maryland Potomac Home Brigade. Lieutenant Hanson Green of the 1st Maryland and a civilian scout from Martinsburg, Thomas Noakes were at the front of the cavalry as guides. When the column moved through the armory grounds entrance, Jacob glanced to the left and noticed the old fire engine house where John Brown and twenty-one followers along with their hostages held out for thirty-six hours against angry town's citizens, area militia companies and ninety United States Marines. The damage to the wooden door where the Marines had used a ladder to ram a hole in it was still quite visible, reminding him of the severe consequences that took place on these grounds in October 1859.

Jacob noticed the column turning right and passing some of the vacant armory buildings. Jacob leaned forward and said to William, "May God's speed be with you."

"And also with you," William nervously replied as he continued to look toward the bridge and mountain.

Once on the pontoon bridge, Jacob glanced at the Maryland and Loudoun mountains and saw fires burning, signifying the Confederates occupied the hills in great force. He thought of his family while the column moved slowly and cautiously across the makeshift bridge. Jacob wondered if he would ever have the opportunity to see them again. War was a dangerous game with many uncertainties, and he didn't desire to become a casualty or a prisoner-of-war. Prisoner-of-war camps were just as bad as being wounded or dying and would reduce his chances of ever returning home.

Once the Federal cavalry reached the Maryland shore, they didn't hesitate or pause, but instead paced their horses into a full gallop across the rugged and narrow Sharpsburg Road, which ran northwest on a narrow strip of ground between the mountain and the Chesapeake and Ohio Canal.

After about a mile, the road headed over a ridge of the mountain. In this area, a campfire was burning. A single musket shot rang out. It must be a Confederate sentry along the road firing a warning shot, Jacob thought. Jacob pulled out his pistol and prepared for the worst. When they arrived, the Confederate sentry had fled. Jacob heard the shrieking sound of a horse behind him. He quickly glanced back and noticed that Ed Hughes' horse had thrown him to the ground. Orders were issued before the expedition that there wasn't to be any pauses to assist anyone should they become a casualty or lose their horse. Jacob decided to disobey orders. Jacob wheeled his horse around and sped back to help his comrade. Jacob stretched forth his hand and Ed took it and jumped onto the saddle. Again, Jacob pushed his horse at a full gallop toward Sharpsburg.

When near Hagerstown, Maryland, the Federal cavalry captured an ordnance wagon train, belonging to Confederate Lieutenant-General James Longstreet's First Corps. Without hesitation, the Federal cavalry hurried their prize north. It all ended when they arrived at Greencastle, Pennsylvania fourteen hours later.

With little rest, Jacob immediately telegraphed the War Department for orders since he was without a command. As Jacob was waiting for a reply, he noticed William looking at some of the spoils of war in one of the captured wagons.

"We made it," Jacob said walking over to William.

"I know. For a while I had my doubts and thought the rebels would begin to blast us as soon as we were on the Maryland side of the river. I really believed we'd all be killed or have to return to the Ferry and surrender."

"I guess now, you can take time and write Lydia Rose and your family a few lines to let them know of your welfare," Jacob said, smiling at William.

"I guess you can do the same."

"Yes, that's true. For now we are safe. Much more so than our comrades at the Ferry. I don't know if you received word, but Harpers Ferry surrendered a few hours ago and Colonel Miles was wounded."

"I am sorry to hear about Colonel Miles," William said shaking his head in frustration, continuing, "then we did the right thing in getting out as quickly as we did."

William and Jacob's conversation was interrupted when a soldier approached and handed Jacob an envelope.

"Sir," the private said saluting, "I have a telegram from the War Department for you."

Jacob opened the envelope. His eyes quickly scanned its contents. He quietly folded the paper, knowing its seriousness.

"What did it say?" William asked in a curious tone.

"I am to report to General McClellan. He is somewhere between Frederick City and the gaps of South Mountain in pursuit of Lee's army."

"Maybe they're retreating for the Potomac,"

"No, I really think Lee might be trying to concentrate his army. There will be another great battle and men will die before he leaves Maryland."

"How do you know?" William eagerly asked.

"There's no way Bobby Lee is going to cross the Potomac without putting up a fight. His confidence in his rebel force must be pretty high about now with their win at Manassas."

"Then it's good-byes." William somberly answered stretching forth his hand.

Jacob took William's hand and then embraced him saying, "You must take care of yourself and stay alert. I don't want to hear of you becoming a casualty or prisoner.

Lydia Rose needs you. She will have one good man to spend the rest of her life with."

Jacob turned and silently walked away with the intention of carrying out his orders and finding General McClellan. He began wondering if Benjamin was with Lee's army and would they do battle against each other in the coming days. He dreaded the thought of meeting Benjamin on the field of glory.

Chapter Forty-Eight

In the late early evening hours of Tuesday, September 16th, Jacob slowly rode along the Boonesborough Pike in the direction of Sharpsburg. There were many Federal soldiers marching along the way. When the road came to an area of descent toward Antietam Creek, he noticed multiple batteries of artillery. Some of the artillery pieces were heavy ordnance such as the 20-pound Parrot guns. Jacob paused and glanced off to his right and noticed a two-story brick Federal style house with an imposing white Greek Revival portico, seated on the crest of a ridge near Antietam Creek. When Jacob inquired of an artilleryman standing near a caisson where General McClellan's headquarters was located, the soldier pointed to the Phillip Pry house.

Jacob slowly rode in the direction of the house. Thoughts of a major battle were on his mind. What role would he play in the upcoming conflict? Even though he had courageously fought Indians in Kansas, this fight would be different for him because thus far in this war, he had never lifted his weapon against another individual in anger.

After Jacob dismounted, he commanded an orderly to take his horse to the barn and see that the animal was fed and watered. As Jacob ascended the rock steps toward the front porch, the sound of galloping horses attracted his attention. Jacob turned and noticed a large party of cavalrymen arriving in front of the house. Out of curiosity, he paused and waited. Some of the officers dismounted. Jacob recognized a small individual in stature. It was General McClellan in the lead walking rapidly in his direction.

"Sir, Captain Jacob Martin reporting as ordered," Jacob said, saluting the general.

"At ease Captain Martin."

Jacob handed General McClellan his orders from the War Department and remained quiet as he read its contents.

"There isn't any time to assign you where I feel you might be needed, so instead, I will place you on my staff as a courier until this is decided."

"I understand from some of the boys along the way the rebels are across the Antietam," Jacob curiously replied.

"Yes, Bobby Lee is there. Actually early this morning, I thought he was going to retreat back across the Potomac, but once the haze lifted from the field, I noticed rebels along the ridge at Sharpsburg. But that's good because while I was in Frederick City, we intercepted his plans and now we'll have the opportunity to cut him to pieces. Come with me," General McClellan said in a confident tone.

"Are we attacking this afternoon?" Jacob asked.

"No, Franklin's Sixth Corps isn't up yet and no one has received any orders yet. Are you West Pont?" General McClellan asked, looking with anticipation toward the crest of the hill.

"Yes sir, class of '56," Jacob answered, glancing back at the general.

There was a tree near the Pry house along the crest of the hill. Jacob quietly noticed General McClellan looking at an officer dozing on the ground under a tree and another sitting idly nearby. Once General McClellan and Jacob were closer, both officers rose to their feet and waited until the general was near.

"General," the one officer that sat idly by said, as he saluted.

The other officer rose and brushed off his trousers, saluted and was standing near the first officer. Jacob noticed both officers were major generals by the two stars on each of their shoulder straps.

"General McClellan," the second officer addressed.

"General Sumner and General Hooker," General McClellan said, Continuing, "Gentlemen, please follow me."

Everyone followed, pondering on what General McClellan had on his mind. It was evident to all that the general had been out on a reconnaissance because of the dust covering his uniform. Would he give battle to Lee and the rebel forces or allow them to cross the Potomac without another fight?

Once the other three officers and Jacob entered the Pry family's dining room, General McClellan said, "Tomorrow we fight the battle that will decide the fate of our republic." With that statement, General McClellan had everyone's attention, continuing as he pointed to various locations on a map spread out on the dining table, "The rebels are on very good defensive ground, especially near the Harpers Ferry Road and the heights along the Boonsborough Pike. I have spent the morning observing their positions, examining the fords across Antietam Creek, even on some occasions, drawing fire from their batteries. Bobby Lee knows he holds the best defensive ground and he has no intention of crossing the Potomac without a fight. Therefore, I intend on giving him a battle on these grounds tomorrow once the boys are in place."

General McClellan glanced around the table, noticing Generals Hooker and Sumner's expressions to see the reaction to his statement.

All were silent. General McClellan continued looking at the map and pointing at the hills and ridges south of Sharpsburg, "At this lower bridge, I have ordered General Burnside to move forward with his corps and occupy the heights in rear of the bridge to protect our left from any Confederate forces that might be arriving from Harpers Ferry. This is good defensive ground. If that doesn't happen then my intentions are that General Burnside should attack Lee's right." Pointing on the map to the Hagerstown Pike and a heavily wooded area where a white building stood, General McClellan continued, "While using your men, General Hooker, I want you to cross the upper bridge and attack the rebels on their left. I want you to move down the Hagerstown Pike."

"What is the terrain like?"

"From what I can tell, it is deceiving. The terrain is full of little hollows, wooded areas, and still full of crops. On some of the field, my view was hindered."

"Sir, what do you want me to do?" General Sumner asked.

"For now, your men will stay on this side of the Antietam and provide support for General Hooker."

"It will take me some time before I can get my boys across the creek and into position. When did you plan for me to attack the rebels?" General Hooker asked looking up from the map.

"First light," McClellan ordered.

Generals Hooker and Sumner quietly nodded their heads in agreement.

"If that is all, then gentlemen, you may be excused and begin your movements. May God's speed be with you," General McClellan ordered as everyone saluted.

Jacob quietly turned to leave. A courier handed General McClellan a telegram. General McClellan swiftly ordered, "Captain Martin, wait, this message pertains to you."

Jacob turned with an astonished expression. He slowly approached the commanding officer.

"It's from the War Department. You have been promoted to the rank of major in the United States Army. Congratulations Major."

"Thank you sir," Jacob replied, saluting and departing once more.

When Jacob descended the stone steps of the Pry House, he commanded an orderly to bring his horse. He was excited with receiving a promotion and more pay, but he knew his new rank would bring more challenges and responsibilities.

The soldier arrived with the animal, Jacob mounted and swiftly rode to a ridge west of the house. He patiently looked across Antietam Creek through his spyglass toward Sharpsburg, studying the enemy's defensive position and wondering what the Confederate's strategy and tactics would be for the upcoming engagement. Each battle seemed to get more bloody and more vigorous in nature with the cost and sacrifice of life much greater. Confederates were along the ridge. Again, Jacob pondered. Was Benjamin on the ridge he was gazing at? Did Benjamin know he was a father? Would Benjamin and I live to see each other? Tomorrow would tell.

Chapter Forty-Nine

Throughout the night, Benjamin wasn't able to sleep, knowing men in his regiment would die once the first streaks of day began gleaming. There were only twenty-two men that answered the call of duty after the serious fighting on South Mountain, which took place several days ago. The tiny regiment had eleven killed or wounded since entering Maryland.

A foggy mist hung over the field. Wet drops of drizzle fell upon Benjamin's face, making the air feel chilled and damp. He thought of many of the men of the 8th Virginia, who were almost naked because of the worn and tattered uniforms covering their thin bodies. Before crossing the Potomac near Leesburg, some of the men in the army and his regiment were either barefooted, sick, or not fit for duty and were sent to Winchester. Others in the army refused to cross the Potomac and fight in the north. They were only interested in defending their homes in the south. Hunger and exhaustion made straggling among the various ranks as contagious as disease. Mostly green corn had been the diet of the soldiers on the march from the Potomac River to this place along the banks of Antietam Creek. Even with thin ranks, he witnessed two dead Confederate soldiers hanging from a tree after disobeying orders by picking apples to eat. After the driving march from Hagerstown and the battle at South Mountain, Benjamin believed the army should retreat across the river because it wasn't really supplied and ready to take on another major engagement. He was greatly concerned for the men that remained and their welfare.

Skirmishing between the two armies had already begun the evening before about a mile away near a place known to the locals as the East Woods. Throughout the night, pickets were close enough to fire at each other. Benjamin knew a much larger and well-supplied Federal army was lingering across Antietam Creek and would surely advance on them at first light.

Benjamin's small regiment was brigaded with the 18th, 19th, 28th, and the 56th Virginia. No more than 270 men filled the ranks. They were under the command of Brigadier-General Richard B. Garnett. Benjamin liked General Garnett because he was a brave and hard fighter. His leadership was inspiring to the men because he was always at the forefront of the action taking the same risk as his men. As the rays of light began to slowly appear, the brigade was positioned on Cemetery Hill, along the Boonsborough Pike in support of the Washington Artillery of New Orleans.

While sitting around the campfire, like other Southern soldiers, Benjamin was frightened and willing to accept his fate when battle came. He knew very shortly there would be a mighty and fierce battle to the death. He took a stick lying nearby and stirred the embers, looking at several of his men writing a few lines of a letter home to their loved ones. He noticed one of the soldiers had tears streaming down his cheeks, possibly having a premonition of his fate. His thoughts returned to his home and Rachel. By now, she must have heard of the desperate fighting along South Mountain on Sunday, and also the two armies assembled along Antietam Creek to possibly fight again. She must be worried not knowing his fate or welfare. Because of the rapid movement of troops and in enemy territory, there hadn't been much time for writing. Not being able to get word to Rachel troubled Benjamin. Once this affair was settled, he would write her a few lines to ease her mind.

About a mile west of Benjamin's position, he heard the thundering sound of artillery beginning to open in rapid succession. Was fighting about to commence all along the line? As gunners of the Washington Artillery raced to man their cannons and begin the artillery drill, the number five man raced from the limber to the gun with ammunition. Benjamin rose to his feet and called out to his men to form ranks. Now off in the distance toward the Hagerstown Pike, he listened to the artillery response from Colonel S. D. Lee's Confederate artillery battalion on a ridge near the white church and Jeb Stuart's horse artillery on Nicodemus Hill. The day of sacrifice was just beginning; the battle of Antietam Creek was in its genesis.

"I guess it's time to start the killing. When will it all come to an end?" James commented as he loaded his musket.

"Not till the last drop of blood is shed," Benjamin concluded gazing across Antietam Creek.

"I've seen enough fighting and dying to last me a life time. I just want to go home for a spell and see my wife and boys. That's all, nothing more. I haven't seen them in almost a year now," James somberly said pulling his wife's photograph from his pocket and kissing it.

"My friend, one of these battles will decide it all. Maybe this will be the one and the fighting will come to an end. Let's fight with that kind of determination."

Shortly off in the distance, Benjamin watched General Garnett with a few staff members walking onto the ridge near the artillery. Garnett paused and looked through his spyglass at the Federals assembled on the opposite side of Antietam Creek to determine their design and intentions. Were they preparing to rush across the middle bridge on the Boonsborough Pike in their direction, Benjamin wondered? Suddenly, a courier swiftly rode to where the general was standing. Benjamin noticed the general and courier exchanging conversation. General Garnett turned and pointed in his direction. The courier hastened toward Benjamin.

When the officer brought his horse to a halt, he swiftly asked, "are you Lieutenant Kelly?"

"Yes sir, I am," Benjamin calmly answered.

"My name is Captain Leon Daniels. Because of the heavy fighting along the Hagerstown Pike, we have had some of our couriers killed and wounded by the severity of the action over there. Since you and your men are not engaged at the moment, I've been sent by headquarters to draft some officers to fill that gap. So, I'm choosing you. Climb on!"

Benjamin was astonished and paused, looking at his friend James Bell.

"Go on! Hurry!" James shouted, gesturing with his hand.

Benjamin mounted the horse behind the officer and they raced into Sharpsburg.

When Benjamin and the courier rode onto the main street in Sharpsburg, he witnessed a disordered state of affairs and overturned wagons with dying and wounded soldiers cluttering the street. Horses reared in panic at the sound of artillery shells crashing into homes and splintering trees. The pungent smell of sulfur filled the air. Benjamin noticed the provost guard striking stragglers in an effort to hurry them along toward the sound of battle. Federal artillery shells sent bricks, shell fragments, and shards of glass in every direction. Benjamin noticed a lady standing on the porch of her home, braving the dangers of battle to give cold water to wounded soldiers as they passed.

Captain Daniels noticed a horse with a saddle racing by.

"There's a horse for you," the Captain shouted.

Captain Daniels and Benjamin gave chase. When Daniels rode alongside of the horse, Benjamin reached for the reins and brought the frightened animal under control. He quickly mounted the other horse and followed Captain Daniels to a tent in a grove of trees on the south side of town along the Shepherdstown Pike.

The campsite was General Lee's headquarters. Once Major Daniels and Benjamin brought their horses to a halt, they swiftly dismounted.

Benjamin was quite thirsty. He walked over and took a drink from a pail of water to remove the taste of gunpowder from his mouth and to quench his thirst.

"And Lieutenant, what is your name?" an officer asked as he slowly approached with a limp while smoking a cigar.

"Benjamin Kelly from Company A, 8th Virginia Infantry," Benjamin answered, noticing the officer was wearing a carpet slipper on one foot instead of a boot.

"I see. Have you been over that ridge yet today?"

"No sir, I haven't. I just arrived."

"Well from what I understand it's like stepping into Hell fire. Plenty of good men are dying over there. And before the sun sets today, the precious blood of thousands of them will be poured onto this ground."

As the officer walked away, Benjamin watched him mount his horse and with staff members rode away toward the village.

"Who was that officer?" Benjamin asked Captain Daniels, as he approached, sipping water from a tin cup.

"You didn't know who he was?"

"No, I couldn't tell. Like all of us, he doesn't look his best."

"That's General Longstreet."

"As many times as I have seen the man, I didn't recognize him."

Benjamin watched General Lee emerged from his tent with several other officers. Immediately, the request went out for a courier. Inexperienced at such duty, Benjamin was eager to learn. Without hesitation, he stepped forward.

"Lieutenant," General Lee said pointing westward, "you will accompany me."

Benjamin noticed the general's hand and arm were still bandaged and in a sling from an accident, which occurred before the army crossed the Potomac. Benjamin assisted General Lee onto his horse and took the animal's reins, leading him.

The sound of battle increased. Benjamin, General Lee, and his staff were approaching a hill on the outskirts of Sharpsburg where the general could get a good view. By now, the morning was hot and muggy. It was difficult for them to see because the battlefield was covered with a white hazy curtain of smoke from the constant barrages of artillery and musketry.

Benjamin gazed at General Lee, as the general intently and calmly watched the action through his field glasses. To Benjamin, General Lee appeared quite unconscious of the enemy shells exploding and bursting around him. He didn't fear for his life. Benjamin, like the others, turned his attention toward a Federal division marching across the field in the direction of the West Woods, which was along the Hagerstown Pike. It was a splendid sight because the Federals were divided into columns of brigades about seventy yards apart. The sun had burned off the mist and was now shining brightly down on the parade-like formation.

The Federal troops were General Sedgwick's men. Everyone watched as Sedgwick's men made a left flank movement near the Mumma farm, bringing them into attack position on General Stonewall Jackson's front along the Hagerstown Pike. Thus far, Jackson's men had suffered the brunt of the Federal assaults and it appeared they were about to receive another one by a fresh division.

Benjamin noticed Colonel S. D. Lee rapidly approaching. Once he reined his horse in, Colonel Lee frantically said to General Robert E. Lee, "Sir, General Hood sends his compliments. We are hard pressed. Unless General Hood receives reinforcements, the day is lost."

"Don't be excited about it, Colonel," General Lee calmly said, "Go tell General Hood to hold his ground. Reinforcements are now rapidly approaching between Sharpsburg and the ford. Tell him I am now coming to his support."

"General, your presence will do good, but nothing but infantry can save the day on the left," Colonel Lee swiftly answered.

Colonel Lee quietly saluted and began to return. General Lee called out to Colonel Lee. He pointed to General McLaws' division at the double quick, heading toward the West Woods to meet the anticipated threat from the Federals. Benjamin's confidence was renewed and he felt inspired to serve under such a leader as Robert E. Lee.

As Benjamin gazed over the field of battle, he knew the fight was far from undecided, but matters looked grim for the Confederate forces. They had beaten back repeated attacks on this side of the field. How many more could they withstand before their lines of defense collapsed under the superior Federal army?

*   *   *   *

In the early morning hours, as artillery began their cannonade along the area of the Hagerstown Pike and the West Woods, Jacob watched some of the early fighting from a bald hill on the eastern bank of the Antietam near the Pry house with General McClellan and his staff. Several civilians had raced to the scene with the first barrages of artillery and expressed their hopes and prayers it would be the end of Bobby Lee's ragtag army. Jacob noticed a well-dressed lady standing with an officer of high rank who supported great mutton chop whiskers. The muffled sounds of continuous volleys of musketry filled the air. Everyone was looking through their glasses westward where white smoke and haze was quickly lifting skyward. All eyes were on the white church along the Hagerstown Pike and the Confederate artillery on a ridge eastward from the road. The Federal forces could not be seen and the Confederate soldiers were barely visible.

It was 6:00 o'clock in the morning when Jacob glanced at his timepiece. General McClellan was standing with Major-

General Fitz John Porter of the Federal Fifth Corps. General McClellan ordered Jacob to his side and sent him to seek out General Hooker and discover the progress of the Federal First Corps. Without hesitation, Jacob raced to his horse and dashed north along the road until he came to Antietam Creek. He crossed the creek in the vicinity of the upper bridge near Pry's Mill.

The fighting between the blue and gray continued savagely throughout the morning hours. Jacob continued to make trips to and from General McClellan's headquarters, carrying orders to the various corps commanders from the commanding general. It had been tedious and dangerous duty. Now there was a lull in the fighting on the Federal army's right flank along the Hagerstown Pike and Miller's cornfield after Federal attacks and counter attacks by the Confederates.

It was 10:30 in the morning according to Jacob's timepiece. He paused and gazed through his spyglass across the field of glory from the area of the North Woods. The pungent stench of gunpowder irritated his nose and caused his eyes to water. His throat was raw and his lips were cracked, but minor physical problems were nothing compared to what he witnessed. Jacob was stunned by the devastation reaped upon this area of the battlefield in the four hours of heavy fighting it had endured. This section was reduced to shambles and ruins after the intense battle throughout the morning hours between the blue and gray. Thousands of men covered D. R. Miller's cornfield; not a cornstalk was left standing. The fence line along the Hagerstown Pike, and around the white church near the West Woods was littered with the dead and wounded. It was more shattering to the mind than anything Jacob could have imagined or conceived. He helplessly watched as men from both sides lifted their hands in agonizing pain and cried for help, but it was unsafe to venture into the area where the battle had claimed so many lives. Jacob noticed about forty rebels lying in perfect formation on the ground where they had been shot down. With the uncivilized killing today, the price of life was cheap. He watched soldiers carrying a comrade on a litter to a field hospital. The young boy shrieked and jerked in convulsions with blood pouring profusely from a mortal abdominal wound.

Jacob turned his horse around and noticed a woman kneeling beside a wounded Federal soldier. He paused. He could not recognize her, but watched as she held his head in her right arm and raised a canteen to his lips to give him water. Suddenly, the soldier violently jerked and the water trickled down his lifeless face.

When he rode closer, he was amazed. It was Amanda, who he had arrested in Washington City as a Confederate agent.

"He was just alive. Now he is gone," Amanda sadly said as she looked up at Jacob. "I felt something hot pass through my sleeve. It must have been a stray bullet. It must have struck him in his chest."

Amanda laid the soldier's head on the ground and examined her sleeve. She said while holding it up for Jacob to see, "There, it did pass through my sleeve."

"Amanda, I thought," Jacob surprisingly said when he was interrupted.

"I know, you want to know what has happened," Amanda stood and approached, continuing, "I was an agent for the Confederacy, but also for the Union."

"You were playing both sides of this war. Why?"

"Maybe, the risk, the challenge, and the adventure. But, when I thought about it all, I really had no life as a spy until you came into it. Then it all changed."

"But, I was the one who had you arrested and even now you don't appear too upset that I am wearing Yankee blue."

"Don't ask me why, but I found out after my arrest that you were the responsible person. For some time, it troubled me. "

"Really?" Jacob said in a surprised tone.

"Does Sarah know you were a double agent?"

"No. She does not know the truth and does not know I played both sides of the war. She is too loyal to the Southern Cause. If she knew all that I did, she would kill me."

"I don't believe that she would kill you. You are her mother."

"No, like many others believed, you too, are wrong. Actually, I am Sarah's older sister. Our mother passed away shortly after Sarah was born and I am the only mother she has ever known."

"Does Sarah know?"

"No."

"Where is she?"

"I don't know, but if you see Sarah, please do not tell her what I have shared with you. She does not know the truth about anything that I have confided to you."

"What happens to you now."

"By now, Sarah believes that I am in a prison somewhere in the north. And I want her to keep believing that because as far as spying goes, I am finished." Pausing and looking into Jacob's eyes, Amanda continued, "I was serious when I told you that I was going abroad."

"You must find safety. This is no place for you," Jacob said as a random shell exploded in a hollow nearby.

"I will stay as long as I am needed here on this field of battle," Amanda insisted.

"You are a courageous woman."

"I meant what I said to you in Washington City. You'll know where to find me."

Jacob dismounted and took Amanda by the hand and gazed into her eyes. He said, "I know where to find you."

Jacob took Amanda into his arms and embraced her. He stepped back and mounted his horse. Once more he looked at Amanda and could only hope and pray for her safety. Then he put spurs to his horse and rode toward Antietam Creek.

Chapter Fifty

Benjamin was with Generals D. H. Hill and Robert E. Lee and other staff officers. They were on the crest of the ridge overlooking a farmer's sunken lane, where General Hill's 2,500-man division was entrenched. The Confederates were harden veterans of many battles and well discipline. Benjamin, and Generals Lee and Hill were watching the Federals advancing. General Lee rode along the crest of the ridge offering words of encouragement to Hill's men. When he came to Colonel John Gordon of the 6th Alabama Infantry, Gordon boasted, "The men are going to stay here, General, till the sun goes down or victory is won."

After acknowledging Colonel Gordon's promise, Generals Lee and Hill moved onto a knoll on the east side of the Piper farm and north of the Boonesborough Pike. There General Longstreet joined them. Benjamin remembered him as the same officer he had spoken to upon arriving earlier at Lee's headquarters. Benjamin helped General Lee dismount where he joined Longstreet and was ordered with the rest of the staff to the backside of the slope. Benjamin returned to the crest of the ridge with a spyglass in hand. Hill stayed mounted, but apart from Longstreet and Lee. Benjamin heard Longstreet cry out to Hill, as he pointed in the direction of a puff of smoke from an artillery piece on the east bank of the Antietam, "There is a shot for General Hill." At that moment, both legs were cut off below the knees of Hill's horse. It was the third one that he had lost that day.

Hill's men were still in the process of tearing down the fence and piling it up on the northern side of the lane when Confederate skirmishers were seen by Benjamin fleeing over the ridge from the Roulette farm. Benjamin observed Federal infantry moving across the field in parade like fashion four lines deep. Officers mounted on horses were exhorting their men as bands followed playing patriotic airs. The alignment in the soldiers' formation was perfect, bayonets gleaming and banners fluttering in the breeze. It was like a parade instead of advancing to do battle. There was no protection of any kind for the attackers. When near the crest of the ridgeline, the Federals halted and fixed bayonets. Afterward, they dashed across the field.

Benjamin noticed the Confederates in the sunken lane lying on the grass. They appeared patient and ready for the on-coming Federal column. Every weapon was loaded and ready. When the Federals crossed the ridge and came near the Confederates, red flashes of musketry from Hill's men made a crashing sound. Benjamin silently watched as hundreds of Yankees in the attacking front line fell to the ground wounded or dead. Within a short distance of each other, Confederates stood to their feet and continued to pound the Federal line with volleys of musketry. Artillery now added to the devastation. At first, the Federals were stunned, but under fire they reformed and tried again. The firing continued and the progress all along the Federal line was halted, but Benjamin was sure more soldiers would be drawn into the whirlpool of death.

The fighting continued for some time along the sunken lane in an effort to breach the Confederate line. Confederate casualties were heavy. By this time, there were few couriers left because many of them were already carrying out orders that had been issued by the generals.

A boy soldier of about fifteen years old arrived and said to Benjamin, "General Longstreet wishes to speak to you."

Benjamin quietly gave the soldier the reins of General Lee's horse and approached General Longstreet.

"As I understand, General Anderson has arrived at Sharpsburg with his division. I want you to go and find General Hill and tell him General Anderson's men are on the way. They will be directed across that field," Longstreet commanded while pointing in the direction of the Piper farm.

Without hesitation, Benjamin departed and swiftly headed toward the area between the sunken road and a fifteen acre apple orchard, where he believed that Hill might be directing the fight. When closer to his destination, it became increasingly dangerous, but he had endured battle many times before and knew the expectations from his own experiences. As Benjamin approached the area near the orchard, artillery shells began to explode nearby and tear up the ground, throwing dirt into his face. The scene was confusing because it was hazy from the foggy white smoke of multiple volleys of musketry, heavy cannonading, and · men screaming in terror as shell fragments struck them.

Unexpectedly, Benjamin's horse cried and rolled to the ground on its side, trapping him. The horse was instantly dead and Benjamin frantically fought to free himself from the animal's lifeless body. Blood mingled with dust covered his uniform. For a brief moment, he was confused from the fall. As he continued to struggle to break free, he noticed a cannon shell bouncing across the ground in his direction. Fortunately, it didn't explode, sending its fragments in every direction. Unhurt, Benjamin worked himself free of the horse. Immediately, he pulled out his pistol and glanced around. He jumped to his feet and raced for the shelter of the sunken lane near the area where Rhodes' Brigade was entrenched.

When Benjamin leaped into the sunken lane, the first person he noticed was Colonel Gordon. He had been wounded twice, but was still on his feet, encouraging his men.

"Where ya comin' from?" another soldier asked.

"I am a courier. I was sent to find General Hill and let him know that help was on the way, but my horse got shot out from under me, and with all that lead flying, I took shelter where I could find it."

"Well Lieutenant, welcome to hell. Look at all of those dead and dyin' around ya. If we stay here, dat's jist what's gonna happin' to us."

The fire from the fighting was devastating. After listening to the soldier's testimony, Benjamin glanced around his surroundings. Dead and wounded were lying in multitudes, stacked on each other as far as he could see. Men with blood streaming down their faces and with red handkerchiefs wrapped around their blackened foreheads tore open cartridges and continued to rapidly load their muskets and fire. Another soldier, an officer nearby loudly cried out in pain. Benjamin quickly noticed the man and saw that he didn't have any eyes in his sockets. Another soldier was saying the Lord's Prayer with his final gasp for breath. Only a few appeared to be unharmed. He turned his attention once more to the ghastly drama of fighting. When Benjamin attempted to aim his weapon, he was struck in the face by wood splintering from a fence rail caused by a bullet fired by a Yankee's weapon. Blood trickled down his cheek, but he kept up the fight.

While firing, Benjamin noticed out of the corner of his eye a Confederate soldier crawling along the edge of the bank near him. At first he didn't pay any attention because the Federals were upon them and he wanted to keep up a steady fire. Several times, Benjamin fired his pistol, but it began to click. He was out of ammunition. Benjamin rolled over on his back and removed the magazine from the weapon. The uninterrupted popping of weapons and the thudding sound of bullets striking rocks and striking the fence was a continuous sound. He placed the new bullet magazine into his pistol. When he turned, he noticed the soldier was lying in front of him in an effort to shelter him from harm.

"You need to be under cover, not exposed, or trying to protect me," Benjamin shouted over the noise of the battle.

"My wound is mortal," the soldier whispered gasping for breath. "I won't be going home. I just ask that you would take the letters in my haversack and send them to my wife along with a few lines regarding my death."

"You'll be doing that instead of me," Benjamin reassuringly said looking at the soldier.

"No, I won't. My time has come to an end," the soldier answered reaching for the items.

Suddenly, a bullet struck the soldier's body. Benjamin noticed the shocked, lifeless expression on his face. Benjamin took the letters and placed them in his shirt for safekeeping. He knew if the soldier hadn't used his body as a shield for him, that same bullet would have killed him instead.

Things looked very critical. The crushing sound of men's bones being broken by Minnie bullets splintering them, and their shrilling cries were unnerving. Benjamin tried his best to shut it all out and at the same time keep up a constant fire. While firing his weapon, Benjamin said to the soldier beside him that had greeted him when he first arrived, "See if that dead officer over behind you has any ammunition. I'm running low!"

When there wasn't an answer, Benjamin repeated the order, but again there was only silence. Benjamin turned and noticed the soldier's eyes were staring at him. Benjamin knew he too was dead.

*   *   *   *

Major-General Israel B. Richardson with General Sumner's 3rd division was late leaving camp with their three brigades. Jacob found them riding near the Roulette farm. Still, eager to see action, and with no orders to carry, he caught up with Brigadier-General Thomas F. Meagher's brigade, which was all Irish and made up of the 29th Massachusetts, the 88th, 63rd, and 69th New York Infantry.

"Sir, may I follow along and be of assistance to you sir," Jacob anxiously asked.

"Well Laddy, where did you come from?" General Meagher asked glancing at Jacob.

"I am supposed to be returning to General McClellan's headquarters, but at the moment, I have no orders to carry," Jacob answered looking at the general for his reaction.

"Well if you want to disobey orders and get into the fight, that's up to you. I must admit Laddy, I admire your bravery, but as I understand, it's bloody hot where we are going."

"Yes sir. Is that the 69th over there?" Jacob asked, pointing.

"Yes. And if any man tries to run, your duty is to shoot him."

The brigade was commanded to halt. Jacob observed that every man was ordered to remove his knapsacks, bedrolls, and canteens. The only items left were rifle and cartridge boxes. Each regiment received a last minute talk of exhortation and prayer before continuing. Jacob noticed the determination on their faces, the quiet confidence of success, and the knowledge that every man knew his responsibility as a soldier. They were determined to meet their fate. When all was ready, the advance resumed.

Jacob rode closely behind the 69th regiment as it followed the 29th in line. Drums were beating the march, the emerald battle flag bearing the gold shamrock and harp fluttered in the breeze. He knew these Irishmen were veteran fighters and wouldn't run under the rigors of battle.

Orders were given once the brigade reached the crest of the ridge overlooking the sunken lane. Immediately, they fired two volleys and then rushed the Confederates with the bayonet. The brigade was armed with smoothbore rifles, firing buck-and-ball cartridges, which were effective at close range.

The Confederates instantly responded. Jacob noticed the blazing flashes from a firing crashing volley of musketry that shattered the Federal battle line. As the Irish brigade's battle line recoiled, he noticed several soldiers trying to desert the effort. He pulled his sword from its scabbard and struck the one soldier with the blunt end of the blade shouting, "Get back in line or I'll have to shoot you."

The angry soldier glanced at Jacob. He pulled his revolver and fired once, hitting the other soldier in the leg that was still running.

By now the Irish brigade was charging the sunken lane, but were repulsed.

Jacob noticed General Caldwell's brigade approaching at the double quick. As they neared, the 29th Massachusetts suddenly charged forward. The fire of the Confederates began to slacken. The charge of Federal soldiers was too much for the Confederates as they began to leave the sunken lane by twos and threes.

Jacob rushed in with the Federal soldiers and began to fire into the remaining Confederate soldiers still wanting to fight. He had one Confederate officer lunge forth in an attempt to pull him from his horse, but the rebel was quickly shot dead. The Confederate line wavered greatly until it began to totally collapse. Jacob continued to fire at the Confederates as they either fought back or tried to escape the onslaught.

*   *   *   *

Benjamin and the rest of those soldiers that remained in the sunken lane began firing from behind the dead bodies of their comrades. He was again running low on ammunition. He continued to experience the sounds of bullets making their thudding sounds while striking dead bodies. This fight was like nothing he had experienced thus far in the war. Now as he looked around, the Federals were not only firing from the crest of the ridge to his front, but also they were firing down the lane where his comrades had recently deserted. The volleys of musketry were too much for Benjamin and the other Confederates soldiers that remained. Casualties were appalling. Men were perishing by the multitudes. Benjamin noticed Colonel Gordon taking another hit. This time the officer fell to the ground with his face in his cap. Would they have to fight until death relieved them of this horrifying experience or would they live to have the opportunity to surrender?

Shortly, the order was passed rapidly down the lines to abandon the sunken lane. Benjamin knew with the intensity of the Federal fire and their increasing numbers being added to the fight that it would be by the blessings of God to come out of this fight unscathed. He looked before proceeding, only to witness large numbers of Confederates being shot down as they left the shelter of the fence-railed breastworks and raced up the steep road bank for the rear. Instead of panicking, Benjamin crawled along the edge of the lane. Many of his comrades were shot in the back and at times, fell upon him with their full weight, hindering his efforts. All along, bullets kicked up dirt in his face. Everything was confusing and disorderly. His comrades' unbearable screams, loud cursing, and shouts of dying defiance gave him the determination to get out of this battle alive. Inching forward, he felt the sting of something passing through the leg of his trousers. He knew it was a passing minnie ball.

Benjamin glanced over his shoulder and witnessed the continuation of the slaughter. He was breathing heavily, exhausted, but full of determination. He thought he might possibly be away from immediate danger. He had to take the risk of danger or be faced with capture and end up in some prisoner-of-war camp, which would be just as bad as being killed. Swiftly, he rose to his feet and raced for the cornfield and ridge. Bullets hissed and whizzed by his body, but like many, he didn't look back.

Soon, Benjamin was over on the crest of the ridge. Exhausted, he looked for his photograph of Rachel. It was gone from his haversack with some of his other personal effects. He must have lost it while in the sunken lane. He looked back at the sunken lane, which by now was filled with Yankee soldiers. For now, he was safe and could seek some safety, but for how long, he did not know. He was disappointed and demoralized by the events that transpired in the sunken lane. The center of Lee's army had been penetrated. What next? With their diminishing numbers would they be able to hold off the Federal onslaught?

It was the first time Benjamin had ever panicked or given thought to running away from battle, but all was lost and to stay in the sunken lane meant certain death. It was hell just as the soldier had proclaimed earlier and the fight had not ended for him or any of the rest of the army. There were still many hours of daylight left. Would the army be beaten by sunset? Would he still be alive to see another sunrise?

* * * *

With the Confederates giving up their efforts, Federal soldiers poured into the sunken lane and began to express their jubilation by tossing their hats into the air, waving arms, and shouting. Knowing their celebration might be too premature, Jacob wheeled his horse around to find General Richardson. He found the general near the center of the line urging every man into the fight.

"General, do you have anything that I should relay to General McClellan?" Jacob asked saluting the senior officer.

"The center is broken. My men are pushing the devils back toward Sharpsburg."

Jacob wheeled his horse around and galloped down the backside of the ridge toward Antietam Creek.

While resting and changing horses back at the Pry house, Jacob walked onto the bald hill and used his spyglass to gaze across the battlefield. Again, he saw the devastating effects of war only this time he took part in it. Jacob knew the day's fighting wasn't finished. Off to the south of the Boonesborough Pike, he could hear the rumble of thunder from artillery. As he continued to look across the sloping fields along Antietam Creek, Jacob wondered if Benjamin was alive or dead. When he removed the spyglass, he looked down at the ground and pondered on when all this would end.

Chapter Fifty-One

The next morning, both armies still remained on the field. Neither was willing to give in to the other. During the late afternoon of the previous day, Burnside's Federal soldiers of the Ninth Corps pushed the thinly held Confederate lines back into the very streets of Sharpsburg. Victory appeared certain, but reinforcements under General A. P. Hill arrived from Harpers Ferry and saved Lee's Army of Northern Virginia from complete destruction.

Throughout the night, many of the dead and wounded remained on the field unattended because it was too dangerous to try and remove them. The cries never ceased for water or death to put an end to the agony they suffered.

On Thursday morning the 18th, General McClellan issued specific orders, not to precipitate hostilities. He was expecting reinforcements and wouldn't make any movements until they came forth, but still Confederate sharpshooters and Federal pickets carried on a brisk exchange of fire.

Behind the front battle lines, Jacob was riding near the Poffenberger's barn that was being used as a makeshift hospital. He heard the cries and moans of the wounded. Jacob dismounted and walked toward the barn. When he glanced into the dwelling, it reminded him of the horrors of war that he had witnessed after the fighting around Richmond. Jacob walked through the entrance and looked around to see if perhaps Benjamin was among the wounded. When satisfied Benjamin wasn't among the suffering, he turned to leave, but not before pausing to watch a surgeon remove a soldier's leg.

The surgeon had his assistant place a cone-like funnel over the suffering soldier's nose and face. While the assistant placed some chloroform on a cloth and over the funnel, the surgeon adjusted the flaming light in several of the lanterns. The soldier breathed and slowly lost consciousness. When ready, the surgeon wrapped a tourniquet with a screw-like device around the soldier's leg, just below the right shattered knee. He nodded to his assistant and began to quickly cut through the soldier's flesh with his surgical saw. Once the leg was removed, he packed the stump with bandages. When the surgeon turned around to get another instrument, he was void of expression. The assistant took the soldier's leg and tossed it through the window into a pit where many other limbs were lying to be buried later.

After witnessing such a gruesome event, Jacob rushed from the barn and immediately emptied the contents of his stomach. He had to get away. Again, he mounted his horse and rode toward the sunken lane, the site of some of the heaviest fighting the previous day.

As Jacob rode by the Roulette homestead, the evidence of war was apparent everywhere he looked. Horses were greatly disfigured, overturned artillery caissons, and small arms equipment were lying everywhere.

The most appalling scene was when Jacob came to the sunken road where the bloated, blackened bodies of Confederate soldiers were still lying stacked upon each other. It was a ghastly scene, nothing he had ever witnessed. The carnage was beyond words. As far as Jacob could see in this lane there lay so many dead rebels that they formed a line which one might have walked upon as far as the eye could see. They lay just as they had been killed and their blood was still soaking the earth. The smell was offensive and the vultures circled overhead. As he glanced at the expressions on their dead faces, some had that hollow, somber expression while others appeared horrified. They met their death with great pain. Others appeared to be just sleeping.

Jacob noticed a Federal soldier going through the haver-sack of a dead Confederate soldier lying on the ground along the bank of the sunken road. He watched as the soldier looked into another haversack and again removed some items. This same soldier now removed a timepiece. Jacob walked over to the soldier.

"What are you doing?" Jacob asked in an irritated tone.

"What does it look like," the soldier snapped as he continued his plundering.

"This is against army rules of warfare. I command you to cease this activity at once," Jacob ordered.

When the soldier ignored Jacob's command, he drew his revolver and cocked the hammer, shouting, "Now back away or I'll blow out your worthless brains where you stand."

The soldier stood and noticed Jacob's rank. He coldly answered, "But sir, these things won't do the Johnnies any good now that they are dead."

"Soldier, don't you have any pride about you. If that were you lying there on the ground dead, would you want somebody picking your pockets and stealing from you?"

Jacob noticed another officer of lesser rank approaching. He turned and commanded, "Lieutenant."

"Yes sir."

"I want this man placed under arrest and turned over to the provost marshal."

"Why sir?" the officer asked.

"This man is nothing more than a thief. I caught him plundering the pockets of the dead."

"But sir, Private Gentry is a good man. He obeys com-mands and he is one hell of a good fighter. On more than one occasion yesterday, he showed his true valor while fighting the Johnnies."

"Lieutenant, are you disobeying an order?" Jacob angrily demanded.

"No sir. I will carry out your order."

The officer pulled his weapon and called for several other soldiers to assist him with the prisoner.

Jacob turned and began to walk along the edges of the sunken lane in the direction of the Roulette farm lane, looking and pondering on what he was witnessing.

*   *   *   *

Along the area of the sunken lane and Piper's farm orchard, an informal flag of truce had been requested between the blue and gray to tend to their wounded, which still cried in agony. Benjamin took the reprieve to go and look in the area where he was fighting the previous day. While slowly walking in that direction, he heard the unbearable cries, the low moans, and angry curses from men that wore the blue and gray. Sometimes, a soldier would just be praying for God's intervention or just struggling to make an effort to join the living once more. He looked to his side and there lay his horse that was shot out from under him the previous day.

When Benjamin arrived along the sunken lane, he was appalled at the carnage. Dead men still gripped their weapons. One in particular still had a cartridge wrapper between his teeth. He was in the process of reloading his musket when he was struck dead. The grass was colored with the crimson stain of their dry blood.

Benjamin turned and noticed a soldier sitting quietly along a tree. He walked over and gazed at the figure. He was dead. The soldier was holding a piece of paper in his hand. When Benjamin looked to see what was on the paper, he realized it was a photograph of his wife and son. He must have pulled the photograph from his pocket near his moment of death to gaze one more time upon the ones he loved the most in life. Benjamin tried to remove the photograph from his hands, but his grip was still to tight. He thought of Rachel. She most likely knew of the horrors of the devastating fight and the cost and sacrifice of life that was given on this field yesterday. She must be worried, not knowing his fate. He needed to get word to her that he was alive and well.

*   *   *   *

Jacob noticed a ragged and dirty Confederate officer, whose face was still blackened with gunpowder near the area of the Roulette family lane near a tree. When he approached, he thought it would be good to see emotionally how the other side was holding up.

"Johnnie, would you like to trade some coffee for tobacco?" Jacob asked placing his hand in his haversack.

"I have nothing to trade," the soldier answered in a whisper as he continued to look across the field of devastation.

Even though Jacob didn't recognize his appearance, he did recognize the voice.

"Benjamin?"

Benjamin turned and said, "Jacob."

Both Benjamin and Jacob were silent as they looked at each other.

"This fight was costly." Benjamin said removing his hat and wiping his forehead. "I knew we weren't prepared to fight this battle. We didn't have enough of anything, supplies, men or weaponry after fighting along South Mountain. My regiment went into this fight with less than fifty men. You people are able to re-supply and fill your ranks quicker than we are. Many at home are against conscription and those that do fill the ranks either run off and surrender when given the opportunity by your people to do so." Benjamin paused and looked at the dead lying in the lane, continuing, "But yet soldiers such as myself and these brave men lying here in this lane are willing to carry the burden and fight the war." Benjamin turned and looked at Jacob continuing, "You know why? Because we believe in the Cause we are fighting for. And every one of us will probably die fighting to preserve that freedom, our rights."

"It doesn't have to be that way. You can get out now and go home. I'll take you in as my prisoner and see you are paroled, and then you can return to Rachel. She needs you more than Jeff Davis does."

"What do you mean? Has something happened to her?" Benjamin asked in a concerned tone while his expression was turning tense.

"You don't know?" Jacob swiftly asked.

"Know what?"

"Rachel has given you a son."

"Well, I'll be," Benjamin joyfully answered as a smile radiated across his face.

"His name is Benjamin. The same as yours. Congratulations soldier," Jacob said stretching forth his hand.

Benjamin paused, looked down at the ground and then again at Jacob. He said, "Jacob, I know as surely as I am standing here that you still love Rachel. Over the last six weeks, I have believed that she felt the same."

"The relationship that Rachel and I had is gone. Yes, I will not lie to you and say that I don't have feelings, but they are not the same anymore. We were like brothers and I will not come between you and Rachel. Benjamin, I am moving on with my life and that life does not include Rachel."

"I guess I will have to trust you on that one."

"I want you to go home and love Rachel and cherish her all the days of your life," Jacob said.

A Federal soldier came walking by saluting and saying, "Sir, the truce will end shortly. They are asking the Johnnies to return to their lines."

"Thank you private," Jacob replied, returning the soldiers salute.

Once more, Jacob turned his attention to Benjamin and pleaded, "You must get out of this fight while you are still alive and un-harmed. Please, let me take you in as a prisoner."

"No Jacob, I can't do that," Benjamin replied in a stubborn tone.

"Why?" Jacob quickly insisted.

"Look at them, "Benjamin said as he again pointed to the dead soldiers in the sunken lane, "They are as thick as sheaves. These men lying in this lane have given everything they could give. Their lives. As much as I love Rachel and want to see my new son, I'll not betray the trust of these men who yesterday fought so gallantly beside me here in this place. There is still a lot of fight left in this army, and a lot of men still believe in the Cause."

Jacob silently nodded, turned and began to walk away.

Benjamin called out, "Jacob."

Jacob turned and looked at Benjamin, waiting for him to speak. Instead, he noticed Benjamin pulling his weapon. Still, he remained silent.

"I still haven't forgotten you are a spy and that you betrayed my trust. I could easily kill you right here at this moment."

"I don't think you will. As good of a shot as you are, you could have easily killed me last month at my homestead when you had the chance to, or at the river, but you didn't."

Benjamin nodded in agreement and answered, "That's true and as far as I am concerned the score isn't settled."

"When will it be?"

"I don't know, but not today. Not at this moment."

"Benjamin, listen to me. You must return to Rachel and your family."

Benjamin was quiet as he glanced over the battlefield at all of the destruction of war. His heart was stricken with grief and despair over such enormous loss of life. Tears began to fill his eyes. He turned and said, "No. Not right now. For some reason, I can't, even though it's in my heart to do so. No Jacob, you and I will live to fight another day on opposite sides on some battlefield such as this. Just before this great fight, I noticed the harvest season was soon to begin. Now it won't happen because these fields have been destroyed and devastated by war and stained with the blood of fighting men. They lay everywhere, dead. But I guess in some way the harvest has happened. It's all around us. By the mercies of God, we were not a part of *The Bloody Harvest*."

Both Benjamin and Jacob quietly and somberly gazed upon each other, not knowing how much more bloodshed and fighting they were to experience before this war would end. They stretched forth their hands and shook, turning and departing and going their separate ways. Even though this had been the bloodiest single day of the Civil War, both knew the war would not end, but continue to spread its blood, devastation and heartache.

Jacob watched for a long time as Benjamin walked away. Before leaving, he looked around the battlefield once more and agreed with Benjamin. Over the last several days the harvest had come. It was truly *The Bloody Harvest.*